FRIENDS OF ACPL

THE FLAMING ARROW

"CHE-LOO STOPPED, AND LISTENED INTENTLY"

The
FLAMING ARROW

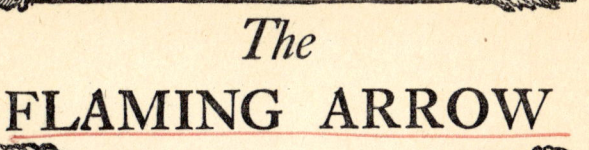

BY
CARL MOON

WITH FRONTISPIECE BY THE AUTHOR

NEW YORK
FREDERICK A.
STOKES COMPANY
PHILADELPHIA

Copyright, 1927, by
FREDERICK A. STOKES COMPANY

All rights reserved
Published September 8, 1927
Second Printing November 21, 1927
Third Printing, July 12, 1928
Fourth Printing, October 26, 1931
Fifth Printing, August 28, 1935
Sixth Printing, February 7, 1939
Seventh Printing, October 20, 1943

Printed in the United States of America

TO MY SON
FRANCIS MAXWELL MOON
THIS BOOK
IS LOVINGLY DEDICATED.

CONTENTS

CHAPTER		PAGE
	Foreword	ix
I.	Unexpected Delay	1
II.	The Wounded Guest	15
III.	A Spider on the Wall	28
IV.	An Unwelcome Task	40
V.	The Witch-Killer	55
VI.	The Flight of an Owl	70
VII.	The Dawn Woman	84
VIII.	Chá-za, the Fool	102
IX.	A Test of Skill	121
X.	A Flame to the Arrow	141
XI.	In the Dark	157
XII.	Three Against One	177
XIII.	Sign of the Black Witch	199
XIV.	The Rattlesnake	221
XV.	The End of Many Things	239

FOREWORD

When the Indian Summer sun drops down
Behind the western hill,
And lazy smoke from the chimneys rise,
And twilight peace o'er the desert lies,
While all the world is still,

'Tis then old men may tell us tales
Of days long, long ago:
Of strange romance, and legends old,
And wondrous deeds of warriors bold.
All true?—well, maybe so.

THE FLAMING ARROW

The Flaming Arrow

CHAPTER I

UNEXPECTED DELAY

Of power and skill may the hunter boast;
Of mighty deeds may the warrior sing;
But the gods may smile and lay them low
With a feather plucked from a bluebird's wing.

IN the low evening light of a mid-September sun, three Indian hunters ran in single file along the bank of a shallow bush-grown canyon. Their gait was the long lax-muscled stride that swings the runner forward with least effort, and covers surprising distance in an allotted time.

Since late morning they had trailed a wounded buck, and by shrewd maneuver had driven him into the cover of the canyon that now led steadily upward into ground more and more difficult for the weary beast to traverse.

Before them low hills began to appear, and to their right, a little distance away, a great solitary mesa rose like a giant block against the flat horizon-line beyond. The hunters felt the mesa to be uncomfortably near.

At the time of our story, before the coming of the white man, there was not, in all the broad region from Pah-qui to the setting sun, an Indian village of the stone-house people more famous or better situated than Pau-lan'-tee. Its strength and fame were due to its unique location as much as to the skill and bravery of its warriors.

From its terraced houses, on the summit of this lofty mesa, it calmly surveyed the desert world beneath, and often, in the dusk of twilight, could look from its sheltered doorways on a dozen camp and signal fires, twinkling like fallen stars far out on the bosom of the darkening earth.

Some of these fires were of enemy, and some of friendly, tribes, but Pau-lan'-tee looked with equal indifference on them all.

To the north and east of the mesa stretched the open desert; to the south and west the land was scarred by many deep washes and wandering canyons with bush-grown hills and sage-covered plains between.

Farther westward the rough ground rose rapidly into the foothills of a lofty mountain range, and amid these hills and wooded slopes the Pau-lan'-tees hunted the abundant game.

The three hunters, who were of another tribe, had hoped to take the wounded buck before arriving so near the home of the Pau-lan'-tees, but the endurance of the big animal had proven better than their judgment. And now the low descending sun warned them to end the chase as soon as possible, as the arrival of complete darkness, before the kill, would send them to camp empty-handed.

The leader, and eldest of the trio, a man known for his great skill on the trail and in the hunt, stopped in the center of a small patch of smooth ground, and all three dropped to earth, and rolling over with their faces to the sky, relaxed every muscle. Thus at intervals had they taken telling advantage of the wounded buck who could use no such means to restore his ebbing strength.

After a brief rest they arose, but the leader did not immediately resume the chase. With a gesture southward he spoke to the elder of his two companions.

"Lō'-mah, your way is along the left bank." Then turning to the other, "Che-loo', you run with the greatest speed. A little way and this canyon turns to the north. It is for you to cross the bend and head the game into the rough ground toward the setting sun. There we make the finish. The deer must not be taken too near the great mesa. We of Pan'-gua are friends of the Pau-lan'-tees, and it is a law among us that we can run game across another's hunting-ground if it has first been seen, or wounded, in our own, but we will not kill our meat at the very doors of the mesa people. That would make bad talk, and it has come to my ears that even now there is bad talk of us among some of the Pau-lan'-tees. Now we go."

Without reply the two hunters obeyed the orders given them. Our interest is now with the young Indian whom the leader addressed as Che-loo'.

He was above the average height of village men, and his nineteen years, half of which had been spent in the hunt, had brought his well-muscled body to a more mature build and strength than his age would seem to warrant. His apparel and trappings were, with one exception, extremely simple. His moccasins were plain, their only adornment a small button of blue stone that fastened the upper flap across the ankle. His fringed leggings of doeskin were supported by a stout belt from which was suspended a sheathed hunting-knife.

His upper body was free of clothing, giving full play to the muscles of chest and arms as he ran. Suspended diagonally across his back was his bow-and-arrow case. Though all else was plain and unadorned, on this essential trapping the owner had lavished time and rare materials with all the pride of a true hunter. Woven designs, in beads and dyed porcupine-quills, ran its full length, while from the upper part of the bow-case brightly stained eagle feathers mingled with the long fringe. The quiver was equally well adorned, and was finished at the lower end with a row of feathers from the bluebird's wing. To Che-loo' the hunt was the joy of life.

As he ran, the young Indian watched the trend of the canyon, and as he rose into higher ground he noted the northward curve. To cut across the great arc it made would surely bring him ahead of the deer, which had, since mid-afternoon, been running no more than three or four good bow-shots ahead of its pursuers, but he saw that his way would bring him nearer to the great mesa than he wished to go. He might encounter several Pau-lan'-tees on their way home from their fields or the hunt, and he would have neither time nor wish to explain his presence.

He had met very few of the mesa people, and he decided to make every effort to avoid being seen, and to hide if necessary.

Immediately before him lay a long low ridge, and as he came to it he crossed a well-worn trail leading toward the mesa. On the lower side of the ridge many great boulders dotted the wide slope and he welcomed these, as they would afford excellent cover should he have need to hide.

He was now as near the great mesa as he would have to go, and was beginning to feel that he had passed all danger of being seen, when he saw before him a still broader trail and at the same moment heard voices of women who seemed to be approaching from a thicket of tall mesquite-bushes down the trail to his left. He dropped behind a large boulder and waited.

To face Pau-lan'-tee men was one thing, but Pau-lan'-tee women—he would not face them even if he were to risk the loss of the wounded buck. And now he heard still another voice, that of an old man, querulous and loud. As the voices drew near he began to doubt the security of his hiding-place, as the boulder was beside the trail, and though large enough to shield him from view, the passing Pau-lan'-tees might chance to look behind it.

Crawling backwards on hands and knees, he gained the cover of a thick clump of bushes that stood a few feet behind him. As he began this retreat his knee pressed heavily down on the end of his quiver, loosening one of the bluebird feathers. Unnoticed by him it lay like a bit of blue sky on the dark sand beside the boulder.

From behind his new hiding-place, where he could see without being seen, Che-loo' anxiously watched the trail, hoping that the women with their aged companion would pass quickly that he might not be long delayed. This sudden interruption in the chase filled him with impatience, and he wondered what his companions would say if he failed to carry out the instructions given him.

An old man came into view. Che-loo' recognized him at once as one who had visited his village of Pan'-gua some years before. He was known as Cha'-za, the Fool. The old man was bent forward under the load of a buckskin bag that the young hunter guessed contained pinyon nuts gathered by the two women.

Mumbling to himself, with occasional shouts to the women, who seemed to be but a short distance behind him, the aged Pau-lan'-tee passed the great boulder and continued his way toward the mesa. Not so the women. At the boulder they stopped, and after a word stepped around it to the shaded side, facing the hidden hunter, and leaned wearily against its sloping surface.

Impatient, yet half curious, Che-loo' peered through the branches of his screen at the women who innocently, though effectually, blocked his way. Though without fear of man or beast he had always feared woman, but had mistaken this fear for dislike. Aside from his mother, he believed he heartily disliked them all, and avoided them on all occasions. For this his mother had scolded him roundly, believing that he meant to avoid the home and communal life that all good warriors of the village people should aspire to.

The effect was the opposite of the mother's intent, and he avoided the village maidens all the more, and spent more and more time with his traps and in the hunt. His physical appearance was no aid to him in this avoidance of the young women of his own age, as they all secretly wished to attract his attention, and arouse his interest, for they believed him to be the most handsome and most desirable of all Pan'-gua men. Of this he was ignorant, and supposed his many

UNEXPECTED DELAY 7

chance meetings with them to be common to all men who must suffer women to annoy them.

Just now he watched the two Pau-lan'-tee women, complaining within himself against the ill luck that had placed them in his path. Both were young, but unlike in almost every other particular. One, a typical pueblo, or village, girl, was plump, of medium height, with flat though pleasing features. Her eyes were brilliant, and seemed to dance with mischief that even bodily weariness could not wholly subdue. A half-smile, as though habitually there, played about the corners of her mouth, and seemed ready to break into a ripple of laughter on least provocation.

The other, a girl of seventeen or eighteen, was unlike any woman the young hunter had seen. She was tall, and although well-formed, appeared slender beside her companion. Something in the splendid mold of her face, or in the easy movements of her body, caused Che-loo' to give her more than ordinary attention.

There was frank admiration in this attention, but it was of the kind he had always had for any fine animal, or a beautiful sunset. Vaguely he felt that this Pau-lan'-tee woman was pleasing because she could not be offensive, but beyond this slight interest his impatient thoughts did not go.

The smaller of the two women called loudly to the old man.

"Cha'-za, we rest a while before the steep trail comes. Put down the bag. We can take it on from here. It is but a step to the mesa now."

The voice of the speaker, in spite of a certain note of command, left the impression that she hoped the old man would not obey it. Clearly the bag and its contents belonged to the women, and old Cha'-za had volunteered to carry it for them. This act Che-loo' attributed to the man's weak mind.

Cha'-za paused and, turning about, shouted his reply in a voice that would have carried many times the distance to the boulder:

"Cha'-za has the bag, and Cha'-za will keep it, and he will eat the good pinyon-nuts, and laugh at Mah-wee'-nah and En-tay', for they will have none."

At this the girl who had called to him laughed loudly, while the old man continued on his way up the trail mumbling to himself.

"Not always is Cha'-za the fool," continued the girl. "For me he would carry nothing, but for you —ah, he is like all men. For you, Mah-wee'-nah, he would carry all you ask. He would carry you to the mesa-top if you tell him to. I should like to see him do it; that would be funny." And again her laughter rang out and echoed among the rocks.

"What would you do, empty-headed one, if you could not tease, and say foolish things? I do not think men do more for me than for you."

The words of the last speaker came clearly enough to the ears of the young hunter, but he could not have repeated one of them, so astonished was he at the sound of her voice. Something about it caused him to feel uneasy, though not unhappy. It was low-keyed and soft and made him think of the fur of the young panther, or the sound of summer wind in the sage. Suddenly he felt that he could never face a woman with a voice like that. He wished more than ever that the two would go and go quickly, for the sun was fast

UNEXPECTED DELAY

sinking below the horizon and he knew that he should, by now, be with his companions at the capture of the wounded buck.

The first speaker made some comment, but he gave no heed to her words. Then her voice suddenly rose to a higher key as she exclaimed:

"Look, Mah-wee'-nah! The feather of a bluebird! It is a good omen—but see, no bluebird dropped it here. There is a little thong attached, and a bead of white stone."

As he watched the two women bending over the object of their interest, Che-loo' realized what had happened, and groaning within himself at this added ill luck, that might serve to detain the women longer, he wished he had been more careful of his loved bow-and-arrow case.

"It is for you, Mah-wee'-nah, this good omen," went on the speaker, "for it is you who have need of it to drive away the evil spell of the eyes of Dou-gow' that, you say, has put thoughts of fear in your heart."

"En-tay'! You are not to say his name like that. Some one might hear! You are to say that to no one, you have promised. It may be I am foolish, and that there is no such evil to fear of him—but I will keep the good omen," continued the soft voice of the speaker as she fastened the feather in her hair. "It belongs to some man, for it is from a bow-case or ceremonial belt, so I will wear it to the mesa-top, and then I will throw it away for another to find."

"You know I shall speak to none about your fear thoughts," replied the other meekly. "But the little feather—you will not throw it away, foolish one. Will the terrible man who has lost it know that the feather you wear is his? If you throw it away the good omen will be—"

Here the voice of the speaker ceased abruptly, and again broke into an exclamation. "Look, Mah-wee'-nah! There are more blue feathers behind the bushes yonder!"

To the surprise and alarm of the young hunter, the Pau-lan'-tee girl was pointing directly at his hiding-place. He looked quickly down at his quiver and noticed, with dismay, that its blue-fringed end projected to a point that made it visible to the sharp eyes of the speaker.

Annoyance and confusion seized him, and he wished that he could sink into the earth. Then, in sudden anger, more with himself than the women, he realized he must show himself before they could walk to his hiding-place and find him crouched like a rabbit in a trap.

With flushed face he rose to his full height, and coming from behind the bush took a step toward them. Then he stopped, as if caught in a flood of embarrassment that rendered him incapable of motion or speech. Words filled his thoughts, but he could not utter them.

The same difficulty had settled upon the talkative En-tay', and it remained for her companion of the soft voice to open the conversation if there was to be one.

"Does a Pan'-gua, who is a friend of the Pau-lan'-tees, have to hide from them?" she asked quietly.

The voice held no note of anger or surprise, and it partly restored the confidence of the bashful hunter.

"I did not hide for fear—or to spy on you. I hunt with my two friends. We followed a deer that we wounded on our own hunting-ground. It came this way and we—I did not want to be seen by your people, for we would have to make much talk of it, and it was late. I hid here that you might not see me when you went along the trail."

It was the longest speech he had ever made to a woman, made with a certain dogged persistence and in a low, even tone that left no doubt of the simple truth of his words. His eyes fell to the ground before the quiet gaze of the girl who had spoken to him.

"You should not wear bluebird feathers on your bow-case. They are too easily seen" she remarked with a smile; and then, as if suddenly remembering the feather in her hair, she removed it and held it out to him. "This must belong to you."

This act caused the hunter to do a strange thing, so strange that he pondered it afterward, and could not explain to himself why he did it. Stepping toward her he exclaimed:

"No—no! you will not take the feather from your hair. I will not let you do that. It, it—you must keep it, unless you wish to quarrel with a Pan'-gua who is your—who is a friend of the Pau-lan'-tees."

Then, abashed by his own boldness, he dropped his eyes to the ground, and studied the toe of his moccasin that now moved back and forth in the sand.

For a moment the Pau-lan'-tee girl hesitated, then with a smile she replaced the feather in her hair, tying it securely with the bit of thong.

"I will wear it, because it is a good omen, and it is said we anger the Shiuana [gods] if we cast away a good omen, or give their sign no heed."

Again silence fell on the three. Under the expectant gaze of the two women, panic seized the young hunter, and without further word, or backward glance, he bounded off like a deer toward the canyon, and disappeared in the thick brush.

For a moment the astonished women looked after him, then En-tay' leaned back against the great boulder and laughed long and loud. She seemed unable to stop the laughter that bubbled up within her, and though joined by her companion the mirth of Mah-wee'-nah was not so great.

"Oh, my good friend, did you ever, ever see man so strange, so foolish or so handsome?" gasped the laughing En-tay'. "What a look in his big eyes. At me he looked, at first, and there was anger in his face, then he looked at you, and—oh, poor little me. No longer did he look at me. I became nothing. None look at En-tay' after they have looked at Mah-wee'-nah. Poor hunter man, when he looked at you his eyes were like the eyes of the scared rabbit that is held in the trap. Was he not foolish when he ran away?" and again the speaker laughed loudly.

"He was foolish, but no more foolish than you," came the unexpected reply of Mah-wee'-nah. "You were like one who is dumb. He had words to say, but you—I think he cast a spell on you, for you, En-tay', who can always talk, were all eyes and no tongue."

This brought En-tay"s laughter to a sudden end, and a new light came into her eyes.

"So, lovely one, you would tease me, poor little me, about this handsome hunter. You turn such words on me—because for one thing. It is that you like him. You liked him much; it was in your face that you—"

"Stop the wagging of your tongue, silly one," inter-

UNEXPECTED DELAY

rupted Mah-wee'-nah. "Come, we must go. It grows late, and old Cha'-za is half-way up the mesa."

"Oh, of course we must run quickly, and say no more of how you like this hunter of Pan'-gua," assented En-tay' with mock seriousness. She knew every mood of her lifelong friend, and knew when she could and could not tease her. "Yes, we will say no more of the handsome one, or about the feather that you wear for him in your hair—so that the gods will not be angry with you for throwing away their good omen. It is for the Shiuana you wear it, but never, oh never, for a handsome, foolish Pan'-gua hunter."

Mah-wee'-nah stopped short on the trail, and turned angrily on her tormentor.

"What do you think I should have done, foolish one? Throw away his feather before his eyes, and make him angry? Is that the way we of Pau-lan'-tee should treat a stranger of Pan'-gua?"

"Oh, never, never!" replied En-tay', and her voice was as deep and as solemn as she could make it. "That would be evil, a very evil thing to do—but you told him that you would wear it because you must not make the gods to be angry, and now, now you say it is because you would not make him angry. Now that he is gone, and so cannot be made angry, I think maybe you will give the feather to poor En-tay', that she may wear it always."

But Mah-wee'-nah made no move to comply with the suggestion. "It is not for him that I wear it, but because it is a good omen. I need it for that," she added in a low voice.

The teasing En-tay' glanced quickly at her companion, then impulsively put her arms about her.

"No more will I tease my Mah-wee'-nah. I am a wicked one to forget about the fear thoughts that have all day been in your heart. The little feather is a good omen, and you will keep it until the moon-god is again new. It will keep the witch away, and turn the evil eyes so they can no longer make you to fear." Then, as the two resumed their way along the trail, the speaker lowered her voice almost to a whisper, though they had the trail to themselves. "You should not fear the evil eyes of that old Dou-gow'. He is but the Governor, a tapop, and does not all power belong to your father Ah'-mot, the great Cacique? The eyes of Dou-gow' are for all women whom he thinks are good to look upon. I have heard my father say that."

"It is not for me that I have fear of him," replied Mah-wee'-nah. "It is for my father." Then the soft voice dropped to a whisper. "I have heard words that men say, when they did not know that I heard, and I know that Dou-gow' has done great evil to many men. But of this we must not talk. Even the rocks may have ears when there is talk of the evil."

On a hillside, beyond the canyon, Che-loo' found his two companions in the act of skinning the great buck, and in reply to their good-natured bantering about his delay, he made no mention of the two maidens of Pau-lan'-tee. It had only been an old man, called Cha'-za, the Fool, who had delayed him, and long before the evening meal had been roasted above their camp-fire, he had forgotten his embarrassing experience on the mesa trail.

CHAPTER II

THE WOUNDED GUEST

> The solemn Council speaks the final word,
> And thus may set, unwittingly, in force
> A bold decision, like some mighty bow
> That sends a flaming arrow on its course.

IN the cold blue of the desert night, shortly before the dawn, four Indian men, wounded and weary, staggered up to the outer wall of a small pueblo village that stood silent and dark under the starlit sky.

Three of the four were the Pan'-gua hunters who had captured the buck near the great mesa. The fourth was of different tribe, age, and character. Although his hair was streaked with gray, his rather handsome face bore few marks of advanced age, and his body was still that of a strong and active man.

Of them all his physical condition seemed most grievous, and it was evident, from his childish groans and incoherent mutterings, that reason had left him. He moved between those who supported him like one who walks in a dream.

The heavy silence of the sleeping village was suddenly broken by the long lone howl of one of the village dogs, whose keen scent had given him advance notice of the approaching men. At the wall the men stopped and the leader of the three hunters spoke in a low voice to Che-loo'.

"Go quietly to your father, and tell him of this. None but he and the Cacique must know of it. We wait here until we have word where to take our wounded friend."

Che-loo' left his two companions with their charge, and hastened to a door that opened off of the silent plaza, quieting the village dogs with a low command as he ran. Pounding on the door with his fist he called in a guarded voice:

"Mat'-so, my father, open! It is Che-loo'."

In a moment the heavy wattled door swung silently on its thong hinges, and when the young hunter had stepped within the dark of the entrance, he quickly told his father of the men by the wall; of the wounded guest, and briefly did he mention the evil that had befallen them all.

By the end of the account his father was ready for any needed action, and as the two stepped into the night he spoke in a low voice.

"It is well you come quietly. I will give word to Ne-chō'-ba to meet us in the Council-house. Bring the men there."

"I do not have place in a clan. Can I too enter the Council-house with our Cacique?" questioned the youth.

"If a man have my word, he can enter, without name or place—before Ne-chō'-ba or the Council. If you spent more time in the village you would have knowledge that the Governor of Pan'-gua is next in authority under the Cacique. Go bring the men."

Then, seeing that his son staggered as he turned to obey, and that a crude bandage bound his shoulder, he added:

THE WOUNDED GUEST 17

"You are hurt. Are you able to bring the men?"

"I am able. The wound is but a scratch. It is only weariness that I feel," came the reply.

He returned to his companions, and silently they led the muttering stranger into the village and to the Council-house, where a small fire was growing under the swift hands of Mat'-so. He took charge of the situation and when the wounded men had entered, he closed and softly barred the heavy door.

"I have set Ne-chō'-ba awake. Soon he will be here," he announced quietly.

All were silent while he gave close attention to the wounded guest, who continued his childish mumbling, and not until he had made him comfortable on a pallet of skins was attention given to the others.

At a low knock on the door, the bar was lifted by Mat'-so and an old man entered. He was tall and slightly stooped with age. His long white hair made a thin frame of silver for a face remarkable for its strength and character. It was apparent that his bright, deep-set eyes windowed a mind still keen and alert. To him had been handed down the leadership and attendant dignity of a long line of forefathers through whom his hereditary office had come, for he was the Cacique or tribal head of the Pan'-gua people.

As he entered the Council-house, his thin hand shielding his eyes against the unaccustomed glare of the fire, he nodded to the men seated about it. Then his eye caught the figure on the pallet of skins, and the habitual calm of his face broke into an expression of strange excitement, an expression new to those about him.

"Ah'-mot! It is Ah'-mot—the Cacique of Pau-lan'-

tee! The Cacique of Pau-lan'-tee!" he exclaimed, in the slow repetition of amazement.

Then recovering himself with an effort, he strode to the muttering figure and bent over it. A glance told him that the wounded guest had, for the time being, lost his reason, but that he had been made as comfortable as possible.

With commanding gesture, he turned to the others.

"Tō'-bah-yan! Lō'-mah! What means this? How does the great Cacique of Pau-lan'-tee come to be wounded, and alone in your care?"

"I will tell," replied the first of the two men addressed. "Three days ago, as you know, Che-loo', Lō'-mah, and I, Tō'-bah-yan, went out to hunt. On the day that has just passed, at the time of the long shadows of morning, we entered the Black Canyon of Ash-ni. The wind had been very great all night, blowing much sand over the desert. Within the canyon all was quiet. We walked forward for some time. From behind a turn ahead of us came voices that we knew to be of our great enemies, the Apaches, though the place was far from Apache camps.

"Quickly we crawled, without noise, to the end of the turn and looked. We saw three Apaches coming toward us—they were forcing the Cacique of Pau-lan'-tee to walk with them. His arms were bound to his back, but he was able to walk fast.

"We said to ourselves, this is bad medicine, an evil thing. The Apaches have captured the great Cacique of Pau-lan'-tee, and will take his life from him. We will take him from these desert dogs."

Here the narrator was interrupted by the loud snoring of Che-loo' who, from sheer exhaustion, had rolled backward on the floor and was sleeping heavily. His father gently turned him over on his side and the speaker continued.

"As they came toward us we saw blood on the Cacique's head. This made us shut our teeth in anger, and with our knives we ran upon the Apaches. One of them, that was near the Cacique, raised his war-club quickly over the head of his captive to kill him before fighting us. Then Che-loo' leaped with his knife quick, like a cat. He struck the Apache down before the club could fall."

At this the face of the Governor lit with pride as he looked down at the face of the sleeping youth on the floor. Ne-chō'-ba nodded his silvery head as he uttered a grunt of approval.

"Then we fought hard," continued Tō'-bah-yan. "When there was an end of fighting we buried the Apaches in the sand, and hid the place with dry earth and leaves. This we took from the belt of one of the Apaches." And here the speaker held out a small buckskin bag to the aged Cacique.

The old man opened it and drew out two rings and a carved bracelet of bone, a beautiful necklace of rare turquoise with a large polished pendant that shone in the firelight like a bit of brilliant blue sky.

"These things belong to Ah'-mot," remarked the Cacique quietly. "I know them of old," and he returned the ornaments to the pouch and placed it in his own belt for safe-keeping.

"When we had bound our wounds," continued Tō'-bah-yan, "I left the Cacique with my two companions, and followed the trail of our three enemies back up the canyon to see if there were more Apaches. Not far away I came to a place where the Apaches' tracks met other tracks, and I saw that these had been made by Pau-lan'-tee moccasins. In many places the trail had been hidden by flying sand, but at this place I plainly saw the tracks of four men of Pau-lan'-tee, one of them the Cacique whom we had saved. These tracks of the mesa men joined the footprints of the Apaches, and—though it is a very strange thing I tell, I speak truth—there had been no fight between the men of Pau-lan'-tee and their great enemies the Apaches. The tracks of Ah'-mot showed plainly that he alone must have made fight. The marks of his feet were like those of one who jumps around quickly.

"Then I followed, for some way, the tracks of the three Pau-lan'-tee men who had turned back toward the mesa after giving their Cacique into the hands of the desert dogs, for I would see if they ran or walked. They had walked. Then I knew that these three men had planned this evil thing against their own ruler.

"I returned to my friends and they had dug for water in the canyon bed, and given drink to the Cacique and bound up his head, but he seemed to know nothing, except to make strange sounds as you have heard him make here. Then I said to my companions, it is a long way to our village, and the Pau-lan'-tee mesa is not a half-day's journey away, but we must bring the Cacique to our people as quickly as we are able.

"I told them of what I had found on the back-trail, and that it was plain that some evil had come to pass in Pau-lan'-tee, that mesa men should wish to destroy their own Cacique. We agreed we must come quickly to Pan'-gua and let no one know of what had come to

THE WOUNDED GUEST

pass, as only the wise men of our Council could judge of the matter.

"After we had rested and eaten, though the Cacique would take no food, we followed the canyon bed, that no eye should see us. After we had walked some time we saw footprints in the sand. They were tracks of Gool, the Witch-killer."

At mention of the name a low exclamation, that might have meant anything, escaped the ruler of Pan'-gua, and Mat'-so sucked in his breath like one who hears bad news.

"You know the tracks were those of the Witch-killer?" asked the Governor.

"His tracks are well known to me," replied the narrator, "though for many days he has not been seen south of the great mesa. His moccasins are sharp, and he pushes out with the toe as he walks."

Mat'-so nodded as though satisfied with the other's judgment, and remarked:

"There is no evil in the matter if the weazel-eyed Witch-killer did not see you while you were with Ah'-mot, the Cacique."

"He could not have seen, "affirmed Tō'-bah-yan confidently. "We stopped when we found his tracks, I climbed the canyon rim, and looked with care far over the land to the four winds, but no man came to my eye. From that place to the walls of our village we saw no man. That is all, umo. My talk is ended."

For a time Ne-chō'-ba looked thoughtfully at the floor, and the silence within the room was broken only by the wounded guest whose intermittent mutterings broke through his restless sleep.

"You have done well," he remarked at last, and he

bid the two hunters take their slumbering companion with them and go to their homes, cautioning them to keep strict silence regarding all that had taken place.

For some time after the men had departed, the aged Cacique and the Governor sat in silence, gazing into the flickering fire with troubled thoughts of the unexpected difficulty that confronted them.

"Mat'-so, this is very bad medicine that has come to pass, and great trouble may grow out of it. It is a matter for prayers to the Shiuana; a matter for our star-gazers, and our wise men to think upon. I am full of years, but I have not seen an evil like this. When day is come, the Council must be called, and nothing said until we are within the circle. Ah'-mot will need the care of a woman who can cook what he may need, and bring it here in secret. Your woman, Ot-si'-pah is that one, for you have taught her the wisdom of a silent tongue. She alone, beside the Council, must know of this matter. Is the wound of Ah'-mot a great one, that he should mumble as a child?"

The Governor, who while the other was speaking had been gazing intently at the face of the injured guest, turned to the Cacique.

"The wound is but small—not made by a heavy blow. There is no other wound. It comes to my thoughts that there is some evil magic that has taken away his mind. The spell—if it be of some witch unknown, to us—may not be easy to heal."

"The coming day may bring to light all you need to know," suggested Ne-chō'-ba reassuringly. "But if the spell be of a strange witch, we may have to take Ti'-ee, the witch doctor, into the matter." Then, after a pause, he continued:

THE WOUNDED GUEST 23

"What think you of this evil that has come upon our Pau-lan'-tee friend?"

The dark face of Mat'-so expressed both anger and disgust as he made reply.

"For you and me there is no mystery in it—but what we do about it may decide between friendship, and the blood of battle. To my mind it comes clear that Dou-gow', the Pau-lan'-tee Governor has done this thing. The three men who secretly gave Ah'-mot into the hands of the Apache dogs are men of Dou-gow''s clan —evil men, like himself, who do his bidding in all things. He has made secret agreement with the Apaches, who are glad to say they will carry off the Cacique, and send him on the Long Sleep, with his fine necklace and rings for their pay. Always has Dou-gow' used secret ways to destroy men he hates, and he hated and feared Ah'-mot, for the Cacique has stood against his evil wishes. None know that better than you, Ne-chō'-ba.

"As for us people of Pan'-gua, do we forget why we left behind us our pleasant homes on the great mesa of Pau-lan'-tee, to come here, like rats in the night, to live in the desert? Was it not because of Dou-gow', and that he hated you, just as he is now angered against the Cacique of his own people?

"The blood of the snake runs in the veins of that evil one, and the blood of his own people is scattered along his trail. He has sprung from black earth, and bad medicine came into the earth with him. He has two thoughts for putting Ah'-mot out of his way. For one he wants the daughter of Ah'-mot for a wife. This the Cacique would never look upon. And the other is that he has the bold hope of being made Cacique himself, as Ah'-mot has no living son.

"Now that he believes the Apaches have sent Ah'-mot on the Long Sleep, he will make great show, before the Pau-lan'-tees, of searching the land for him. He will put sorrow in his evil face, and none will fast more surely than he, when the time of all hope has past. If he can turn the matter against us, in any way, he will do it, but I believe that thought has not yet come to him. No village within three suns' journey of the great mesa will go unsearched, and we must see that Ah'-mot is not found here if they make search of Pan'-gua."

"Not until Ah'-mot has again come to his right mind," interposed the Cacique. "But we must be warned in time, if Dou-gow' comes here, for we have but one place where our guest could be hidden, should they come while he is under the spell."

Mat'-so nodded understandingly.

"Dou-gow' will know that the Pau-lan'-tee people may look with suspicion upon the one who might profit most by the Cacique's disappearance, and he will not make haste to rule with the Cacique's hand. In that we will make profit, for we will have time to learn much that will warn us what to do. Dou-gow' is hated by many of his people, and feared by all."

The Governor ceased speaking, and Ne-chō'-ba nodded his approval of what had been said.

"Your thoughts run in the direction of my own," he replied. "This matter has put us in a trap that is of our own making—though the Shiuana may have willed it. The Chin'-di [evil one] himself leads Dou-gow'. Each year we have said this devil man will soon be

THE WOUNDED GUEST 25

found out by his brothers, and the mesa people will throw him from their village; but each season he has gained new power in their Council. He was shaman, then war captain, and now he is Governor. We must clip his wings before he flies higher. An eagle fights more deadly than the hawk.

"We must keep Ah'-mot here; there is no other way. By ancient pact, and unending friendship, he is our brother. By every way known to us, we will make effort to bring him to living health. Our men should have taken him back to Pau-lan'-tee, and told truth of all they saw and did. To tell them that now would be empty words, for they believed they acted with wisdom. Now it is too late. Ah'-mot could not make so great a journey. To send word to Pau-lan'-tee that he is here, wounded in the head, would put all against us. Our talk of Apaches would sound like a lie, to all but Dou-gow', and he would cry lie the loudest, for none would believe that a Pau-lan'-tee, even one so evil as Dou-gow', would make pact with Apaches. We could accuse no one, as we do not know the three mesa men who betrayed Ah'-mot, though I think I could name them all.

"It would be a hard thing to make the matter clear, even to our good friends among the mesa people. When Ah'-mot is recovered—ah-ēē'—then will the evil one have his head in the trap—his day will come to darkness. If Ah'-mot should go on to the Silent Others, the secret of his coming here must be buried forever in Pan'-gua."

Then into the voice of the aged Cacique came a new note as he continued:

"Now, Mat'-so, we must learn who the three mesa

men are, and we must know if the Pau-lan'-tee people suspect Dou-gow'. This may not be easy to learn, but the way is before us, and it is for us to take it. Now are we in the dark, and our hands are tied—until we know whom to accuse, and who of the Pau-lan'-tee people may be with us."

The two fell silent again, and after a time, as if to lift their thoughts a little above the near tragedy of their predicament, the Cacique remarked:

"Mat'-so, your son Che-loo' is more swift in action than we have thought. I have known him as one who is slow. Is it not said that he is lazy?"

"He is slow, except in the hunt," replied Mat'-so. "In the hunt he works long and with skill."

"He has been counted one who is a sluggard in the village," went on the Cacique bluntly, "but now we find him quick in fighting and without fear. This to me is a new thing."

"To you it is a new thing," replied the Governor, "but I know him to be like two men in one. In the village he is quiet, and dislikes work in the fields—I say to him, 'You are slow and lazy like a fat old squaw.' But when he is on the hunt, or when he is angry, then he is like that," and he snapped his fingers with quick gesture. "He has great strength, and there is no man in Pan'-gua whom he cannot throw to the ground. With ease can he do it."

Ne-chō'-ba made a low sound in his throat that was meant to indicate mild surprise. Then, recalling the matter that confronted them, he said:

"Day is near at hand. Call the men of the Council. Then tell your woman to make food for Ah'-mot. It

THE WOUNDED GUEST 27

may be he will eat when sleep has left him. I wait here."

Alone in the Council-house with the injured guest, the old man arose and, walking to the figure on the pallet, looked long at the face of his wounded friend, who had at last relaxed into a more peaceful sleep. Then, lifting his right hand above his head, and staring before him like one who looks out across a far horizon, he spoke slowly and in a low clear voice:

"Pyat-yama, father of the Sky People, ruler of the Star Brothers, look down upon us earth-born. San-ash'-ty, our Earth Mother, lend us your eyes of wisdom, that the evil may not blind us. From the ancient One-of-all-knowing, there has come to the fathers of our people, in the estufas of old time, an ancient teaching—that kindness done a stranger who comes wandering to our door is a good thing that brings no evil. This one is no stranger—he is friend.

"Bring to us the sacred fire of your understanding, to light the feet of our feeble going; the strong bow of your wisdom for the arrows of our thoughts, as we come to the circle of our Council—to the many words of our smoke-talk. Come to the aid of us feeble earth-born!"

Then, as the broadening dawn glowed more distinctly through the semi-transparent sheets of gypsum that served as the room's only windows, he slowly turned to resume his seat by the dying embers of the fire, his lips moving with the words of an ancient song that he chanted under his breath.

CHAPTER III

A SPIDER ON THE WALL

The evening shadows o'er the mesa lie,
And towering buttes are gilded by the sun.
The last winged shafts of light, like arrows, fly
To hold in check the night till day is done.

IN the mellow light of evening, at the close of the day following the return of the three hunters, Che-loo' made his way out of the village, and leisurely climbed to the top of a small though lofty plateau that stood a short distance away. At the summit he seated himself near its edge and let his gaze wander idly over the wide desert below him.

His manner was preoccupied, and his eyes moved indifferently over the familiar landscape. Few people of Pan'-gua, aside from the two men with whom he always hunted, understood Che-loo', but there was reason for the common misunderstanding. He was a lover of adventure, and his dislike for the inactivity and petty labor of village life gave him the reputation of being lazy and indolent. He reasoned that these duties, so tasteless to him, should fall on those who would not, or could not, bring in the meat and pelts of the hunt.

Then, too, there was in his face a certain charm of expression, faintly feminine, that had often led the unsuspecting to underestimate both the power of his muscular body and the activity of his mind.

It was, doubtless, a wrong appraisal by the Apache warrior that led him to sudden ending at the hands of the young Pan'-guan, and this had saved the life of the captive Cacique, and turned the short battle into an easy victory for the three hunters.

Just now the thoughts of Che-loo' dwelt on a puzzling question, to which he could find no reasonable answer. After being awakened, and escorted from the Council-house by his two companions of the hunt, he had slept like the dead until the sun had passed far into the afternoon. But when he had risen, rested and refreshed, and was standing alone near the entrance of the village estufa, he had, by merest chance, overheard his name spoken by an aged member of the Council. The words of the unseen speaker came sharply to his ears:

"The Council has decided on Che-loo', son of Mat'-so. It is a strange thing to select a youth for so important a matter—but Ne-chō'-ba was set upon it, and he is a judge of men."

Che-loo' had waited to hear no more, but had turned away with a feeling of guilt at having overheard words that were evidently not intended for his ears, an act wholly despicable in the eyes of his people. He had been curious to know what it was that the Council expected of him, and he had gone in search of his father, who would be able to tell him what he wished to know.

Though he had searched his father's cornfields, and the village streets, the Governor could not be found. On his return to his home his mother informed him that his father had gone away on a secret mission, but had left word that he, Che-loo', must go alone to the mesa-top, at sundown, and there wait for him.

This strange instruction merely added to the mystery, as it was not like his father to select a place outside the village for their conversation, though it might be of strictest secrecy. Che-loo' was of an independent type of mind that did not hold in profound respect all the thoughts and actions of the older men of the tribe. Having spent most of his life in the hunt, he had given less heed than most of the young men of the village to the solemn teachings and example of the elders.

While obedient to all commands given him, he held to his own way of thinking, and secretly chafed under many of the fears and superstitions that held most of the older men in bondage. Fear, in any form, he despised.

Throughout the remainder of the afternoon he had pondered continually the words of the man in the estufa. What could it be that the Council had appointed him to do? The uncertainty was a new experience, and it irritated him. He well knew that, according to tribal custom, the Cacique had appointed some one member, doubtless his father, to tell him of the matter, and that he must wait patiently until that one volunteered the information.

Never before had the Council taken any notice of him. Its dealings had always been with older men, especially when choosing any one man to perform a special task, and this, the unseen speaker had said, was an important one. A hundred conjectures had thronged his mind, all more or less connected with the mystery surrounding the wounded Cacique of Paulan'-tee, but he suspected they were far from the mark.

Within his usually calm and careless mind there was turmoil, unquieted by the heavy silence about him. Before him, in the fading light, lay a vast wilderness of parched, wind-swept plains, scarred here and there by deep barrancas and outcroppings of rugged rock. Far away to his right, the blue horizon-line of long, flat-topped buttes cut sharply the edge of the darkening world from the bright gold and fading rose of the western sky.

Some distance out from the foot of the mesa a small pool of living water—a rare sight in so barren a region—lay like a bit of golden sky mid the tawny sands of the desert. Fed by seeping waters from the higher ground immediately to the north, the seepings that nourished the pool seemed to pour into it just enough water to take care of the rapid evaporation and the needs of the little village of Pan'-gua that squatted on its southern brink.

Beyond the town stretched the cornfields that appeared from the mesa-top like tiny square patches of green sewed to the rough soil-garment of the Earth Mother.

The village was of pueblo type, housing a tribe of four or five hundred souls, and now, in the light of day, it had the appearance of having stopped, in some romping journey across the desert, to drink from the pool, and that it intended to move on as soon as its thirst was slakened.

The houses, erected terrace-fashioned about a large square court, or plaza, had been hastily built. On most of the roofs, where the usual chimneys of clay and pottery should have stood, crudely lined smoke-holes served as a temporary necessity. Logs that had been notched at regular intervals, served in lieu of ladders that would require more time to construct. These leaned against such houses as boasted a second story, and served as a means of ascent for those who dwelt in the upper chambers.

A large circular estufa, or ceremonial chamber, rose at the far end of the plaza. This windowless, lozenge-shaped structure had its entrance through the roof, and access to it was had by means of a flight of stone steps that led up from the ground.

In spite of the appearance of careless and temporary construction of the houses, the weathered logs, and projecting ceiling-beams, the deeply worn pathways, and the size of the large mound of ash and refuse beside the village, told plainly enough that it had occupied the site for several years. Only one of the buildings seemed to have been erected with any thought of permanence and that was the large square structure at the northern end of the village that served as a semi-secret Council-house, and now sheltered the wounded guest.

Che-loo' wondered if the great Cacique of the mesa was recovering, and what would happen if he did recover. Surely there would be strange trouble as well as great rejoicing in Pau-lan'-tee. He could not fathom just why any of the mesa men would want to destroy their ruler, especially one who had always been loved and respected by his people.

Some movement in the village now caught his eye and he looked down expectantly. Two men, small in

A SPIDER ON THE WALL 33

the distance, emerged from one of the narrow passages between the houses, and made their way toward him. He watched them with keen interest. One he easily recognized as his father, but the other, a much older man, walked with head bent forward and he could not see his face. As they neared his lookout Che-loo' rose to his full height, that they might easily see him silhouetted against the sky. The two men saw the movement and looked up.

Surprise came over the face of the youth, for he now saw that his father's companion was Ne-chō'-ba, the Cacique. The aged ruler never left the village, except on very important occasions, and surely this was no occasion that could demand his presence.

Though he climbed slowly, that he might not hasten his companion, the Governor reached the top some moments ahead of the older man, and spoke a familiar word of greeting to his son, who came forward to meet him.

"Ra-ua'. You came alone, Che-loo'?"

"Yes," replied Che-loo', "as you commanded."

He wanted to ask his father why the Cacique had come, but he knew better than to display curiosity. The aged Ne-chō'-ba now came up, nodded in a friendly way to Che-loo', and though breathing hard against the exertion of the climb, he spoke to the Governor.

"This is no Council-house for me, Mat'-so. The way is too steep."

"Yes, old chin-dogs hunt in the valleys where the way is easy for stiff legs, and leave the good hunting of the hills to young whelps who can climb with strength," replied Mat'-so banteringly.

"I had not thought to call you a whelp, but since the words come from your own mouth—so be it," countered the Cacique quickly.

Whereupon both men laughed, Che-loo' grinned respectfully, and all three seated themselves on the ground.

Meanwhile, unseen by the others, a fourth visitor, who had been secretly watching the two older men, had arrived at the foot of the plateau on the side opposite the one up which the others had climbed. Here he prepared to ascend the almost perpendicular wall, for on that side there was neither trail nor sloping approach.

His furtive glances, as he looked carefully about him, and the extreme caution displayed in his movements, told that he was not expected by those seated in supposed seclusion on the mesa-top. His appearance was repulsive in the extreme. His misshapen body, that of a tall man had he stood erect, was bent forward at the waist as though bowed by the heavy load of a large hump that rose between his broad shoulders.

His long black hair, matted with grease and dirt, dropped in heavy shreds over his large sullen face like bars over a prison window. Two sharp yellow teeth, protruding slightly on either side of his mouth, pressed downward over the lower lip like the fangs of a wolf. His eyes, large and black, looked out from a mind that seemed capable of craft and cunning. Over his distorted body a great buffalo-hide hung like a ragged mantle, its uneven edges flapping about the middle length of bare arms and legs.

In his right hand he carried a stout cottonwood staff

that he used as an effective aid to his ambling gait, and doubtless as an equally effective weapon when the need arose, though it was well known that in a girdle, beneath the mantle, was carried a more formidable means of defense—a long obsidian knife of keen edge with handle of curiously carved bone.

Such was the appearance of the creature known to most of the tribes of the region as Gool, the Witch-killer. There were, in the land, many witch-doctors and shamans, but above them all this creature had been set apart both by reputation and title. He was believed by many to possess powers little less than those of the gods, and it may be there were a few who would have liked to send him on the Long Sleep had they dared. About him many fearful legends had been spun. Some of these might have been true, and some were too grotesque for any but the most gullible to believe.

That he was familiar with the haunts and devious ways of ghosts and witches, and that he knew the charms and spells that could put most of them to route, was believed by all.

Such was his reputation, and such the superstitious fear in which he was held, that no village in the region, either desert or pueblo, denied him admission, and the doors of few Council-houses were barred against him.

Yet with all the tales that were told of the Witch-killer, and despite the dire suspicions held by the people, no death or special act of violence could be directly charged against him. There were, it is true, many accounts of strange occurrences in which he might have had a hand. There was the unnatural death of the dread Cush'-di, a vile and murderous chief of the Apaches, whose great body was found at the foot of a cliff without visible wound or bruise, his killing-knife in its sheath, his war-club in his closed fist. When account of it was noised abroad, all of the wise ones nodded their heads and whispered, "Strangled by the Witch-killer."

Then there was Pan-yōh'-ga, the brown-head, an evil man and self-imposed ruler of the little pueblo of Zun-ovi. He wanted many wives, against the law of all pueblo land, and it was said he cast a spell on all women who refused to marry him, and some had mysteriously disappeared. In the light of a cold dawn, Pan-yōh'-ga was found hanging by his reddish brown hair to the top of the kiva ladder, with strange witch marks on his throat, his long knife resting harmlessly in his belt.

Tales of many such happenings were spread by traders from village to village, and from camp to camp, and the people, ever suspicious, found it convenient to lay them all at the door of the powerful hunchback. Many of these disturbing things could not well be charged to one man, be he witch or Chin-di, but wherever old squaws were gathered together to clack their tongues over their pottery-making, or old men smoked idly in the village estufas, the name of Gool was often whispered in the recounting of these fearful doings.

When prayers were made at the shrines, to the Shiuana who protect the earth-born from the Chin-di, the timid ones often placed an extra prayer-stick before the altar as a secret protection against the Witch-killer.

A SPIDER ON THE WALL

And now, as he cautiously made his way up the precipitous side of the mesa, his powerful arms reaching out to grasp a projecting crag, or secure the aid of stout root or branch, and his long muscular legs bracing him above some precarious footing, he had the appearance of a huge brown spider crawling up a wall.

On the mesa-top, all unmindful of the hunchback, Mat'-so and Che-loo' waited for Ne-chō'-ba to speak. As if more from habit than necessity, the old man lifted the blanket that had been twisted about his waist, and drew it over his shoulders, though no chill had yet come with the evening air.

For a time the aged ruler looked thoughtfully out over the desert, grown dull under the fading light, and Che-loo' studied his seamed and placid face while he waited with suppressed impatience. He knew that from the Cacique would come the reason for this very unusual meeting, and perhaps the answer to his long query as to what the Council had appointed him to do.

Abruptly the old man spoke.

"Che-loo', the fight against the three Apaches was good fighting. You fought as a warrior should fight —with skill and without fear."

The unexpected compliment brought a look of pleased embarrassment to the face of the young Pan'-gua. It was the first time the Cacique had addressed him by his given name. Always, before, he had called him Mat'-so be-gey—son of Mat'-so. For the aged ruler to use the given name of a young man, when addressing him, was a distinct mark of honor, an open admission of manhood. Afterward, a youth thus recognized was considered a man. As Ne-chō'-ba paused, Che-loo' felt there was need of reply.

"It was a fair fight. There were three Apaches against three of us," he affirmed.

The Cacique made a deprecatory gesture with his hand.

"You fought with older and more experienced companions, and your enemies were desert men who fight for the love of killing, and they fight with great skill. It has been said that you are slow—and lazy. Now we find that you can be very quick when there is need, for Tŏ'-bah-yan tells us it was you who saved the life of the Cacique of Pau-lan'-tee."

As he said this he looked down toward the village, and added reflectively, "We hope that his life is saved to him, though he still talks like a child and there is less strength in him." He paused and then turned back to Che-loo'. "The gods have marked you with great favor that you should have been the one to do this deed. Of old a pact was made between the ancient ones of Pau-lan'-tee, and the fathers of our people, that they should fight as brothers, and share all dangers against a common enemy. As the ancient ones of old time look down upon us from the land of the Silent Others, they know that we keep the pact.

"It is thus they have marked you to do greater things. We expect much of one who is young and without fear; one in whom the Shiuana have hidden swiftness and skill. No longer do we expect him to wander about the village in idleness, or do no greater thing than make traps and hunt. There is a thing that is often a stranger to youth, a thing of which you will soon have great need." The old man paused that the words to follow might have greater emphasis. "It is wisdom—a gift of the Shiuana—that teaches men to think quickly, say little, and to know when to give battle and when not to fight. With the coming of day Mat'-so and I sent a runner to the Black Canyon to learn if any men of Pau-lan'-tee had found the tracks made by you and your companions.

"If the runner has found fresh tracks that follow yours, he will make two signal fires on the first mesa above the canyon, as soon as the light of day is gone," and the old man pointed a lean finger toward a low black line far out in the desert. "If no fresh tracks are found, he will cover those made by you and your friends, and will build one fire. We will be warned, if there is danger and know what to expect.

"If footprints made by you and your companions are found beside those of the Cacique of Pau-lan'-tee, whom the mesa men could easily track, word would go quickly to Dou-gow', the Governor, that Ah'-mot had been taken away by men of Pan'-gua. That," he remarked slowly, "would mean great trouble."

In the fading light the three men fell silent, Che-loo' to ponder the rather solemn and disturbing words of the Cacique, and the others to fix their gaze expectantly on the distant mesa that grew more and more obscure as darkness fell.

A few paces from where they sat, a head was slowly lifted above the abrupt edge of the mesa, and a face peered through the open branches of a sage-bush. The Witch-killer had at last reached the top and had worked his way to a point where he could both see and hear. He seemed content, for the moment, to do no greater evil than give eyes and ears to the three men seated before him. Beneath the matted hair his eyes gleamed with satisfaction, and a twist of his wide mouth, that might have been a smile on any other face, lifted his upper lip to disclose more of the yellow fangs.

CHAPTER IV

AN UNWELCOME TASK

When shadows are dancing, the Chin-di dance,
In the gloom of night, on the kiva wall,
And pallid smoke of the sacred fire
Crawls up the air, like a serpent spire,
Beware of the spell of the Poy'-yō's call!
There's ill in the Poy'-yō's call.

AFTER a long moment of waiting, the silence that had fallen on the three Pan'-gua men, seated before him, baffled the hunchbacked spy. He had not arrived at the top of the mesa wall in time to learn what Che-loo' and his two companions were so quietly waiting for; but the Witch-killer had patience.

A cricket chirped drowsily from beneath a sage, and far out on the plain a li-olki trilled the plaintive notes of its twilight song. Above Pan'-gua a flattened veil of blue smoke lay suspended in the motionless air, and the barking of the village dogs sounded remote, like faint, detached echos.

Before the eyes of the three watchers a tiny fire, twinkling like a red star, appeared on the far mesa, and grew into a steady point of light. Several moments passed, but no second light appeared beside it. At last the one blaze was extinguished, and only a dull remnant of the afterglow remained to illumine the plain.

AN UNWELCOME TASK

Ne-chō'-ba made a low sound in his throat, very expressive of relief and satisfaction.

"Ah-ā!" he exclaimed. "Early this day Kiz'-di, the star-gazer, found two wing-feathers of telo the hawk on the estufa roof. A good omen comes from telo the hawk. The Shiuana are yet with us," he went on with uplifted voice. "Their ears have been open to our prayers. Even though Ah'-mot sleeps much and is weak, he still lives. Great danger has been close to us, and may yet be near, but an arrow may clip the hair and not spoil the head. All is well for the day—and it yet may come about that the Cacique of Pau-lan'-tee will set the three dogs of his people into their own trap. Mat'-so, I will return to the village before darkness covers this path you call a trail, for I am neither owl nor cat."

As Ne-chō'-ba arose to his feet the sullen face of the Witch-killer dropped silently down over the edge of the wall. Che-loo' also arose to go, but at a signal from his father he resumed his seat.

The aged Cacique slowly made his way alone down the trail, and the sound of his cautious steps had not yet become inaudible when a noise, as if made by a piece of falling earth, came sharply from the cliff on the opposite side of the mesa.

Mat'-so jumped to his feet and, stepping to the point from whence he believed the sound had come, peered searchingly into the darkness. Not far below him a great figure silently flattened itself against the mesa wall and became an obscure part of its shadow.

"A squirrel or mountain rat," called Che-loo'.

"It may be," replied his father as he resumed his seat, but he seemed unconvinced.

The Witch-killer, satisfied with what he had overheard, and realizing the noise he had accidentally made had aroused suspicion, cautiously moved downward into the protecting darkness that now veiled the foot of the cliff. He had heard little, but that little was of great importance, and he knew he could make good use of it. He thought of the noise of the falling bit of earth. That was bad, and, if sufficiently suspicious, the Pan'-gua men might search for tracks on the morrow at the foot of the mesa. He believed he knew of a way to prevent such search.

"So!—Ah'-mot still lives, though he sleeps much and is weak," he mumbled under his breath. "The news is worth the climb, though it near cost me my neck."

The repulsive face became thoughtful, and he stood for some moments contemplating the words of Ne-chō'-ba. Then he grunted sarcastically. The words of Ne-chō'-ba are empty words. So—he thinks Ah'-mot will set the three dogs of his people into their own trap," he continued, quoting the words of the old Cacique. "None but I could tell him what spell was used to send Ah'-mot on to the Silent Others—none but I and the Chin-di Dou-gow'."

Then carefully cupping his hands, he placed them to his mouth, and in a falsetto voice he made a succession of low yet penetrating sounds, weird and unearthly, but seemed to compose themselves into a connected strain, half song, half cry. It lasted but a moment, and ended in a long-drawn note that gradually faded into silence.

"They may look for tracks when they hear

AN UNWELCOME TASK

suspicious sounds—but they will not go where the Poy'-yō calls."

Thus whispering to himself, he recovered his cottonwood staff, and with incredible swiftness, moved away into the desert.

For some moments after he had resumed his seat, Mat'-so remained silent, and sat intently listening. Then hearing faintly the distant footfalls of Ne-chō'-ba, and being assured that he had reached the plain in safety, he turned to his son.

"Che-loo', the Council has chosen you as one to do an important thing. It is like the turn of an arrow that may bring life or death, fighting or peace. While Ah'-mot, the Pau-lan'-tee Cacique is with us, we are near to great trouble. He should be with his own people on the great mesa, but before we can let them know that he is with us—we must—"

The weired cry made by the Witch-killer rose in the still air, sharp and tremulous, cutting across the low speech of the Governor like a thin blade of sound.

"Poy'-yō witch!" whispered Mat'-so hoarsely. "It comes from the foot of the cliff, down there. An evil omen—and comes at an evil time." And Che-loo' saw the dim bulk of his father turn in the darkness and point with extended arm.

He knew well the fear that must be written on his father's face, and was glad that darkness hid it. Although he had never expressed it in words, Che-loo' had always felt within him a strange disgust for the fears that most of his people had for witches, yet he knew that the older men believed they had sufficient cause to fear the dread Poy'-yō that had, according to their account, brought on the great thirst and illness that had swept the land at the time of his birth. He could not bring himself to the belief that anything but man, and the great Ah'-hool, god of all, had power for good or evil.

Many times had he gone, in secret, to places where he was told witches dwelt, and had found nothing. Such places had a strange fascination for him; they tried his bravery, and this he was always putting to the test.

And now, as they sat in darkness on the mesa-top, he felt shame for his father, who was ever fearless in all other matters, and wondered that he should believe that the strange sound had been made by anything but the voice of a man, a man shrewd in the knowledge of ghostly sounds.

It seemed a time to let his father know that he did not share his fears.

"That was not a witch, that made that sound. Witches don't make sounds—or do anything," he explained rather lamely, for it wasn't just what he had intended to say.

"Then you are more of an empty-head than I had thought," replied the Governor, whose fear put an edge of anger in his voice. "Are you, then, wiser than old men? Wiser than our shamans, and star-gazers that you know so much? You are young and know little. You know nothing of the great evil the Poy'-yō witch has done all village people. Unless sacred meal, and hair of the puma, are burned on the firestone, before the coming of dawn, great evil will come upon us all." His words, spoken with solemn emphasis, left no doubt of his beliefs and fears.

The Governor made as though to rise to his feet.

AN UNWELCOME TASK 45

"We can go on with our talk—unless you fear to stay here," suggested Che-loo' quietly.

If the older man had had any thought of returning immediately to the village, his son's reference to fear made that impossible now, for he knew he could not appear less brave than his own child. He dropped the subject of witches, and picked up his former conversation where it had been interrupted, though a marked uneasiness betrayed itself in his voice.

"You know that the Cacique of Pau-lan'-tee was given into the hands of the Apaches by three men of his own people?"

"Yes, Tō'-bah-yan told us about the tracks," replied Che-loo'.

"Our Council must know who the three men of Pau-lan'-tee are—must learn what the people of Pau-lan'-tee think of the matter—must know if they suspect Dou-gow', their Governor. These three things are for you to learn. Our Council believes we may need to take the whole matter before the Pau-lan'-tee people, if Ah'-mot does not soon regain his right mind. To do this, we must know what men to accuse of this great evil—accuse them openly that they may be tried before the Pau-lan'-tee Council.

"We of Pan'-gua cannot have our enemy, Dou-gow,' made Cacique of the mesa people. This he may become—if we cannot set this evil matter straight. My son, keep in your thoughts what I am about to tell you, for they are heavy words." The Governor dropped his voice impressively. "Dou-gow' is an evil man; more evil than any you have known. He is wise and cunning, and has the heart of the Chin'-di. We know that it is Dou-gow' who has tried to destroy Ah'-

mot, his Cacique, for he hates and fears him. It is known to you that, for many generations, we of Pan'-gua lived on the Pau-lan'-tee mesa near the great village.

"We were happy, we liked the Pau-lan'-tee people, they were as brothers to us—though they were great in number and we were small. We spoke the same tongue, their men took our women, and we took Pau-lan'-tee women for wives, though the clans were separate.

"Now the snows of nineteen winters have fallen since we came here to live by the pool in the desert. For many summers we have said we will go back to the mesa to live, but Dou-gow' has always been against our return, and it was Dou-gow''s evil work that forced us from the great mesa. Always he has hated Ne-chō'-ba, as he has hated his own Cacique.

"The clan of this evil one is the Badger clan, the largest among the Pau-lan'-tee people, and he is the head of it. It is from this clan he has his power. Of the Pau-lan'-tee Council half are of the Badger clan, and they dare not stand against Dou-gow', for they fear his word among his people. He has a tongue for loud and solemn talk—that makes lies sound true. More of that I need not tell now."

Mat'-so paused; and taking advantage of this, Che-loo', who had sat in astonished silence, asked:

"Why am I chosen as the one to do this thing?"

If his son's voice held a note of complaint, the Governor chose to ignore it.

"Ne-chō'-ba has said you are the one to go, and the Council has agreed with him. Ne-chō'-ba has given reasons, and they sound good. He has told the

AN UNWELCOME TASK

Council that an older man would cause suspicion just now. Dou-gow', and the guilty ones who help him, will be suspicious of all, until the matter is quiet. You act lazy, look young and harmless—in that, your weakness is your strength. We know you have quickness in action, and are strong when there is need. The Shiuana have used you to save the life of Ah'-mot—in this they point to you to do a greater thing.

"You will go to the mesa as a trader. We will give you fine buckskins, and sky-stones of good blue, to trade for Pau-lan'-tee weaving. If you have care of your actions, and remember you are no more than a trader, the people of the mesa will give small heed to what you say or do, for their thoughts are on their Cacique, and some will talk much.

"Open your ears to all talk, for by it you will learn much."

Che-loo' suddenly found that he had no interest in this spying mission, and no desire to undertake it. If there were adventure in it, a chance to shoot, hunt something, or use his muscles in a contest of strength or skill, he might enjoy it; but to go on an old man's errand, to talk and listen and bring home gossip, like some long-tongued squaw of the village—his heart sank within him at the thought.

He well knew he must keep all this to himself, but he decided to make further protest.

"This kind of work is not to my liking," he ventured; but the complaint was made in so low a voice his father either did not hear it, or chose not to give it attention.

"But there is a hole in the moccasin—as we say," continued the Governor, "for you have a weakness.

You may believe it is strength, but it is a weakness, that may bring you great trouble, and might bring your trip to Pau-lan'-tee to bad ending." He paused.

"My ears are open," said Che-loo' respectfully.

"You fear nothing," continued his father, "and to be without fear is not always to be brave. The brave use wisdom. There is a time when it is better to seem fearful than to fight. At such times he who is only fearless, may fight like the fool, and in the end, lose all. The head is the weapon that decides the fight.

"You have another fault. It is a small one, but in Pau-lan'-tee it might make big trouble for you. It is a little trick you do with the voice. It is like bad magic, for you make a noise in your throat that sounds like the voice of another speaking at a distance."

Che-loo' was glad the darkness hid his face, for he felt embarrassed and did not care to have his father know it.

"It is but for fun I do that trick," he replied. "I have found no harm in it—only children have fear of it."

"Leave this magic in Pan'-gua. It will do no good in Pau-lan'-tee," commanded his father. "It is a little thing to you, but it is a strange thing for strange ears, and is more like an evil of the Chin'-di than of man. It is like the voice of a witch. Even though you go to the great mesa as the son of the tapop of Pan'-gua, it would not save you if the Pau-lan'-tee people thought you were a witch, and they might see that the strange sounds were made by you.

"Among the mesa people, when one is tried and found to be a witch, he is sent on the Long Sleep, if he be of the tribe. If he be of another village he is

AN UNWELCOME TASK 49

stripped of all clothing, bound and beaten, and sent back to his own people, a thing of shame without food or weapon. My eyes have seen this thing. You say you believe witches have no power. In that you talk child's talk—but remember that no people know more of ghosts and witches than the people of Pau-lan'-tee.

"When you are there, do nothing that can bring anger to Dou-gow', and if you learn he suspects you, return quickly to Pan'-gua; he is an evil one to cross, and you would gain nothing if he sets his mind against you. Openly he would do nothing, for he knows that most of his people are friendly to us; but you have seen he has secret ways of dealing with those whom he would put out of his way. I have told all you need to hear."

"When am I to do this thing?" inquired Che-loo'.

"This night all will be made ready for you. With the coming of tomorrow's sun, you will go."

Mat'-so rose, and the two walked down the trail in the dim starlight. Che-loo' felt strangely uneasy. He greatly disliked the task that lay before him, yet he well knew he would undertake it, and do the best he could to carry out the orders given him. No village man ever thought of disobeying the Council.

Perhaps he could hunt on the way to the great mesa, as it was almost a two days' journey—but there was the trader's pack, he had forgotten that, and traders' packs were heavy. The pack would be to his back what the task was to his heart, a great burden. No, he would have no chance to hunt, though he would have his good bow and arrows.

For a time the father and son were silent, each occupied with his own thoughts and the steep uneven trail. As they neared the village the Governor spoke:

"Ne-chō'-ba has said he will have words with you tonight, in the estufa. We go there after we have eaten."

Later in the evening, as they crossed the plaza on their way to the estufa, the faint sifting sound of a medicine rattle, and the low guttural chant of Ti'-ee, the witch-doctor, came from the closed and darkened Council-house. Every effort to destroy the evil spell that held the mind of the wounded Cacique in its mysterious grasp, was being made, but evidently without effect.

High on the flat roof of his dwelling, Kiz'-di, the star-gazer, sat motionless, with face lifted toward the heavens, silently seeking such aid as the great Shiuana might impart through the signs of the Star Brothers.

The rising moon sent a diagonal flood of white light across the broad plaza, cutting, in sharp silhouette, the long black shadows cast by the eastern wall of houses. Straight lines of silvery smoke from the evening fires arose in the still air above the roofs, like pale quaking spectors against the dark western sky.

A group of boys stood within the shadow of the estufa talking and laughing. The Governor ordered them away gruffly, saying they had better be in their homes where they belonged. Che-loo' believed the gruff attitude of the usually kind Governor was in some manner due to the faint disturbing sound of Ti'-ee's rattle and incessant chant.

The shrill voice of a termagant squaw called out into the darkness from a fire-lit doorway far down the

AN UNWELCOME TASK

village, and some thieving dog, that had evidently run counter to a well-aimed missile, yelped loudly, and held to a running repetition of lesser yelps that rapidly grew faint in the distance.

The high peevish cry of a sleepy baby retained, for a moment, its place among the varying sounds, and the answering croon of a cradle-song came faintly from the soft voice of a weary mother.

These sounds were all familiar enough, though to-night they came to the ears of Che-loo' as parts of a vague restlessness with which the whole village seemed burdened: a disquieted state that might portend some grave occurrence.

Though outwardly calm and indifferent, an attitude he well knew how to assume, he was moved by strange emotions, unfamiliar and disturbing. It could not be fear, he told himself, for though he had seen fear in others, he was sure it had never taken hold of him.

But just now, as he was about to enter the estufa to receive final instructions from the Cacique, he was suddenly possessed of a desire to run away into the night, and lose himself far out in the great desert he loved.

His father did not enter the estufa with him, but remained at the foot of the flight of stone steps that led to the entrance, and Che-loo' knew that he would stay to guard the passage that no one might interrupt the meeting within.

He found Ne-chō'-ba alone, seated over a little fire that blazed and crackled in the fire-pit. As he entered, the Cacique lifted his white head and motioned his caller to be seated opposite. For some time he looked steadily into the face of the youth before him, though it seemed to be with unseeing eyes. From the expression on the old man's face, Che-loo' was aware that his thoughts were far away from the things immediately about him. Suddenly, as if recovering himself, Ne-chō'-ba poked the fire into a brighter blaze, and spoke.

"You go to Pau-lan'-tee with the coming of day. While there you will stay at the house of one called Cha'-za."

Che-loo' was amazed by this instruction, and wondered if he had heard aright. As the old man paused he asked:

"Not the one they call Cha'-za, the Fool?"

"The same," came the reply. "He is called Cha'-za, the Fool—but it may not be a right name. Cha'-za is a friend to me and to Pan'-gua. He has two houses, one above the other. Many traders who visit Pau-lan'-tee stay in the upper house. If Cha'-za acts the fool, treat him as the fool. If, when you are alone with him, he acts the wise one, treat him as one who is wise. Cha'-za is full of years and his own ways—seek not to change him. It is not a time to send you to the house of one who stands too high in Pau-lan'-tee. A low mark does not catch the eye of the marksman."

Ne-chō'-ba fell silent for a moment, and looked searchingly into the face of Che-loo'. When he spoke it seemed to be with some hesitation.

"I must trust you with a secret; a secret known only to few men." Taking a charred stick from the edge of the fire, he made a small black circle on the estufa floor. Within the circle he made a straight line and a shorter line beside it. "That," he said, pointing to the longer of the two lines, "is Pau-lan'-tee. The short line is Pan'-gua as it stood beside the great vil-

AN UNWELCOME TASK 53

lage on the mesa. The circle is endless friendship between the two villages, a protection against a common enemy. None but the oldest members of the two Councils know of the sign, or what it means, for it is the mark of an ancient pact."

Ne-chō-ba rubbed the sign from the floor with the soft sole of his moccasin, and handed the charred ember to the Che-loo' commanding him to make one like it. When this had been done to his satisfaction, and the last sign erased from the floor, the old man continued.

"When you are alone with Cha'-za, and are sure that no eyes but his can see, make for him this sign. He will quickly ask what it means. Tell him what I have told you, and say that Ne-chō-ba gave the sign to you. Cha'-za was, one time, a member of the old Council. From the time you show him the sign he will do much for you, and will tell you who, among Pau-lan'-tee men, are friends and who are enemies. Tell him nothing of Ah'-mot, or that you know anything about him. Can you hold this secret, my son?"

"I shall keep it," replied Che-loo' simply.

Ne-chō'-ba arose and Che-loo' knew their brief talk had come to an end.

"Mat'-so has told you what you are to learn for us. May the great Ah'-hool guide you, and the Shiuana be with you." With this parting valediction the old man waved his hand toward the entrance, and Che-loo' stepped out into the night.

There was one little matter of his own that he would attend to before sleep came to his eyes, and he was glad to have the bright moonlight to aid him. While his father made ready his trader's pack, and burned sacred meal and puma-hair on the hearthstone, Che-loo' would visit the foot of the mesa wall, and look for the tracks of the Poy'-yō witch. He felt sure he would find footprints made by pointed moccasins whose owner pushed out with his toes when he walked.

CHAPTER V

THE WITCH-KILLER

A tuft of hair from a puma-hide;
The wings of an owl, some blackened corn;
A panther's claw to a feather tied,
Are Chin-di things—of Witches born.

SOME little time before the three hunters, Che-loo', Tō'-bah-yan, and Lō-mah' discovered the foot-prints of Gool on the sandy floor of Black Canyon, the Witch-killer had secretly, though closely, watched them as they led the half-conscious Cacique of Pau-lan'-tee toward Pan'-gua. From a hidden spot on the canyon's rim he had taken careful note of the appearance of the wounded men, and particularly of the condition of the ruler of Pau-lan'-tee.

As he peered into the canyon, the hunchbacked shaman rapidly drew his own conclusions as to what had probably taken place, and by the time Tō'-bah-yan climbed to the rim of the gorge and scanned the surrounding country he was far away, taking long and hasty strides toward that part of the canyon the wounded men had left behind them.

He took care to keep a short distance from the rim, and to travel over rock ledges and hard ground where his moccasins would leave no trail. He was in evident haste and moved with fixed purpose. His tracks that had been discovered in the canyon-bed by the three hunters, had been made before he had sighted the wounded men, and the matter could not be undone. He was aware his footprints would be found by them, but he would now see to it that no others were left to tell of his movements.

He kept his eyes fixed on the ground, only raising them from time to time to make sure he was not being watched. The cottonwood staff was carried under his arm, for fear that its prodding would leave a telltale mark along the way.

After walking some distance he suddenly stopped and bent low to study several footprints that appeared at his feet. Then with great caution he moved backward, covering even the slightest mark of his own feet that he might leave no imprint among the tracks on the ground. Farther on he came to other tracks, and gave considerable time to the examination of each print, now kneeling that he might make more careful calculations, now looking away across the country as if to gage directions by some distant landmark.

He looked long at one particular mark in the sand, then mumbled half aloud:

"Ma-te'-lo, the cripple,—and the others? Ay,—any child of the mesa might guess. Dou-gow"s work was near undone. He leaves Ah'-mot to the Apaches—the Apaches go on the Long Sleep, and Ah'-mot goes to Pan'-gua."

Then he arose suddenly, as though some new thought had lifted him to startled attention, and his eyes narrowed. "Ah—ah! It may be, it may be!" he muttered, as he rapidly made his way into the open desert and turned his face southward.

The high wind of the early morning had died away,

THE WITCH-KILLER

and the sun hung in the middle of the afternoon sky. Its rays beat down from a clear heaven and the hot sands of the plain sent back its dancing shimmer of heat. In the quivering atmosphere distant mesas seemed to shake themselves free from the earth for a space, to remain suspended in the air like a mirage. Far out in the plain a vertical column of sand-whirl slowly drifted, like a gray ghost, across the desert, to be suddenly dispersed by a counter current of air.

All unmindful of the pounding heat of the sand and sun, the Witch-killer kept an even gait and steady course throughout the long decline of the day. The sun had just dropped below the western buttes when he reached the top of a low, bush-covered hill, and entered a camp of rude huts.

It was the largest of three camps that sheltered the Che'-pahs, a small desert tribe, and had the distinction of including among its half-hundred dwellings the large square hogan of its tribal chief. This man, Sho'-ya by name, had the reputation of being both uncommonly wise and brave. Though small of stature and mild of voice, he had, on more than one occasion, proved to be a cunning and disastrous foe to both the Apache and Navajo, and thus a valued ally of both the Pau-lan'-tees and Pan'-guas, who shared his fear and hatred of the two marauding tribes of the north.

Sho'-ya took great pleasure in being chief of his people, but deep in his heart lay another ambition. He had been a small shaman, or medicine-man, before he had been made chief, and his secret dream was that he might one day be known far and wide as a great witch-doctor.

There was but one man he both admired and heartily

envied, and that man was Gool, the Witch-killer. No one was more welcome to his hogan, and in his desire to gain such crumbs of the art of curative magic as the great shaman might give him, he was willing to give in return almost anything he possessed.

He was known among his own people as a man of few words, but in the presence of the hunchback he was talkative, and had gradually become aware that the Witch-killer looked to him for much of his news of the surrounding country. With friendship among most of the pueblo tribes, and three camps that were usually on the move, the Che'-pah chief was a most fruitful source of information.

In his desire to please this great shaman, all else became secondary. Gool was a familiar figure among the Che'-pahs, and as he made his way to the hogan of the chief no particular attention was paid him.

As he entered the dwelling of Sho'-ya, the latter was about to seat himself beside a large steaming pot that contained the evening meal. Opposite the pot the wife of the chief, a short fat woman of flat greasy face and shining smile, was busy with a shallow basket of thin maize-cakes that she was about to place on the ground beside the stew.

Both looked up as the Witch-killer entered and the eyes of Sho'-ya lighted with pleasure as he recognized the bent figure of the great shaman.

"Ha-la'-ni, umo! [How goes it, aged one?]" he called out in his mild voice. "You smelled the pot afar off, and come to it as it leaves the fire. A good omen for me and a good meal for you."

The hunchback, with what was obviously intended for a smile, nodded to his host and then to the fat wife, who, becoming suddenly embarrassed, all but slid the corn-cakes from the woven plaque. The Witch-killer placed his staff against the wall and squatted on his heels beside the chief, while the robust squaw disappeared behind a curtain of hides that partitioned a corner of the hut from the remainder of the room. She emerged presently, her round face a little less greasy, and she brought forth another flat basket containing dried berries and pinyon-nuts, a special treat in honor of the distinguished guest.

The business of eating left no place for words. No verbal compliments were paid either cook or cooking, but the more certain compliment shown in the noisy consumption of food seemed to please the smiling hostess. The process of eating was simple and effective. A flat maize-cake was lifted in the hand, deftly rolled into a thick tube, and dipped into the pot. The thick gravy, and often bits of juicy meat, were thus lifted from the stew and noisily masticated.

Not until the meal had ended did the Witch-killer drink, though the long journey in the heat of the day must have given him a great thirst. Now he drank copiously from an olla offered by his hostess, and with a brief "hoa," moved to the side of the hut, where he seated himself on a panther-pelt and leaned his crooked back against the wall. Sho'-ya followed and seated himself where he could face his guest.

"The light of seven suns has passed since I was here," remarked the Witch-killer. "You were going to the great mesa to have words with Dou-gow'."

"Yes," replied the Che'-pah. "I went to the mesa two suns following the one you were here."

He paused, secretly hoping to turn the conversation

to a subject more interesting to himself, yet not daring to attempt it until he had learned the real cause of the great shaman's visit.

"The Cacique of Pau-lan'-tee should give great feast to the chief of the Che'-pahs who have so long time been his friends," remarked the hunchback.

"I did not see Ah'-mot," replied Sho'-yah. "My words were with Dou-gow', the tapop, and Klee'-tso, the war-captain."

"It is a strange thing you visit Dou-gow' and do not see his good friend Ah'-mot, the Cacique." There was a mild note of surprise in the voice of the Witch-killer.

"It is plain you do not know well the mesa men if you think Ah'-mot and Dou-gow' are friends," replied the Che'-pah. "No one knows when Dou-gow' is friend and when he is enemy. If I were the Cacique of Pau-lan'-tee—never would I close an eye in the presence of Dou-gow'."

The Witch-killer looked keenly at his host, gave a non-committal grunt, but made no comment. Believing his guest was after some particular information regarding the Pau-lan'-tees, the little chief knew the matter must be disposed of before the grim and learned shaman would have anything to say regarding the power and ingredients of certain and various charms, medicines, and similar accessories of the black magic about which he longed to inquire. After a few moments' silence he went on at a venture:

"Dou-gow' said much that was not to my liking. He said if I was wise I would no longer look upon Ne-chō'-ba and the Pan'-guas as my friends. He said it would be well if I told my people not to visit Pan'-gua at the time of their corn dance that comes with the new moon. Such talk was not good to my ears, but of that I said nothing."

Again the Che'-pah fell silent and hoped that his guest would be satisfied with such information as he had given. The Witch-killer looked speculatively at his host, and for some time neither spoke.

"Has Dou-gow' no reason for such words?" inquired the hunchback at last.

"He gave reason," replied Sho'-ya. "When we were alone he told me some great star-gazer of his people had told him that he, Dou-gow', would soon rule the Pau-lan'-tees, and then it would be well for the Che'-pahs if we were his good friends."

During this recitation by the Che'-pah, the face of Gool remained as impassive as a mask. No change of expression gave indication of the thoughts that passed within his mind. When Sho'-ya paused, he lifted his eyes questioningly as if to ask, "What more did he say?"

"Dou-gow' believes I have an empty head," continued the Che'-pah. "I am a long-time friend of Ah'-mot, the Cacique, and it is with him I have made the pact of friendship. His people like him, and he is not an old one who is soon to go on the Long Sleep, yet Dou-gow' would have me think that he is to be made Cacique in Ah'-mot's place. It is a law of the stone-house people that a cacique remains a cacique so long as he lives. It is Dou-gow' that has an empty head, not Sho'-ya. His words say that I, who am a chief, must not be friends of the Pan'-guas."

The mild voice of the speaker hardened a little, and his eyes took on a glint of anger as he continued, "Ne-chō'-ba is my long-time friend. My people hunt where the Pan'-guas hunt, and have always been free to drink from their pool, and welcome to the shelter of their village. Is a Che'-pah a snake that he would turn to bite his friends?

"Always have the Apaches wanted the pool and the good hunting that is found toward the setting sun. This they could not have so long as the Pau-lan'-tees and the Che'-pahs are friends of Ne-chō'-ba. If we turn away from him—quickly would the Apache dogs swallow up the poor Pan'-guas without great effort. Am I one to throw meat and drink to desert dogs who would turn to bite me as soon as they have eaten my friends?"

In the rising anger that accompanied his words, the voice of the little chief became metallic, and his eyes narrowed. This did not escape the hunchback, but he reflected none of the fire or temper of his host.

"Dou-gow' may be very wise, and may have far vision for things your eyes do not see," suggested Gool evenly.

The Che'-pah looked keenly at his guest. The conversation was not going as he had wanted it to go. He fell silent, that he might ponder the meaning of the Witch-killer's words. He knew that the great shaman and Dou-gow' were on friendly terms, but just how friendly he did not know. It was like him to say much in few words, and his remark might indicate his thoughts.

"If Dou-gow' becomes ruler of Pau-lan'-tee, continued the hunchback," it may be he will make a pact with the Che'-pahs, and let them live at the foot of the great mesa. They would have water, and hunt where

THE WITCH-KILLER

the Pau-lan'-tees hunt. Is that not better than all Pan'-gua hunting?"

If the Witch-killer intended this as a suggestion welcome to his host, he was soon aware that he had made a mistake.

"Am I a suckling whelp to crawl at the feet of this house-living wolf on the mesa? I, Sho'-ya, will never make pact with Dou-gow'. If he goes against Ne-chō'-ba, one of his own kind who speaks his tongue, and prays to the same gods he prays to, would he not turn, with least cause, against a Che'-pah? Ah-ēē'! Sho'-ya may appear to be without ears and eyes, but this Pau-lan'-tee tapop will learn better."

As the speaker paused, Gool, as if to change the subject, arrived at the real cause of his visit.

"When I was here I gave to you in trade three nee-che beans. You must trade them back to me. I have need of them. I will have more before the time of your ceremony."

A look of almost childish guilt came into the face of the Che'-pah.

"I have but one of the beans," came the reply.

"Where are the others? You said the beans were for your fire ceremony. Have you had so great a time within the seven suns since I was here?"

"Two of the beans I traded to Dou-gow'. He wanted them quickly, and gave me two large sky-stones for each bean," confessed the Che'-pah honestly.

"Then the Pau-lan'-tee tapop knows of the magic of the nee-che beans?" inquired the Witch-killer.

"He says he has heard of them, and that he wants them as protection against the Black Witch that brings sickness to the mesa. Some shaman told him that drink made from the beans gives visions of the Shiuana, and the visions give great power to the one who drinks. I asked him if he knew the evil magic in the bean. I gave him warning that half of one bean would send the eater on to the Silent Others, and that one quarter would make him who eats it like a child who is drowsed into a long and evil sleep that none can wake him from. But there was in his face a look that made me think he knew all I had said."

In the silence that followed the Che'-pah's last remark, the sound of heavy breathing came from behind the hide curtain. The chief's fat wife had listened herself to sleep.

"Dou-gow"s face may have said that he knew much, but he knew nothing of the nee-che beans but what your words told him," remarked the hunchback dryly. "No stone-house men know of this magic, because they do not use it in any ceremony."

"In this matter your ears have not heard right," and a boastful note came into the voice of the little chief. To correct the great witch-doctor was a rare privilege, and one he would not overlook. "For many seasons have the Pau-lan'-tee people known of the evil magic of the nee-che bean. I have heard—I do not know if it is true, but it came free to my ears—that a very great evil was done to one who was high among the Pau-lan'-tees. She was made out to be a witch, and it was said that some evil one, in secret, gave her to eat of the nee-che bean, so that when she talked as a child they could say she was a witch."

A sudden change came over the face of the hunchback, but his face was in a shadow and the new expression escaped the Che'-pah.

THE WITCH-KILLER 65

"Who brought words of this witch matter to your ears?" inquired the Witch-killer with as much indifference as he could assume.

"It was long ago—the thing is no longer clear in my thoughts," replied Sho'-ya in evident hope that he might end the subject, and turn to more interesting matters.

The long right arm of the Witch-killer shot forward, and he gripped the arm of his host.

"I would know of this tale of the woman witch. Tell me of the one who brought it to your ears—and what that one said." Although his voice was meant to be light and friendly, the quick mind of the Che'-pah chief saw there was far more than idle interest in both the gesture and demand of the hunchback. He recalled the great trouble on the mesa, thought of the one who had told him of it under vow of secrecy, and was sorry he had been so hasty.

For a long moment he remained silent, trying to decide whether to speak the truth, or concoct a false story. He decided the truth could do no damage.

"There has been, for a long time, among my people one whom we call the Dawn Woman," he began. "She it was who told me of this matter—but she spoke no names. It may be I do not remember all, but what comes to my mind I will tell. It was not long after the time of the great thirst and trouble brought by the Poy'-yo witch, two seasons maybe, when this evil thing was done on the great mesa. I was told that there was in Pau-lan'-tee, at that time, a woman who was known to all as one who was very wise, and good to look upon. Her name was not said to me.

"Some evil one hated this woman, and it may be he

hated her husband. She was made out to be a witch, and I was told that none knew about the nee-che bean but the evil one who gave it to her in secret. The Paulan'-tee Council said she was a witch, and she went on the Long Sleep. It was said that there was great trouble, but of that I know nothing. That is all that was told to me."

As if to make the end of his talk and the subject final, Sho'-ya arose and revived the dying embers of the supper fire, and made a lively blaze of small sticks. As he turned to resume his seat, he found the Witch-killer standing with staff in hand ready to depart.

"You do not go?" asked the Che'-pah in surprise. The thought of losing a long evening that might be devoted to a talk of spells and magic filled him with dismay, and he tried to think of some plausible excuse for keeping his guest.

"Yes, I go," replied the hunchback briefly.

At the entrance he turned and stood, for a moment, looking at his host. A low rumble of distant thunder told of a coming storm. The little chief heard this with delight.

"Where better to spend the night than in the shelter of a hogan?" he asked invitingly.

The Witch-killer looked blankly at the speaker, as though his thoughts were far from such things as storms and shelter. Without further word, he stepped back into the room and, squatting down near the fire, took a small pouch from his belt. Loosening the drawstrings, he drew out four straight pieces of bleached bone, of even weight and length, and a flat circular bit of stone. On the dirt floor he marked a small circle a foot in diameter. In the center of this he placed the

THE WITCH-KILLER

flat disk of stone. Holding the four sticks of bone together, and poised vertically over the disk, he raised them until they were about ten inches above the stone and let them drop. There was a sharp dry click as they struck the disk, and they bounced outward in various directions. Only one of the four lit squarely across the circle.

Sho'-ya watched the performance carefully. He was familiar with the implements the Witch-killer was using, but he could not know for what purpose he was now employing them.

The hunchback carefully noticed the direction toward which the outer end of the one important stick of bone was pointing. It was a little northwest, or in the general direction of Pan'-gua. He picked up the disk and bits of bone and restored them to the pouch. The performance had been executed without a word. If it was done to allay any suspicions his host might have, because of his early departure, it worked successfully. Sho'-ya had forgotten all else but the mystery that lay hidden in the stick of bone that had fallen on the circular line. It may be, the hunchback shaman read this in the mind of his host.

"The Shiuana say where I shall go," he said simply. Then from a second pouch he took a pinch of some grayish substance and, tossing some of it to the four points of the compass, he lastly threw a bit of it into the fire. The blaze gave up a thread of heavy greenish smoke that brought a strange pungent odor into the room.

This, to the Che'-pah, needed no explanation. He knew that the strong medicine was a protection to his house and people, and for this he was thankful.

"Is there need of magic against the Chin'-di?" he inquired.

"Before the Moon God is again new—there comes great trouble to some who live in the land of Ash-ni—but it will not come to the Che'-pahs."

With this announcement, the hunchback turned and strode out into the night, leaving his host to stare at the black opening of the doorway, and ponder the significant words and actions of his departed guest. He felt that the visit had not been a successful one.

Near the opposite end of the camp two women stood by the fire-lit doorway of a lodge, peering up at the sky and discussing the coming storm. The Witch-killer stopped beside them.

"Where is the hogan of one they call the Dawn Woman?" he inquired in a low voice. The women looked up at him, and, startled by his sudden appearance, did not answer until he had repeated the question.

"There is no hogan," replied one of the women. "She is gone, and is to be no longer among the Che'-pahs."

The hunchback looked searchingly into the face of the speaker. Then, half-convinced that she spoke the truth, he asked:

"Where has she gone?"

"We do not know," came the answer. "She took two women and some men with her, and they went away toward the setting sun."

The Witch-killer seemed baffled. Then he reached forth with swift gesture and grasped the speaker by the arm. She winced with pain as the strong hand gripped her flesh.

"Where—has—she—gone?" he repeated slowly, and in his voice was an unmistakable note of warning.

"To—to Pan'-gua—I think," faltered the woman meekly.

The hunchback dropped her arm, and, turning about, looked back in the direction of Sho'-ya's hogan as though he considered returning. The women took advantage of his diverted attention to escape into their hut.

For a moment he stood irresolute in the darkness. A jagged flare of lightning split the heavens from zenith to horizon, and the accompanying crash of thunder jarred the earth, reverberating far out over the level plain like the receding rumble of a mighty drum.

Paying no heed to the coming storm, he made his way into the desert and turned his steps westward.

CHAPTER VI

THE FLIGHT OF AN OWL

Come, Ah'-hool, god of the yellow day;
Come, stars of the cold blue night;
Come light the path of an earth-born child.
The trail he takes is long and wild,
And dangers lurk in the way.

AS the faint white light of coming dawn appeared, Che-loo' was far out in the silent desert moving with long, steady stride toward the rising sun, for his course, for a time, lay due east.

Like a true Indian runner he chanted a song in perfect rhythm to his swinging step. With the trader's load on his back, his gait was not so fast as the one he used on the hunt, but his long stride was calculated to carry him far 'twixt the dawn and the dark.

A refreshing night's sleep had banished much of the distaste he had for the tiresome trip to the great mesa. The sifting *pound, pound, pound* of the sand beneath his moccasins, the cool familiar desert odors, the feel of freedom accentuated by the clear joyous song of early birds, and the unbounded space about him, tended to restore much of the carefree mental attitude so habitual with him.

When he was leaving the walls of Pan'-gua, he had met a young girl with filled olla on her head, returning to the village from the pool. In some manner she had

THE FLIGHT OF AN OWL 71

recalled to his mind the Pau-lan'-tee maiden of the soft voice. This memory brought a fresh dislike for the mission that lay ahead of him. Since that day near the great mesa, he had not thought of her. But the village of Pau-lan'-tee was very large and his business would be with men—perhaps he would not see her, or could avoid her if she crossed his path. For the smaller girl, with the loud laugh, he cared not at all whether he met her or not. He knew her kind, or believed he did, and she was like all others.

But soon the crisp air and changing scene swept all thought of the Pau-lan'-tee women from his mind, and he decided to get as much enjoyment as he could out of the long journey to the mesa. When he arrived, he would get the tasteless mission over as quickly as possible.

As he swung along, his chant growing into a louder song, a belated owl, whimpering in low protest at the increasing light, shot across his path in swift flight to the dark shelter of some distant canyon. The song came to sudden end.

"An ill omen—so Mat'-so and Ne-chō'-ba would say," he whispered to himself. "But old men fear everything. The longer they live, the more they find to fear: signs, omens, spells, witches," and he laughed derisively.

But there was a vague catch in the laugh, and he half wished it hadn't been an owl. He didn't believe in witches; but omens—omens were different. They were signs and warnings from the great Shiuana.

The brilliant burst of the sun, that lifted suddenly clear over the dark rim of the desert, flooded him with warm golden light. Warnings and ill omens were forgotten. Above mere words, above mere thoughts, was the wild free exultation that surged in his breast, and lifted him light on his feet; light in spite of the load of skins on his back. Ah'-hool was a great god, a god of good. Why fear?

He was young and the blessings of the Earth Mother were for the joy of her children. Let old men wag their heads and their tongues about fearful things—he would have none of them. Was he not more free than they? The thought added a touch of recklessness to the buoyancy of his spirits, and the duties of the journey ahead took second place in his thoughts.

Old men would doubtless warn him that such lack of fear would anger the Shiuana, but just now he resented the hampering fears that bound old men as slaves to their mumbled rites and dark ceremonies.

Immediately before him lay a wide stretch of desert, comparatively flat, for only in scattered areas was it broken by low rock formations and shallow arroyos. Far ahead, at a point that he would probably reach when the day began to wane, a lofty butte of dark rock, projecting out into the plain like a giant finger from the higher ground to the north, lay across his path. Here he would have the choice of two well-known trails that led from Pan'-gua to the Pau-lan'-tee mesa.

One of these trails kept to the level of the desert, and made a detour around the point beyond which it again bore eastward along the plain. The other, a shorter and much rougher trail, rose to the top of the wall-like barrier and, keeping to the upper level of the mesas and buttes beyond, cut its direct way through patches of pinyon and juniper-trees, valleys of grease-

THE FLIGHT OF AN OWL

wood and sage, to the last short expanse of plain beyond which the great mesa of Pau-lan'-tee stood.

The latter trail suited Che-loo' best, though he well knew, and in fact had been warned, that traders never took it, as it was not easy to negotiate with a pack. It was also known that both Navajo and Apache hunters, wandering south for turkeys and deer, were often seen in the wooded hills. Because of this it was a fixed rule among village men, always to hunt with two or more companions. But this region of timber and canyons held for Che-loo' a lure that was very strong—the lure of the hunt.

So long was his stride, and so great his desire to be within the shadows of trees and canyon walls before the afternoon heat should come, that he found himself at the base of the great rock barrier much sooner than he had expected. His shadow was in front of him now, but it was short and it would be some time before the sun reached the middle of the afternoon when it flooded the desert with its greatest heat.

Within the shelter of the great rock he removed his pack, glad to rest and eat of the maize-cake and dried meat he had carried in a pouch at his belt. There was no water at hand, but the country about him was familiar and he knew that at the base of a low canyon wall, a little beyond the summit of the great plateau above him, was a spring. There he would slake his thirst and take another short rest before plunging into the rough land ahead.

Let traders use the desert trail if they feared the rough country. That was their business, and did not concern him. He wasn't a real trader, anyway. Thus justifying himself, to his own satisfaction, he ascended the plateau and paused on its summit to let his gaze wander over the desert below. There was a welcome breeze in the upper air, and the outlook pleased him. Within the broad landscape he found beauty in the familiar splashes of color to be seen in the red of sandstone, the blue and purple of the shale and sage, and the yellow of the sand.

The feeling of height was good—he liked lofty places. Turning to the dim trail, he was about to resume the journey when his eye caught something on the ground that held him. It was a footprint, scarcely discernible to an unpractised eye, but the keen vision of the young hunter had been trained from early boyhood by the skilled Tō'-bah-yan.

The dim print had been made by a moccasin of unfamiliar shape, and it was this shape that had caught his attention. He looked for a clearer or deeper print: one that would have more to tell. A few steps farther on, a stretch of softer earth disclosed other prints, and here he found one that easily confirmed what he had suspected. The tracks had been made by pointed moccasins, and on close examination he found that the inner side of the print, next to the toe, was deeper than the rest of the marking. There was no mistake: the tracks were those of the Witch-killer, and they were fresh.

Satisfied with this disclosure, he moved on, but he made a mental note of the fact that the trail must be examined, from time to time, that he could learn if the hunchbacked witch-doctor were headed for Pau-lan'-tee. His presence in the great village, at this time, might have important meaning. He had seen the creature but few times, and always at a distance. The repulsive face, and unkempt appearance of the famous shaman had disgusted him.

He had always taken some measure of pride in his own personal appearance. He despised dirt, whether on his skin or his clothing, and he enjoyed bathing and the feel of foaming lather of soap-weed with which his long black hair was frequently washed.

As for the ill reputation of the Witch-killer, or the fear most people had of him, he gave no heed to either. He suspected that many of the awful tales he had heard were true, for Gool looked capable of doing almost anything, but these things did not concern him. He feared no man, and he felt himself equal to any he had met, be he shaman, hunter, or plain warrior. The confidence of youth and strength gave him calm, if not altogether wise, assurance.

Thirst soon replaced the Witch-killer in his thoughts, and he pressed forward more rapidly to the little canyon with its sheltered spring. A lean half-grown coyote gave way reluctantly as he approached the tiny pool, and trotted up the narrow canyon with head twisting from side to side to make sure that neither stone nor arrow was following him.

Having drunk his fill, Che-loo' again rested within the shadow of the wall, and gazed lazily up at the blue dome above him. How cool and peaceful seemed this high realm of the Sky People, this abode of the Silent Others!

In a moment he arose, impelled by an uneasy feeling —the feeling that human eyes were turned upon him. He looked cautiously about him at the top of the low canyon wall and saw nothing; but that sixth sense, so often acute in the Indian hunter, warned him to be alert. Carefully now he ascended the canyon wall, and with head barely above its level, scanned the immediate country around the circle. Then, apparently satisfied with the result, he secured his pack and resumed the trail.

Had he looked behind a small clump of greasewood, that stood on a hill a short distance from the canyon's rim, he might have seen the owner of the human eyes lying flat on his face as motionless as a corpse. As Che-loo' moved away along the trail, the man came to life, and slowly nodded his head as he whispered to himself:

"Ah'-mot must still live. A Pan'-gua trader goes to Pau-lan'-tee—to trade? Ah—*ah, the young ga-che is a fool, and greater fools are those who send him!*"

Around Che-loo' all was as peaceful as could be. Birds flitted from bush to bush, and off in a small group of pinyon-trees two ravens croaked and scolded. There were no other sounds, no other evidence of life in the surrounding solitude. When in the open he had always hunted with companions. To be alone was a new experience, but he found he enjoyed it.

The day wore on, and the trail with its climbs and descents, its mesas and canyons, disclosed nothing to mar the peaceful journey of the youthful trader. As the afternoon shadows began to lengthen, the trail entered a wooded slope covered, as far as Che-loo' could see, with pine and pinyon trees, with an underbrush of scrub-oak and tangled shrubs. Here was welcome shade, and he was glad to enter the cool shadows after the glaring heat that smote the exposed mesa-tops.

He had penetrated the wood for some little distance

THE FLIGHT OF AN OWL

when a sound caught his ear, a sound that caused him to stop in his tracks. It was the far-off call of the crow; but he knew that no crow had made the sound. The imitation was clever, but not clever enough to deceive the ear of one who himself knew how to imitate the calls of both birds and animals. The sound had come from a direction a little to the right of the trail. He moved forward again, but more slowly and with great caution, his eyes studying the sweep of ground immediately before him.

There was no second call of the crow, and he had begun to believe that the enemy or friend who had made the sound had gone off about his business, when his eye caught a slight movement in some bushes a little distance ahead of him.

Dropping to his knees, he loosened his pack, and cautiously moved it to the side of the trail behind a clump of sage. This was no time to play trader. Fitting an arrow to the string of his bow, that he had carried in his hand since the call of the imitation crow, he lay almost flat on the earth and waited.

Again came the hoarse call of the crow; a good imitation, but it betrayed the human note. The call was distinct and not a great distance away and still to the right of the trail. As he watched the bush that had moved a few moments before, he saw a figure of some kind moving beyond it and apparently sliding backward as though intent on placing a greater distance between itself and the bush. Then it half rose, and, leaping from tree to tree, disappeared among the undergrowth on the left of the trail.

Che-loo"s fingers twitched on the bow-string, for the escaping Indian was an Apache; but he knew the distance was too great for a telling shot. As he lay wondering what the next move of the enemy would be, he again heard the crow-call, and this time it was answered by an even more unskilled imitator some little distance beyond the point where the Apache had disappeared.

The young hunter began to realize that he was in a bad situation, for it now looked as though he had walked into a trap that had been nicely set for him by his enemies, who had perhaps been secretly watching him for some time.

He grimly meditated on the fact that they could scarcely have chosen a better place for the attack, yet he had evidently upset their plans temporarily by thus dropping to the ground and placing himself on guard. The moving bush and fleeing Apache were probably a part of the plan to take him: a bait tended to lure him into pursuit. He was glad he had not exposed himself in any foolish attempt to follow the bait, if such it was. Leaving his pack behind the bush, he began to crawl backward, wriggling himself over the ground like a snake.

He knew that as long as he did not lift his head, he was comparatively safe. A few rods back of him, to the left of the trail, was a dense clump of jack-oaks. Early frosts of the highlands had clipped the leaves that now lay heaped beneath them. The thickly matted growth of the slender stems would afford him much better protection than any of the underbrush near him.

Fortunately, he had had long practise in thus worming his way over the ground when stalking game, and he could move both rapidly and silently. After what seemed to him a long time, he reached his goal and crouched behind it. He was safe for the time being.

He now realized that he had been unwise when choosing this rougher trail to Pau-lan'-tee. Perhaps he shouldn't have been quite so sure of himself. However, he had no fear, for he reasoned that if there were not too many of his enemies at hand, he could outwit them and escape with a whole scalp—but the pack of fine buckskins were not his, and he was responsible for them. He realized now what a fine target he must have made with the large gray bundle on his back. He must have been easily observed at a great distance. He would save the pack if he could; but if not—well, the skin beneath his hair felt very comfortable on his head, and he did not care to have his scalp swinging in the breeze above the door of some Apache's hogan.

To take the life of a man had never been pleasing to Che-loo'. He looked upon fighting an enemy as a duty that must, if necessary, be performed, but he had always been reluctant to shed even the blood of the vile Apache. Many of his people had cause for vengeance against the dread Apache and Navajo, and this aroused their hatred and whetted their desire to kill whenever the chance came, but as yet no such cause had been given him.

He looked toward the bush where he had hidden his pack; a figure slipped behind a tree a short distance beyond it. The man was investigating, and probably thought his intended victim lay hidden behind the pack. Drawing his bow to position, Che-loo' decided to defend his property should the investigator attempt to make off with it. From behind the tree that sheltered the wily Apache, appeared a coarse breech-clout of buckskin, and a long section of bronzed back.

Che-loo"'s bow-string gave a sharp twang, and the surprised Apache leaped from his cover and bounded away with the Pan'-gua arrow pinned diagonally, though harmlessly, through his buckskin loincloth. Angry with himself because of the unlucky shot, Che-loo' again dropped down and waited. But presently his white teeth gleamed and he chuckled under his breath. The shot would at least cause his enemy to appear ridiculous to his bloodthirsty friends, since it would appear that he had been shot from the rear while running away, and he doubted if the Apache knew that the arrow was attached to him.

A slight rustling sound came from a point directly to his right. As he turned his head in that direction an arrow whistled so close to him he felt it brush his hair. In a flash he dropped flat on his stomach. A second arrow, aimed to arch a little lower, struck his heel, clipping off a bit of his moccasin but doing no greater damage.

Quickly he worked his way around the jack-oaks, and was thus, for the moment at least, shielded from another shot from the same quarter. It was now the enemy's turn to curse his luck over a shot that had been spent without damage. As his shot at the thieving Apache had revealed his own position, so now had the two arrows from the man on the right let him know where the second Apache lay. With great caution he lifted his head and looked carefully about him. The blow to his heel, though harmless, angered him. He was now more fully aware of the danger that confronted him.

THE FLIGHT OF AN OWL

All was quiet, an ominous quiet. Far overhead a real crow was making hoarse, discordant calls as he winged his heavy flight over the forest. The occasional drone of a bee accentuated the mock peace, and stillness wrapped the forest as a shroud. To hunt was a familiar occupation to Che-loo', but to be hunted was a new and different experience. He became keenly aware that he could make no false or foolish move. If he could outwit his enemies, or hold them off until darkness fell, he might escape with a whole skin, and, with rare good luck, even take his pack with him.

All this would depend on the number and cunning of his assailants. Judging by the number of imitation crow-calls, he knew that two of the Apaches were somewhere on the right of the trail, and had probably intended to creep up on him while his attention was being diverted by the man on the left.

As his eye moved round the circle, he caught sight of two figures, far ahead, beyond a little clearing to the right. They were stooping low and moving cautiously toward the trail. He could just catch a glimpse of their brown bodies as they moved through the dark forest. Then a third followed a little way behind the others.

They were evidently joining the man who had fled with the arrow pinned to his scanty garment, as they would soon reach the spot where the Apache had disappeared among the trees. This was too many enemies for one man with a trader's pack to defend, no matter how brave and cunning he might be. The three men he had just seen would circle around to the left of the trail, and thus more effectually surround him. For the first time in his life, Che-loo' was baffled. He realized that whatever he was to do toward making his escape must be done quickly, if at all.

The pack would have to be abandoned, as he could not hope to outrun an enemy with a trader's pack on his back. He was thoroughly angry now, angry with himself and his enemies. Ne-chō'-ba had said he lacked wisdom, and surely his judgment had proved correct.

Without the trader's pack he would have no excuse for going on to Pau-lan'-tee, even if he escaped with his life; and to return to Pan'-gua without it would mean to present himself as an object of ridicule. With what shame would he appear before Ne-chō'-ba, who had placed such faith in him, and say that he had permitted some thieving Apaches to rob him! Bitterly repenting of his overconfidence, and the lack of wisdom he had displayed, he grimly decided to die defending his pack, if necessary, rather than return without it. He could go on the Long Sleep but once, and he would make the Apaches pay dearly for his scalp.

Suddenly the owl, that ill omen of the early morning, flashed into his thoughts. He made up his mind that if another ever crossed his path, he would make prayer to the Shiuana for protection.

Some small birds rose from a low bush uttering sharp calls of alarm. He turned quickly and looked searchingly at the ground beyond the bush from which the birds had flown. A figure was worming its way along the ground not sixty paces from him, and in front of his position. The tall grass moved as the man made his tortuous way, but so cunning were his movements no part of his body came into view. A thick bunch of tall weeds seemed to be the objective of this wormlike man, and Che-loo', after looking cautiously about him,

THE FLIGHT OF AN OWL 83

again prepared to shoot. This time he resolved to wait until he could aim at a vital spot. He well knew the methods employed by Apaches in such warfare. They might easily close in upon him with a rush and slay him, with a fair certainty, however, of losing at least one of their number in the fight, but they preferred to approach him slyly, two or three at a time, and attempt to make way with him without receiving injury to themselves in return.

To capture an enemy alive, and bring him to torture, was even a greater delight to them. In this he knew they loved to display their cunning as well as their cruelty.

Now that he had determined to fight it out, Che-loo' felt neither fear nor depression. A grim interest in this game of man-hunt held him like a taut bow-string, ready for action at the slip of the finger. With eyes and ears strained to detect further sight or sound of the two Apaches who were now so near at hand, and an occasional glance over his shoulder for any who might try to approach from the rear, he waited.

CHAPTER VII

THE DAWN WOMAN

Free is the hunter as the wind and the sun,
O'er hill and o'er dale is the wild chase run,
And the stars look down, when his day is done,
At the star of his fire on the hill.

WHILE Che-loo' lay behind the protecting shelter of the young jack-oak trees, in momentary expectation of attack from the Apaches, who seemed to be surrounding him, strange thoughts came to his mind. He wondered what his father would say, and how his mother would feel if he never returned to Pan'-gua. Other men had gone out alone and had never returned, and no word of them had reached the ears of the people. Was he to be like one of these?

He recalled the fresh tracks of Gool, the Witch-killer, on the summit of the plateau, now far back on the edge of the desert, and wondered if the hunchback had anything to do with this ambush of the Apaches. He recalled, with regret, that he had forgotten to look again along the trail for tracks of the pointed moccasins.

His thoughts of the Witch-killer were suddenly interrupted by a slight rustle in the leaves to his right. As he cautiously shifted his position to look in that direction he heard the sharp twang of a bow-string, followed by a loud scream of pain. In blank astonishment he saw an Apache leap into the air and fall prone to earth with face skyward, an arrow buried deep in his ribs. In a moment the slain warrior lay still.

With a wild shout of triumph the man who had wormed his way to the clump of weeds leaped to his feet, and with drawn knife ran toward the motionless figure on the ground. As he did so, Che-loo' stared in fresh surprise; then he too arose and, after looking carefully about him, sprang forward with a shout:

"Ha-la'-ni, Che'-pah!" And in a moment he stood beside the triumphant warrior.

The man whirled around in amazement, and his jaw dropped as he stared at Che-loo'. Then a wide grin spread over his coarse face as he exclaimed:

"Ra-ua, friend! Where you come? How you come here?"

"This is not the only Apache," warned Che-loo' quickly, as he pointed to the lifeless figure on the ground.

"No,—one more," replied the Che'-pah, confidently holding up one finger and pointing in the direction the other Apache had taken. "My three friend track him. This one I got sure." And with this he kicked the slain enemy with the toe of his moccasin. "Long time we track 'em. They no see," he went on, in his stumbling attempt at the Pan'-gua tongue, for he wanted to display his knowledge of his friend's language.

Che-loo' was satisfied to have him talk Pan'-gua or any other tongue he might choose, so relieved was he to find friends where he had supposed only enemies were surrounding him, for he now knew that only two had been Apaches, while those he had seen skirting the forest at a distance, as well as the man behind the weeds, who now stood beside him, were Che'-pahs, the desert friends of his people.

He caught the hand of the Che'-pah, and after breathing on it, held it aloft in token of friendship. This seemed to please the other greatly, and he touched the breast of Che-loo', saying in sudden mock seriousness:

"Pan'-gua man—not much good. Pan'-gua hunter —no can much shoot, but Che'-pah good to poor Pan'-gua. I think Apache hunt turkey, but guess *you* the turkey he hunt!"

The speaker followed this teasing bit of humor with a long loud laugh that rang through the forest where, but a few moments before, all had been held in the grim stillness of the man-hunt.

Che-loo' looked thoughtfully down at the face of the vanquished enemy, the enemy who had come so near slaying him, and was thankful. Evidently the Apache had been so intent on watching him, he had been wholly unaware of the Che'-pah's presence, just as the Che'-pah, intent on slaying the Apache, was not aware that his intended victim was hunting human game.

"Where you come to here?" questioned the Che'-pah again.

Che-loo' explained that he was alone, and on his way to the great mesa to trade.

Again the jovial hunter laughed loudly, for he considered Che-loo' in the guise of a trader as a huge joke.

"You hunter, maybe good hunter, but not trader. You trader like a squaw," and again he gave vent to his mirth.

At another time Che-loo' might have resented this

open ridicule, but at present he was happy, and the homely Che'-pah, with his coarse breech-clout, dirty face and greased hair, was as pleasing to his sight as the handsomest of men, and as welcome as a blood brother.

The sun was low in the west, and Che-loo' realized that he must be on his way.

"I go now," he announced to the Che'-pah. "The forest must be at my back when the day is gone."

"One more Che'-pah camp—way up by desert," said the Che'-pah, pointing in a direction near the one Che-loo' would have to take. "Maybe you see 'em."

Che-loo' nodded; then, recovering his pack, he swung it to his shoulders and lifted his hand in sign of farewell to his friend, who would soon occupy himself with the gruesome task of scalping his enemy. He was glad that the Pan'-gua people did not follow this custom of the desert men.

A little farther along the trail he heard Che'-pah voices, and knew that the three warriors were returning to their companion, as they were rapidly drawing near. He waited to speak with them, that he might learn what had become of the remaining Apache. When they were within sight he shouted greeting, and as they came up smiling broadly at him, he noted they did not seem surprised to see him. He wondered at this, as he was sure they had not known of his presence in the forest.

He told them briefly of the triumph of their brother Che'-pah, and of his own part in the fight with the Apaches. All laughed loudly, as if highly entertained.

"We heard the Apache dog cry out, and our brother shout, so we knew," said one of the three.

"What of the other Apache?" inquired Che-loo'.

For reply the smallest of the trio, a stout fellow with keen little eyes and the heavy jaw of the fighter, turned his back. A fresh scalp was suspended from his belt. Another of the Che'-pahs produced a Pan'-gua arrow and handed it to Che-loo', whereupon all laughed loudly, for it was Che-loo's arrow that had been pinned to the Apache's breech-clout, and it explained why they were not surprised to find a Pan'-gua near at hand.

"You make 'em run—we catch 'em," said the stout man amid the boisterous laughter of the others; and as the three turned to go, Che-loo' made the friendly sign of farewell and took up the trail to Pau-lan'-tee.

As soon as he knew himself to be out of sight of the Che'-pahs, he stopped and, taking some sacred meal from a small pouch he carried at his belt, he scattered some of it to the four ways, and whispered his thanks to the great Ah'-hool for his safe delivery from his enemies. He had learned a lesson he would not soon forget.

After a short time the trail opened into a sage-covered plain, and beyond it the ground became rough, finally breaking down into shallow parallel arroyos and deeper canyons, where in rainy season the water plunged down from the highlands and on into the thirsty sand-hills that lay along the margin of the desert.

Che-loo' climbed to the top of a rock elevation and carefully scanned the country ahead for expected landmarks. Apparently satisfied, he descended and, crossing two of the canyons, made his way to the bed of the third. In a few moments he stood within the deep shadow of an overhanging wall. Removing his pack,

THE DAWN WOMAN

he knelt on the sand and scooped out a hole at the base of the cliff. Presently water began to rise in the bottom of the pit, and when a sufficient amount had accumulated to slake his thirst, he drank heartily, and was about to stretch himself on the cool sand for a needed rest, when the faint though unmistakable odor of a camp-fire came to his nostrils. All attention, he stood erect and sniffed the air. Then he climbed quickly to the rim and sniffed again. He walked cautiously in the direction from whence he believed the telltale odor was coming, and having cut across a sharp bend in the gorge, he dropped to his knees, and crawling to the edge looked over.

Almost directly beneath him, with head bowed dejectedly between his hands, as though weary or in deep despair, sat a boy, who on first sight appeared to be twelve or fourteen years of age. The sharp eyes of Che-loo' took in the surroundings. Near the seated figure lay a flat basket containing remnants of food, and a large empty burden basket leaned against the wall near the dying embers of a small fire. A narrow belt of red cloth, woven with design in beads and feathers, lay where it had fallen on the ground near by, and as it caught his eye Che-loo' whispered under his breath:

"Two of them. One a woman."

He hesitated on the rim, wondering if he should make his presence known to the silent figure below. Although the woman was not in sight, she might not be far away, and he wanted to avoid her.

All was quiet in the hush of the warm September evening. The sun had reached the end of its days journey. From the base of ridge and butte, long purple shadows streamed eastward in sharp contrast to the low rays of golden light that poured through the narrow gaps and passes in the hills. Color in daubs and splashes, squares and stripes lay lightly on the earth like a gaudy garment flung in brief display before the gray twilight could fade it to monotone. Southward the distant ridges of red sandstone stretched away like ribbons of pink and rose whose curves and folds were marked by shadows of delicate violet.

Che-loo' saw, but gave no heed to, this beautiful passing of the Day God. He was deciding between two courses, whether to continue on his way unobserved, or make himself known to the Che'-pah boy below, and have the brief pleasure of camp and company. Company of almost any kind seemed inviting, but thoughts of the woman decided him to pursue his way unobserved. Just as he quietly rose to return to the canyon for his pack, the boy below suddenly looked up, and in surprise jumped to his feet.

There was but one thing to do now, and that was to let the young Che'-pah know who he was, and then continue on his way as soon as the brief exchange of greetings were over.

"Ha-la'-ni — sit-si'-lee? [How goes it, little brother?]" he called out.

The boy continued to look up at him, with eyes squinting against the strong light, but made no reply.

"Does a Che'-pah not know the voice of a friend?" asked Che-loo'.

For reply the youth nodded in a friendly way, and placing a finger on his lips to denote silence, beckoned with his free hand to the traveler to come down and join him. Puzzled by the boy's actions, and half curious as to what they could mean, he hesitated for a moment, then nodded his head in assent. Returning to where he had left his pack, he recovered it and retracing his steps made his way to the bed of the canyon, and was soon standing beside the youthful Che'-pah. The latter held out his hand, and much to the visitor's surprise, whispered the quaint address of the Pau-lan'-tee and Pan'-gua people.

"All is good, Pan'-gua?"

"It is good," replied Che-loo'.

As soon as their hands had clasped and dropped to their sides, the boy made a slight gesture toward the canyon wall at the visitor's back, and as Che-loo' turned he saw a shallow cave in which a woman reclined on an improvised bed of skins and desert grass. Apparently she was asleep.

"My mother," said the boy simply.

Although this was uttered in a low voice, the woman opened her eyes and gazed quietly at Che-loo'. A younger woman would have caused him embarrassment, but this mother was about the age of his own. He dropped his trader's pack to the ground and, stepping to the cave, held out his hand to her.

One look told him much, and it was evident that she would not be many days among the earth-born.

"You are welcome, Pan'-gua," she said quietly. "This is a poor camp, but we are on our way to a better." Like the boy, she spoke the pure language of the stone-house people, and this puzzled Che-loo', as they both wore Che'-pah garb.

"You look Che'-pah, but you speak the tongue of my people," said Che-loo'.

"My son and I are Pau-lan'-tee, though for many

seasons we have lived in the Che'-pah camps," she explained. "I am Dez'-pah, and this," pointing to the boy, "is my son Nah'-lee. You are a trader from Pan'-gua. Let us have word of your people."

The request embarrassed Che-loo', who might reply to any direct question, but to manufacture conversation to a woman was something beyond his experience. For a time he fell silent, studying the ground at his feet.

"What is it you want to know?" he asked at length.

"All you will tell," replied the woman. "Not since they left the great mesa have I been among your people, but I know very many of them, and they were all as brothers and sisters to me. I go now to Pan'-gua, that I may have the sweet waters of your pool. There is an ill feeling for me in the waters of the Che'-pah camps—and my heart leads me to dwell once more among my own kind, who speak the tongue of my people. No more will the streets of Pau-lan'-tee echo to the footsteps of Dez'-pah, and no more will the Che'-pah children shout their greetings through the doorway of my lodge—but the Shiuana lead us where they will." Then, looking searchingly at him, "You are like one I used to know. What are you called?"

"I am Che-loo', son of Mat'-so. I am on my way to Pau-lan'-tee to trade," he announced, and he felt that the brief statement included all that any one might wish to know.

"Mat'-so? Yes, you are like him. Almost my heart grows young as I look on you. You are handsome, just as Mat'-so was when he was young. When he and I were children, we played together on the great mesa, and when he grew to be a handsome man—I hoped he would take me to be the one woman of his house, but he married Ot-si'-pah; she had a flat face, but was good. He is of the Beaver, and she is of the Buffalo clan.

"Ne-chō'-bah was older. He took my oldest sister for his wife—but she has long gone to the Silent Others. Our days on the great mesa were days of pleasure, the hearts of all the people were glad, and the Pan'-guas and Pau-lan'-tees were as one great clan. That is all far away now, like dreams of childhood whispered by ancient lips."

She raised herself to her elbow, that she might more easily look into the face of the young trader.

"This is an ill time to visit the mesa. Your father should have sent an older man. You know the evil that has fallen on Ah'-mot, the Cacique of Pau-lan'-tee?"

It seemed to Che-loo' that the large black eyes of the speaker looked at him with more than ordinary expectancy, and he had the feeling that she might read his very thoughts, and perhaps make him say more than he ought to say.

"I think word about some great trouble on the mesa has come to our ears," he replied evasively.

For a long moment she looked at him, and his eyes dropped under the discomforting gaze.

"That is well said," she remarked. "It may be that you are more wise than your years would tell. The evil that has come to Ah'-mot has caused great trouble on the mesa. A stranger in Pau-lan'-tee would do well to have wide ears and a narrow mouth." Again she fell silent; then suddenly, as though startled by some new thought, she spoke in a low voice, as if to herself. "Yes, it must be,—it must be." Then turning to her son, "Nah'-lee child, go and see if any of our men have returned to their camp. If they are not come, go help the women with the pinyon-nuts. They are in the hills above the canyon. Our friend from Pan'-gua will see that no Apaches send Dez'-pah on the Long Sleep before her time. Go, ushie [little one]."

The boy half reluctantly turned away, for it was plain that he was greatly interested in the Pan'-gua trader. When he had gone, the woman made brief explanation.

"I have words that are not for his ears. There are men and women of the Che'-pahs with us, and they go to put me safely with your people. The Che'-pahs are good. To them I am a great one who is loved by the Shiuana. I am called by them the Dawn Woman, for my face is not so dark as theirs. They have done for me all things I ask, as children would do for a mother who dwells in their hearts. Listen, son of Mat'-so.

"I am not to be long among the Earth People, and the mind of one who nears the Long Sleep is sometimes clear, and may see hidden things afar off. It may be that I see much that is not for the eyes of the strong."

Che-loo' looked up sharply at the wan face of his hostess.

"Have no fear. I am neither wat-li nor witch; none accuse me," she remarked with faint smile. Whatever her weakness, her voice had remained singularly rich and strong. "I have reason for the words I speak to you—great reason. The Shiuana do strange things with us. You are here in answer to my prayers, and of that I will speak. It is well that my words go to the ears of the son of Mat'-so. He was ever honest, no man ever doubted his word; when he made a vow or pact, it was kept. To me it is a wondrous thing that I,

THE DAWN WOMAN 95

Dez'-pah, tell the son of Mat'-so a secret that has been so long locked within me. Now—it must be told.

"Last night we camped beneath trees on a hill. In mid-darkness I looked from my couch at the stars, and I made prayers to the great Shiuana. After my prayers had come to their end, a star fell across the sky like a flaming arrow, from over Pan'-gua toward the great mesa of Pau-lan'-tee it fell—then it vanished. I knew, when I saw this sign in the sky, that my prayers would be answered, and I knew that one would be sent from Pan'-gua to the great mesa to perform a strange thing. You are the star, the flaming arrow from Pan'-gua. The flame has not yet kindled upon you—but when the fire comes to your breast, it will bring great trouble on some in Pau-lan'-tee—and great danger to you. Yes, yes, you are the flaming arrow; my eyes see it. You must make prayers to the Shiuana that they give you eyes to see."

The words of the woman moved Che-loo' uneasily, for he felt they were the words of one whose mind was unstable. As she saw this in his eyes, she realized that he might have vague fear of the mystery she referred to.

"Be not afraid of my words, son of Mat'-so, but take my warning, that ill may not befall you. And now listen well to what I am to say, for I must tell you of an evil that is long past, but I tell it that justice may come, and that I may go to the Silent Others in peace. In Pau-lan'-tee, you will ask for one called Cha'-za, the Fool. Give to him the words I now give to you."

"How is it you know that I am to go to his house?" asked Che-loo'.

"All traders of Pan'-gua go to his house," she replied. "Let my words go to his ears alone, I have good reason." With that she lay back on her couch, and though she closed her eyes she continued speaking. "Two seasons after your people left the mesa to live in the desert an evil thing was done in Pau-lan'-tee—by the same hand that has now been raised against Ah'-mot.

"You have heard of Dou-gow', who is Governor of the mesa people. He was then war-captain, but he wished to be greater. Nothing but evil is in the heart of Dou-gow'. At the time your people went away, there was a woman on the mesa more beautiful than all other women. She was called Tee'-lah. She came to the mesa as a little child, an Apache captive. Her mother, who was captured with her, went on to the Silent Others, and the child grew up as Pau-lan'-tee children grow, but she was more wise and better to look upon. The Pau-lan'-tees took her as one of their own, and thought of her no more as a captive. She grew to be a beautiful woman, and Dou-gow' wanted her for his wife; but her heart was against him.

"At that time there was a man of Pau-lan'-tee whom all men and women looked well upon, and Dou-gow' hated that man for two reasons, for he took the beautiful Apache woman to be his wife, and he was also made Governor. This man was Ko-lee'-pah, and when the Council made him Governor, Dou-gow' made secret vow that he would send him on the Long Sleep. But Dou-gow' began to have fear of Ko-lee'-pah, for he was greatly liked by the people, and a man both wise and fearless. He then decided to bring evil upon the Governor's wife, and what he did—is known to no one but Dou-gow', and to me, Dez'-pah. None but Cha'-za must hear your words of this—until I have gone to the Silent Others."

Che-loo' felt very uncomfortable, and wished he might find some reasonable excuse for getting away from this woman with her strange words, and evil secret. He had heard all he cared to hear of Dou-gow', and he despised mysteries. In the fading light within the shallow cave, the pale face of his strange hostess seemed suspended in the shadows like a specter. He hoped she would not be long in telling him what she wished him to know.

"A little time after Ko-lee'-pah took the beautiful Apache for his wife," continued the woman, "Dou-gow' married a Pau-lan'-tee maiden who believed his smooth words and knew nothing of his evil heart—but very soon she learned. One season, after the time of the new corn, there was born to Ko-lee'-pah a girl child, and he and his wife were happy. Then came whispers, from many, that the beautiful Tee'-lah was acting like a witch. In this there was no truth. All of the whispering came from people of Dou-gow''s clan, but the other men and women of the mesa did not know that. At the end of summer, when Pau-lan'-tee people gather crops from their fields, Dou-gow' chose a day when the Governor and his wife and baby had gone down to their fields. He then forced his own wife, who had learned to fear him, to go secretly to the house of Ko-lee'-pah, and hide owl-feathers and burnt corn in the small timbers of the ceiling. These are things that only a witch would have in the house, for in them is evil magic of the Chin-di. Then Dou-gow' traded with desert men for a bean of bad magic, for it contained bad medicine.

"That no one might suspect him, he asked his old

mother, who lived in another house and was as evil as he, to make a strong tea of the magic bean. This evil bean would cause the eater to mutter strange words, and to act as a child—and at last it would send them on the Long Sleep. No others of Pau-lan'-tee but Dou-gow' and his wicked mother knew of this magic, for it did not come to my ears until later.

"When Dou-gow"s mother had made the tea, she waited by her open door for a time when the beautiful Tee'-lah would pass alone. Not long did she have to wait. In the evening of the second sun she passed the door. With friendly smiles the old woman asked her to enter and taste of the good drink she had made of bark and berries. When Tee'-lah drank of the tea, Dou-gow"s mother made excuse to keep her in the house until the magic of the bean could affect her.

"When the Governor's wife left the house of Dou-gow"s mother, she was changed, and never again could speak but to utter strange words, and people in the street had to lead her to her home. In sorrow Ko-lee'-pah took his little child to the house of Ah'-mot, who had no children, and Ah'-mot kept her as his own. Again more and more people whispered that Tee'-lah was surely a witch, and at last the matter was brought to the Council.

"Then two men of Dou-gow"s clan, who were members of the Council, said, 'if this woman is a witch, we will find proof in her house, for all witches keep evil magic.' They searched the house of Ko-lee'-pah and found the owl-feathers, and the blackened corn. The Council was sorry for the Governor, but an ancient law said that a witch must die. They set a time for the following evening when Tee'-lah must go on the Long

Sleep. When dawn of the next sun came, the Governor's house was empty. He had taken his wife and gone away into the desert.

"None would follow them, as all feared both the Governor and the witch, but Dou-gow' knew that the beautiful Tee'-lah would not live, as the evil bean would send her to the Silent Others. He still feared the Governor might return, although by ancient law of the tribe, any one who sheltered or protected a witch was sent away forever as an outcast. But Dou-gow' still feared the Governor, and he sent one, who was of great strength and stature, to go secretly by night, and follow Ko-lee'-pah. He told this evil one that if he could bring back proof that Ko-lee'-pah had gone on the Long Sleep, he would make him chief over all fighting men of Pau-lan'-tee. The man believed the words of Dou-gow', and he went away in the night armed to slay Ko-lee'-pah if he should find him. But neither this man nor the Governor ever returned to the mesa. Traders of the desert brought word of a new grave, far off in a canyon, and it was believed that it was the grave of Tee'-lah.

"Since those days I have seen the face of one who reminds me strangely of the strong man whom Dou-gow' sent to slay Ko-lee'-pah—and—it may be that he now hunts for Dez'-pah as he hunted for the Governor."

"You speak of Gool, the Witch-killer?" asked Che-loo' quickly.

"I did not name the one of whom I spoke," evaded the woman.

"How is it you know all this that you have told me, and why should men hunt for you?" inquired Che-loo', who was now keenly interested in the woman's strange story.

"I am the wife of Dou-gow'," she replied. "I would not have known about the evil bean, but Dou-gow''s mother went to the Silent Others in great fear and torment. I came into her house as she was about to give up her earth-life, and Dou-gow' was holding her with his hand over her mouth, for she was screaming with fear, and he was afraid her words would be heard. When he laid her back on her couch, she shouted that the Black Witch was after her because she had poisoned the beautiful Tee'-lah. Then she accused Dou-gow', and shouted a warning to him about the Black Witch, and he tried to stop her, but I heard her words. After that she went quickly on the Long Sleep.

"In great fear Dou-gow' told me all, and said I must protect him from the Black Witch that had taken his mother—but if I ever told what he had done, he would slay both me and my child, who was then but a few weeks old.

"I could no longer live with Dou-gow', and I could not leave him and stay in Pau-lan'-tee. I waited for a time when he was away on the hunt, and I took my baby and went away to the Che'-pahs. I told Sho'-ya, their chief, something of why I ran away from Dou-gow', and he told his people to always hide me from any mesa men who might make search for me, and that I was a great one whom the Shiuana had sent to them for their good.

"That is all of my secret, son of Mat'-so. I am near the end of the earth-trail, and I go in peace if I know you will do as I have asked. Will you make pact with me, before the great Shiuana, that you will keep my words, and give them only to Cha'-za?"

Che-loo' hesitated. To make a pact as a vow before the Shiuana, was a deep thing, but a feeling of pity for this strange woman decided him. It was all a new experience, this pity for a woman, but he found himself pleased with the thought of doing her a kindness. "Yes," he said at length, "I make a vow to do as you have said."

The pale woman opened her eyes, and again raised herself that she might look into his face. Her eyes shone with great joy, and her wan face was illumined with a smile. "May the great Ah'-hool be with you always—son of Mat'-so. Before tomorrow's sun is gone you will be in Pau-lan'-tee. There are three evil men on the mesa, more evil than all others. They are Dou-gow'; Klee'-tso, the war-captain; and one Mete'-lo, the moccasin-maker. Keep their names in your mind, and give them wide trail, for they are snakes that bite friend or enemy alike."

Che-loo' rose to depart, and as he silently clasped her outstretched hand, he heard the voices of the boy Nah'-lee and the Che'-pah women, returning in the twilight. The words of the boy came plainly to his ears: "I know it was the Witch-killer. I know his crooked back, and I saw him plainly, on a hill-top against the sky."

CHAPTER VIII

CHA'-ZA, THE FOOL

On the white-walled village, lifting high
A-top of a great plateau,
Shines the last faint glow of the sunset sky;
While up from the plain the night birds fly,
And the world lies dark below.

AS Che-loo' neared the mesa of Pau-lan'-tee he began to have some misgivings as to how he might be received in the great village. He remembered that it was many times the size of Pan'-gua, and this thought disturbed him. He disliked villages, and houses were only meant for winter, when it might be too cold to hunt with pleasure.

Now that he was within a stone's-cast of one of the three well-worn trails that led up to the pueblo, he wished heartily that his disagreeable errand was at an end, and that he was leaving instead of climbing the mesa. It was mid-afternoon, and few people were on the trail as he plodded upward.

From somewhere high above him, several young boys were shouting excitedly. When the noise had ceased he heard the tramp of many feet. A party of men were descending to the desert. As he looked upward he saw them coming around a high bend in the trail, two and two. All were apparently young men, brightly equipped with bow, shield, and spear, as if going to battle.

CHA'-ZA, THE FOOL

He wished he had taken one of the other trails, but he was now too far up to go back without being seen by the approaching men. It occurred to him that this party of young warriors was being sent out to make a show of hunting for their lost Cacique. No doubt one or more such parties were sent out each day to make vain search in the surrounding desert, while he, a lone Pan'-gua trader, whom these men would pass on the trail, could tell them a strange and truthful tale of the great Ah'-mot, and of where he lay hidden. The words of the Dawn Woman came to his mind—"The Shiuana do strange things with us."

He removed his pack and leaned against the mesa wall as the men filed past. Some nodded in a friendly way, while others stared at him blankly as though doubtful of his welcome. Two or three, whom he had met on the hunt, called out, "How goes it, Pan'-gua?"

At the end of the procession were two older men. They stopped as they came to him. One, a small man with broad face, was friendly and held out his hand in greeting. The other, a larger man with prominent nose and cruel mouth, folded his arms and stood staring at the young Pan'-gua trader without greeting or comment. Che-loo' took an instant dislike to the man. Finally he spoke, and his hard voice well suited his face and bearing.

"Pan'-gua traders will find the Pau-lan'-tee people will not make trade when there is great trouble upon them."

"Shh! friend Klee'-tso," broke in the other man quickly. "Do not turn the boy back. There may be some who are not so greatly troubled—and the Pan'-

gua may bring news as well as sky-stones and good Pan'-gua buckskins."

"What are you called?" asked the man addressed as Klee'-tso.

"Son of Mat'-so," replied Che-loo' quietly.

"The son of Mat'-so will be welcome in Pau-lan'-tee, be he trader or not," announced the smaller man, and he started down the trail. The other made as though to say something more, but thinking better of it turned and followed his companion, leaving Che-loo' to continue his upward journey with new and unpleasant thoughts. He recalled the name Klee'-tso. The man was the evil war-captain mentioned by the Dawn Woman.

At the head of the trail he found houses and narrow streets immediately at hand. It seemed, from where he stood, that houses must cover the entire mesa-top. Some boys, playing in the street, directed him to the house of Cha'-za, and he found that it stood less than a stone's-throw from the trail's head.

One of the more courageous of the boys cautiously opened the door of the old man's house and called his name, but there was no response. Che-loo' pushed past him and entered. Cha'-za was not at home. He put down his pack and removed his blanket, which he had worn, belt fashion, about his waist, and explored a second room at the rear. It also was vacant, but he noticed its queer owner had left it neat and clean. Only a weak-minded man could live alone and have a clean house, thought Che-loo'.

"Old Cha'-za is not here," shouted one of the boys from the street door.

"You speak the truth," said Che-loo' dryly.

CHA'-ZA, THE FOOL

The gaping crowd of youngsters about the doorway grew rapidly, for the coming of a trader was ever an interesting event. Suddenly, at their backs, came a shout.

"Dash-i-gee!—Weasels at my door—ah! Weasel pups, and bear whelps! Wait till I crack their—"

The half-fearful shrieks from the flying children cut off the remainder of the old man's threat, and as he came up to his door, swinging his long jack-oak staff there was not a child in sight.

As Cha'-za entered he stopped and stared at Che-loo', then he looked down at the trader's pack.

"I am Che-loo', son of Mat'-so. I come to Pau-lan'-tee to trade," announced Che-loo', as calmly as he could.

"Son of Mat'-so. Son of Mat'-so. Son of the Bear and the Buffalo," repeated the old man, and he wagged his head as though about to set the rhyming words to a tune. He put down his staff and closed the door, all the while wagging his head and mumbling in an audible undertone, "Son of the Bear and the Buffalo."

Paying no further heed to Che-loo', who remained standing in the center of the room, he busied himself at length with some embers that still glowed faintly in the fireplace. With his back to his guest, he finally asked:

"Who of the wise or the foolish sends you to Cha'-za?"

"Ne-chō'-ba" came the short reply. The queer unfriendly actions of the old man, following on the heels of the ill welcome he had received from the man on the trail, began to anger Che-loo'. To remain in the dull confinement of any village was bad enough, but to stay in one whose people were unfriendly was far worse. He would leave Pau-lan'-tee as soon as possible.

Cha'-za slowly wiped his blackened fingers on the sides of his buckskin leggings, and returned to the outer door, beckoning his young guest to follow. Che-loo' picked up his pack and blanket and obeyed. Outside, and but a few steps from the door, a broad ladder led to a second floor above. Ascending this, they arrived on the flat roof of the front room they had just left below. Opening a stout wattled door, that stood ajar, they entered a comfortable room, clean and light.

"It is here you stay," announced Cha'-za. "Food is in my house below. Food for fire is in there," and he pointed toward a small doorway which opened through a rear wall.

After carefully closing the door, the old man again turned to his guest. "Does Ne-chō'-ba send a young chin-dog to bark at Cha'-za, when Pau-lan'-tee is in a trap, like a bear caught by the foot?"

Che-loo' was about to make some angry reply, when something in the eyes of his strange host caused him to speak more kindly. "You think Ne-chō'-ba some Pau-lan'-tee owl that can only fly in the dark?" he countered.

Cha'-za made no direct reply, but with growing respect for his youthful tenant he remarked:

"When a bear is in a trap, it is not a time to feed him berries."

"Look, if you have eyes that can see, and you will know if I am sent as a berry to feed your growling Pau-lan'-tee," commanded Che-loo' angrily, and he picked up a charred stick from the ashes of his fireplace, and stooping down marked on the floor the sign

Ne-chō'-ba had given him. As he looked up he noted a sudden change come over the face of Cha'-za.

"Who tells you to make that sign?" he asked in a low voice.

"Ne-chō'-ba. He told me to make it for your eyes alone," replied Che-loo'.

"What does it mean?" came the next question.

Che-loo' told the old man all that Ne-chō'-ba had said, then he carefully erased the mark. For several moments the old man remained silent as he regarded the youth before him, who now arose and tossed the blackened ember back into the fireplace. Che-loo"s anger had caused him to forget, for a moment, the difference in their ages. More respectfully now, he turned with folded arms and looked calmly into the eyes of his aged host. Cha'-za was wondering why so young a man had been sent to Pau-lan'-tee at such a time, but more particularly why he had been entrusted with the ancient symbol and its meaning.

"Ne-chō'-ba does not mistake a rabbit for a fox," remarked the old man at length. "You look rabbit— but it may be there is wolf under your fur." The changed voice, and the vague compliment, for so it was intended, caused Che-loo' to feel a little more at ease.

Tapping himself on the breast as he spoke, Cha'-za commanded, "Look at me, son of Mat'-so! I am Cha'-za—the Fool. Cha'-za—the Fool." He repeated the words with slow emphasis.

"I understand," replied Che-loo'. "In the presence of others you will be, to me, the fool—but I have it in my thoughts that Ne-chō'-ba sends the sign of an ancient pact—only to the wise."

A whimsical smile tipped the old man's mouth, and

he grasped the arm of his youthful guest and shook him in a friendly manner.

"There is good in your words, son of Mat'-so, but keep your thoughts out of your mouth. You are welcome in the house of Cha'-za. There are more friends than enemies of Pan'-gua in Pau-lan'-tee. The enemies hold the bow, but a bow may break in the hand." Then, turning to the door, "When day is gone, come down to my house. There will be food. Always you will find food and water in my house, and its fire burns for the friends of Ne-chō'-ba."

"I give you thanks," said Che-loo', and he watched the old man cross the roof and nimbly descend the ladder, wagging his head and mumbling the half-sane words of a fool. Plainly enough, Cha'-za was not a fool, and Che-loo' wondered why he wished to be known as one. The marked change in the old man's treatment of him had lifted his spirits, and he now felt more friendly toward his host and his surroundings.

Rabbit, eh? Cha'-za had said he looked rabbit, but might be wolf beneath the fur. The next man who made that mistake might not have age to protect him. He would show such a one how much of a rabbit he was. He decided to take a good look at himself in the next pool of quiet water, and see what it was that had caused Cha'-za to say rabbit. Did the man Klee'-tso, on the trail, have some such idea of him? He wondered. For the first time in his life he was interested in what other men thought of him. Rabbit, eh?

The weight of his strange mission, that had brought him to Pau-lan'-tee, began to impress him, and he felt less inclined to leave the great village until he had made the acquaintance of the three evil men of whom the

CHA'-ZA, THE FOOL

Dawn Woman had warned him. He wondered just how much she knew about them. They might be the three who had given their Cacique into the hands of the Apaches; at least it seemed a good guess. He would try to learn if they, or any one of them, were guilty of this evil. That was the task set for him; but even his youthful zeal did not hide from him the fact that to gain such knowledge would require great wisdom and caution. But now, for the first time, he liked the thought of attempting it.

He could see that his father had spoken truly, and that the enemies of the Pau-lan'-tee Cacique were also enemies of Pan'-gua. In the undertaking that lay before him, he would be pitting wits against the enemies of his people; but he wished there could be some adventure in it, some test of strength and skill.

He closed the door and looked about him. The interior of the room was like the interior of Pan'-gua houses, but had fewer comforts. Pelts of deer and mountain lion were piled neatly on one end of the wide seat ledge that ran around two sides of the room. He would spread some of these on the roof outside his door, when night came, for he had never been able to sleep within walls, except when the extreme cold of winter had driven him in.

In the center of the room a stout round post ran from floor to ceiling-beams in support of the long roof-timbers. Two cooking-pots, a basket, and several woven plaques on which to serve food, were beside the corner fireplace. Against the opposite wall were two ollas, or water-jars. A flat stone lid over one of them indicated that other traders, who had occupied the house, had probably used it for storing meal against the mice and rats.

The outer door, like the one in the house below, was heavy and could be securely fastened on the inside by a stout bar that dropped into forked posts on either side. At the rear door, which opened into a much smaller room, the pleasing odors of dried mint and juniper-bark greeted him. He stepped within and when his eyes had grown accustomed to the dim light he saw that the old man evidently used the room as a storage place.

Great bunches of herbs, rawhide ropes, bird-snares, and an assortment of traps, were suspended from the low ceiling-beams, and a quantity of good firewood was stacked along the wall. Doubtless it was here that Cha'-za would store his winter supply of corn, and of beans and dried mellons. The traps, especially the larger ones, attracted Che-loo''s attention, and he examined them with interest and admiration, for they were well made.

Points of light were coming up through the floor at the back of the room. Where floors were of packed clay over heavy beams, this light could only occur where there was a passageway. On investigation he found a stout mat of tightly woven wattles, and this lay over a square opening in the floor. He lifted an edge of the mat and looked down into the rear room of Cha'-za's dwelling. At first he was not sure that he liked this, as it gave the old man easy, and perhaps unannounced, entrance to his rooms; but after consideration he decided the discovery was welcome, as he might wish to leave his trader's pack behind a barred door, at such times as he was not making trade, and this rear passage would be useful. No doubt Cha'-za would permit him to use it, and he was sure the old man must have a ladder somewhere below, as there were no steps leading up to the opening.

Returning to the front room he continued to the roof outside, and looked about him. Houses, rising terrace fashion to heights of from one to five stories, stretched away for some distance, many of them fronting on the winding little street that passed Cha'-za's door. Beyond these he could see others that fronted in other directions and guessed that many streets ran outward from the plaza that probably lay in the center of the village.

He had heard much of this great plaza in which the Pau-lan'-tee people had, for countless generations, held their many annual fiestas and their great ceremonial dances. Here and there over the flat roofs, amid the bristle of tall ladder-poles, were spots of bright color made by patches of blue corn, yellow melons, and red wild plums that lay drying in the warm September sun.

Turning to things nearer at hand, he noticed that the back wall of Cha'-za's two-story house, like those of the entire row in which it stood, had been built on the very edge of the mesa. This could be seen, as the house that joined it on the side was but one-story high, and across its roof he could look out over the far world which lay below.

As the flat roof of the adjoining house was on a level with the one on which he stood, Che-loo' walked across it to a low guard-wall which ran along the side next to the mesa's edge, and looked over. Immediately beneath him the great perpendicular wall of the mesa dropped dizzily downward. No trails could be built along that side, and no enemy could ever scale the smooth surface of the frowning rock.

As he looked from the great height, far across the desert, now flattened like an endless floor beneath him, Che-loo' felt a strange premonition come to him: a vague warning of dangers to be guarded against. Could the foolish words of the Dawn Woman have had some truth in them? She had warned him of trouble. Tō'-bah-yan, greatest of hunters, had always taught him to give due heed to any sense of danger which might come to him, and to travel any new trail with wide eyes and silent tread.

The low guard-wall seemed none too high, and he stepped back and slowly returned to his own dwelling where Cha'-za's broad ladder took him down to the narrow street. Like a new trail, to be traveled with care, it led him on in its winding course amid old and strange surroundings.

At sundown he entered Cha'-za's house with a keen appetite, for he had eaten sparingly on his journey from Pan'-gua. The old man proved to be a good cook, and over the pot of savory stew the tongues of the young trader and his host loosened with good will.

Since Che-loo''s arrival Cha'-za had thought deeply on Ne-chō'-ba's strange action in sending one so young to the mesa at such a time. Of one thing he was now sure, Che-loo' was not the slow and indolent youth he appeared to be; but the older men of Pau-lan'-tee had never taken so young a man into their confidence, and he knew that he must tell certain of his friends that Che-loo' was both friend and confidant of Ne-chō'-ba, the Cacique of Pan'-gua. That Che-loo' had come for needed information regarding Dou-gow', and the lost

CHA'-ZA, THE FOOL

Ah'-mot, Cha'-za was reasonably sure, but he would have to wait until his young guest made this known to him.

Cha'-za's back room put them beyond easy hearing of the street, and to Che-loo''s relief the old man laid aside his mask of the mumbling fool. During a pause in their talk of trapping and hunting, subjects that greatly interested them both, Che-loo' asked:

"Do the Pau-lan'-tees make Dou-gow' their Cacique, now that Ah'-mot is gone?"

"There will be proof that Ah'-mot will not return before there is talk of a new Cacique," came the reply. Then Cha'-za's voice hardened a little as he continued, "When you again have words with Ne-chō'-ba, tell him the eyes of many Pau-lan'-tees are open, and their ears are not closed."

Mention of Dou-gow' reminded Che-loo' of the strange tale of the Dawn Woman, and he told Cha'-za all she had told him of the former Governor and of how his beautiful wife had been falsely accused of being a witch. As the story progressed the old man sat as if made of stone, but the gleam in his deep-set eyes betrayed an excitement he could not conceal. At the close of the narration sounds of amazement repeatedly escaped him, and when he spoke his voice showed plainly enough the depth of his anger.

"The Chin-di! Always he hides the knife when he strikes, for he strikes in the dark. Ko-lee'-pah—yes, he was the only man who could look into the eyes of Dou-gow' and make him look away. He feared Ko-lee'-pah. The Governor never knew who brought the great trouble upon him, but he knew his wife was no witch, in spite of proof brought against her. You will repeat the words of this to no one," he commanded.

"I have made pact, by a vow, to give the words to no ears but your own," replied Che-loo'. "The woman believes that you also will keep her words while she lives. She will not be many days among the Earth People, for her strength has gone from her."

Cha'-za nodded absently, but said nothing. It was evident that the Dawn Woman's account of Dou-gow"s crime against the former Governor had moved him deeply. Che-loo' wondered at this show of interest in an occurrence that had taken place so long ago.

"The woman gave me warning against three evil men on the mesa," said Che-loo', and he gave Cha'-za the names of Klee'-tso, the war-captain, Dou-gow', and Me-te'-lo, the moccasin-maker. "Is it in your thoughts that such men might send your Cacique away?"

Cha'-za looked sharply at his guest, and after a moment replied, "On the morning of the first day that Ah'-mot was missed from the village, I was in the desert with traps. I saw two of the three men you name walking together in a shallow draw far out from the mesa. Soon they parted, and came by different directions, but Dou-gow' was not with them."

"That was toward the Black Canyon?" questioned Che-loo' suddenly. Then, as quickly, he realized he had blundered, and that he should know nothing of where Cha'-za had seen the two men.

The eyes of the old man looked keenly at his guest, then slowly he replied:

"It was toward the Black Canyon. Until now I have kept word of it in my own head. How is it that you know?"

"I did not know," replied Che-loo', looking down with some embarrassment. "I made guess of it. I know nothing of where the men were."

He saw that Cha'-za did not accept his words, and that he had aroused suspicion in the mind of the old man. He was sorry he had spoken off his guard, for he had come to like Cha'-za and did not care to appear foolish in his eyes. He wished he could tell him all about Ah'-mot, and of the tracks of the three Pau-lan'-tees who had betrayed him. He could see no good reason for Ne-chō'-ba's command not to let Cha'-za know of it. Perhaps he could manage to give him some hint of the three guilty men without mentioning Ah'-mot. He realized that this would have to be done with great care.

Evidently Cha'-za, no matter what he thought of the guess about the Black Canyon, did not intend to press the matter.

"You name one called Me-te'-lo, the moccasin-maker. He will be quick to come to you when he learns you are on the mesa, for he will want to be first to pick from your buckskins that he may have the finest for his moccasins. He knows, of old, that Pan'-gua men bring the best. Have an eye on him when he makes trade with you, and show him no sky-stones, if you have any for trade. He is a greedy man who wants more and more of all things. He has great strength, and likes to quarrel loudly—a bad man in a fight. Many traders fear to deal with him. He is a knife-in-the-hand to Dou-gow'. That is the reason for their friendship. Dou-gow' uses the eyes of Me-te'-lo to spy on others, as the moccasin-maker hears much talk from those who come to him. He will have good weaving to give for your buckskins, as the squaws bring cloth in trade for moccasins. See that he gives you good bargain, and if he talks as one who would quarrel, do not show him anger, and you will have no trouble."

"I shall keep your words in my thoughts," replied Che-loo'. "And I will have need of the moccasin-maker," he went on as he looked down at the hole that had been torn in the heel of his moccasin by theApache arrow.

"When tomorrow's sun is in the midst, I go down to my fields for corn," announced Cha'-za. "There is much to be carried up the mesa, and I need your strong back to help with the loads. There is cutting to be done before the ears are ready, but when the day is old," and here the old man pointed his open hand toward the west, "come down to my fields. They are at the foot of the middle trail. Any child can point them to you. Before I go to the fields I will show you the house of one called Man'-yah. He is a friend to Ne-chō'-ba, and to me. He will expect you, and it may be he will have words for your ears that come better from his mouth than from mine. His wife is a weaver of good cloth, and you may make trade. Tell none that I give you word of this man, and enter his house as one who is not expected."

"It will be as you have said," replied Che-loo'.

As Cha'-za was about to make further comment, there came the sound of some one walking very softly on the roof above. The noise was slight, but unmistakable. Cha'-za made a quick gesture with his thumb toward the street. Che-loo' leaped to his feet and running to the door he opened it and stepped out into the twilight. As he climbed the ladder, leading to his

CHA'-ZA, THE FOOL

rooms, he heard the voice of Cha'-za loudly jabbering the nonsense of the fool from the open door below. On the roof, and but a step from his door, stood a man, and as Che-loo' came up to him the caller stepped forward to meet him, limping slightly as he walked.

"You are the trader from Pan'-gua?" he asked, with hand outstretched.

"Yes," replied Che-loo' bluntly, as he formally clasped the hand of his soft-footed caller.

"I knocked at your door, but you were not within. I am Me-te'-lo. I make moccasins, fine moccasins, and I want fine buckskins. Come to my house when the sun is up. Come early and I will give you fine weaving. Old Cha'-za can tell you my house." As he talked, the man moved toward the ladder, and as the dark bulk of his body came against the open sky Che-loo' saw that he was, as Cha'-za had said, a strong man, and the slight limp would take nothing from the power of his great arms and shoulders.

"I will come," replied Che-loo'.

When the man had passed down into the street below, a feeling of uneasiness, hardly accountable to himself, caused Che-loo' to enter his house and look about him. It was too dark within to see anything but the dim outline of objects against the white walls. Feeling his way to the small room at the back he found wood and built a small fire for light. To save time required by the long whirl of fire-sticks, he descended to the house of Cha'-za for a lighted brand.

The old man had closed his outer door, and was seated by the fire in the back room. As he entered, Che-loo' recalled the passage in the upper floor and asked if he might use it, as he wished to keep his own door barred on the inside whenever he had to leave his pack in his rooms.

"It is well," assented Cha'-za. "A ladder is on the ledge, beneath the blankets. I will leave it against the passage. The maker of moccasins has come, as I had said. He lives on the side of the plaza toward the rising sun, in the house of the green door. It is up one ladder, and the house is wide. What do you do with fire?"

"I am making fire in my house that I may see my bed," replied Che-loo,' as he started toward the door with the burning brand. "When it burns I will come down again, by the passage. It is in my thoughts that my trader's pack should be behind a tight door when I am away in the dark of night."

"You may yet become trader," said Cha'-za approvingly.

By the growing light of his own fire, Che-loo' picked up his pack to remove it to the back room, and as he did so noticed some slight change in the feel of the knotted ends of the outer covering. Dropping the pack to the floor, he examined it carefully. There were unmistakable signs that its contents had been disturbed, though he had not opened the pack since he had bound it up on the morning he had left Pan'-gua. He counted the skins, and found that none were missing. Then he opened the small doeskin bag which contained his sky-stones, and poured them out into his hand. Of two large and beautifully polished stones which his father had given him to trade, one was missing. The two matched perfectly, and being larger than all of the others, he knew he could not be mistaken. To search

CHA'-ZA, THE FOOL 119

further was useless, as the stone could not have escaped the stout thong that had bound the bag.

For a time he knelt on the floor and thoughtfully replaced the bright blue jewels one by one and tied them securely within the little bag. Then retying his pack, he barred his door, and going to the passage in the rear room, he pushed aside the mat, and catching the sides of the opening swung himself down to the floor below, much to the surprise of Cha'-za who, hearing him come to the passage, had risen to place the ladder for him to descend.

Quickly he told the old man of the missing stone. Without comment Cha'-za placed the ladder against the wall beneath the opening, and seating himself by the fire, motioned Che-loo' to sit down beside him.

"It is not the first thing that has been stolen in Paulan'-tee—and we do not know who took it," he remarked at last.

"*I* know who took it," replied Che-loo' coolly. "Either I will have it again in my hand, or I will have its worth from the one who stole it."

"Is it not wise to say you are learning to be a trader, and that to learn this much, has cost you one sky-stone?" asked Cha'-za quietly.

"Does Pau-lan'-tee have no law against those who steal?" inquired Che-loo'.

"Yes, when there is proof brought to the Council, but do you have proof?"

"No," replied Che-loo', and he felt a helpless anger rising within him, "but I shall be the law, when that which is in my care is taken from me."

The old man looked at his youthful guest and saw the anger in the young eyes that suddenly seemed to have grown mature. He saw strength, youth, and cool determination fixed before him. A more violent anger would have suited Cha'-za better, it would be more easily handled. Of all men in Pau-lan'-tee, this determined son of Pan'-gua could not have found one with whom it could be worse to make trouble than with Me-te'-lo. As he studied the face of Che-loo' the old man became convinced that, in some way, the moccasin-maker would be made to pay unless some means were found to make him return the stone.

Quietly he laid his hand on Che-loo"s shoulder. "Son, when the witch of evil is in a man, it makes him to do its will—and when the day of that man is done, it is the witch of evil that sends him on the Long Sleep. Let the thief alone with his witch, and others may strike him for you. Can a gourd of water flood the desert? Can you, a youth of Pan'-gua, stand against the strength of this man, who is high in the Council of Pau-lan'-tee?"

Che-loo' rose, and stood for a moment beside his aged host. He knew that Cha'-za was right, but anger gripped him. "I have no answer now," he replied at length. "I go now, umo [aged one], and I give you thanks for food."

Before the old man could make reply he ran up the short ladder, and replacing the wattled mat over the passage, went on to his front room and unbarred the door. Flinging it open he stepped out, and leaning against the house wall looked up at the silent stars. Only the open sky, and broad free earth, could give quiet to his angry thoughts.

CHAPTER IX

A TEST OF SKILL

The sun swings up in a golden glow
That floods the sage and the sand;
The Indian maidens softly sing
As they take the trail to the bubbling spring,
And the shouts of men from the house-tops ring—
'Tis day in the red-man's land!

NEAR the end of a short street, called Bahn ba-toh', or place of the long wall, stood the house of Ah'-mot, the Cacique of Pau-lan'-tee. The ancient dwelling had housed the Caciques of the mesa for many generations, and its inner walls had doubtless looked down on many secret meetings of the men who either belonged or wished to belong to the great Council, for the Caciques had ever held the balance of power within the envied circle.

Today in the cool comfort of its large living-room were seated two women, wife and foster-daughter of the missing ruler. The wife, a stout woman of middle age, sat on the floor with her back against the wall, her fat hands held listlessly in her lap, as she stared vacantly at the bare toes of her up-turned feet. Her eyes were red with much weeping, and she seemed on the verge of fresh tears. The daughter, who has been introduced to the reader as the taller of the two young women who so effectually blocked the path of Che-loo' on the day he and his friends chased the wounded buck so near the great mesa, sat dry-eyed and calm as she silently shelled blue corn into a shallow basket held in her lap. Behind her a flood of light from the late afternoon sun streamed through an open doorway in the western end of the room, and within its golden rectangle the slender girlish form made pleasing contrast with the stout weeping figure in the shadow.

The wife of Ah'-mot was a weak woman, easily swayed by circumstance, and fearful of every witch-sign, or questionable omen that gained her attention. She looked for disaster where others might find small reason for it, and now, in the tragic loss of her husband, she had given full vent to her abundant grief. She secretly enjoyed her great sorrow and the solemn consolation of tearful friends.

Mah-wee'-nah understood her foster-mother's unstable character and was aware that her own strength and calm deportment were now greatly needed to balance such weakness. The more sincere grief within her own heart was not permitted the ease of tears. In her veins ran the blood of a more stoic tribe, but her loyalty and affection were far greater than those of the weeping woman before her. As a baby she had come into the home and hearts of the Cacique and his wife, and she had given them all the love and devotion that a child of their own might have given, but as she grew to womanhood she displayed more and more of the calm poise, as well as physical beauty, of her Apache mother. Quite naturally she had become the pride and joy of the Cacique, who let it be known that no man of Pau-lan'-tee need seek her in marriage unless he was able to show himself worthy of so great an honor.

As the two women sat for a moment in silence, the

outer door quietly opened and En-tay', lifelong friend of Mah-wee'-nah, entered. Without greeting, and as one accustomed to come and go at will, she crossed the room and seated herself at the feet of the older woman.

"With tomorrow's sun, good friend, there will come good news. You shall see—it will come *sure!*" she announced with forced gaiety. Her tender heart went out to the mother of her friend and she sought in every way to lessen her grief. "When he is found, then you will laugh loudly and you will say, 'Why did I so weep with unhappiness, for he is not lost but found.' Is it not so, Mah-wee'-nah?"

"Yes, it is so. Again and again have I said to her, it is not yet time to be so sad, and all the tears of great weeping cannot help," came the reply.

"You know nothing! You, who are young and have no place for sorrow in your hearts," complained the mother. Then, turning to her daughter, "It is not the father of En-tay' who is lost, and she cannot have grief, but *you,* ungrateful one, are the only child of your father; *you* should care." And she fell to weeping audibly.

"I *do* care, my mother, and I too would be sad and weep if I had no hope of his return to us, but weep I cannot when I have not given him up as one who is gone for always."

Feeling irritated by what she chose to believe was a lack of sympathy, the weeping woman rose and moved toward the street door. "I shall go to the house of my sister, where they understand my great sorrow," she wailed as she passed out into the street. The door gave a spiteful slam behind her.

"It is better so," remarked Mah-wee'-nah calmly.

"Each day she has gone to the house of my aunt, who weeps more loudly than she, and when my mother returns she is better of her grief."

"Come!" commanded En-tay'. "You must get out in the sun. Too long have you been in the house. You have said you would have to go to your father's fields for corn. Let's go now and I will help with the load, and I have much to say, *much* that will make your ears dance!"

Mah-wee'-nah put down her basket and rose thoughtfully, brushing the small husks from her skirt.

"My mother tried to make me give promise to let Dou-gow' bring up the corn we need, but I told her no. He comes here too much, and I will have him do nothing for me or for my mother—if I can have my way," she announced as she prepared to depart.

En-tay' stepped close to her friend.

"You know why he comes," she remarked in a low voice. "I shall not say the words, but I have heard, Mah-wee'-nah. He cannot have you. He shall not have you! He is old and mean, with his ugly eyes of evil. Let him take an old woman to wife—the Chin-di!"

"Hush, En-tay'! Do not say such words. I will not think such a thing. It makes me feel bitter here," and Mah-wee'-nah put her hand on her breast. "Better I go on the Long Sleep than to become—" but her tongue refused to voice the hateful thought so repugnant to her. "Yes, we will go to my father's fields. The house walls choke me, and I want to run away, away off where there are no houses and no weeping, and no eyes of people upon me."

"Now *that* is like my real Mah-wee'-nah," exclaimed

En-tay', delighted. "Come, I will tell my mother I go with you, and I have promised to take my little brother when I went again to the fields. I will give him a little bag and he can help."

Securing a buckskin sack in which to carry the needed supply of corn, they proceeded to the house of En-tay' and, accompanied by the little brother, started for the trail.

"Run ahead, ushie," commanded En-tay' to the boy, and when he had obeyed, she turned to her companion.

"Now—open wide your ears. You cannot guess who is here, in Pau-lan'-tee! It is the handsome hunter from Pan'-gua! And he has been in my house!—a long time—this day. And I know his name—it is Che-loo'! Is it not a nice name to say? And he is the son of Mat'-so, the tapop of Pan'-gua—and there is some great secret about him, for he pretends to come to our house as a trader—but I have eyes and ears. He came to have a long talk of many words with my father." Here the excited speaker lowered her voice. "I was in our back room when he came, and almost I jumped out of my skin, but he did not see me—not then—and I kept very still, weaving a belt on my mother's loom. And once in a while I heard his words and the words of my father, but they talked with low voice. And I heard much the name of Dou-gow' and then the name of Ne-chō'-bah and of Cha'-za. This handsome Che-loo' is some great one, and oh, Mah-wee'-nah, he is so nice to look at! He does not have fear of men as he has fear of us, and he does not talk with the words of one who is young, but says to my father—'No, Man'-yah, my people will do this, and do that!'—just like one man of the Council speaks to another. My father likes him. I think my father met him on the trail when he was going down with Klee'-tso and the men, and this man Che-loo' said to my father—'I do not like your war-captain' and I did not hear what my father said to that."

During the rapid talk of the excited En-tay', her companion, as was her habit at such times, said nothing. She knew that she did not need to ask questions, as she would hear all if she simply kept quiet and gave her talkative friend ample time to tell all she knew.

"Is it not nice that he is here—here on the mesa?"

"It may be," replied Mah-wee'-nah, with small show of interest. "Since it makes you so happy—but what of your Mah-sen'-ka, who plays to you love songs on the reed?"

"Always you turn things on *me*—bad Mah-wee'-nah—! Well enough you know this Che-loo' man has no eyes for poor me. He? *He* must have a tall beautiful woman like you. Yes, like *you*—and he is not one who will have fear of old Dou-gow', or the men whom you say watch you when you walk in the street. I can see in his face that this Pan'-gua man would fear nothing but you. Yes, you he fears *much*. I saw it that day in his eyes. It was fear—fear that he would like you too much."

"Stop such silly talk!" commanded Mah-wee'-nah, but the rebuke was too mild to hide the pleasure En-tay''s remarks had given her, and this did not escape En-tay'.

Mah-wee'-nah was young and the love of life and the will to live it in her own wild free way was ever near the surface of her nature. None but the observant En-tay' knew that within the apparently passive disposition of the half-Apache girl, lurked the burning desire for a greater freedom than the village walls and customs would permit.

The growing conviction that the evil Dou-gow' had some designs upon her, and that she was being watched by his spies, had weighed heavily upon her heart, and now the mysterious loss of her father, and the society of the weeping mother, whom she had constantly consoled since the Cacique's disappearance, had oppressed her almost to the limit of endurance.

The words of the lively En-tay' were, just now, particularly welcome, for they brought something new, something more normal, and as the two walked down the trail in the warm glow of the low evening sun, she felt a weight lift from her breast, and a quick response to the gay humor of her companion.

This young Pan'-gua hunter, of whom En-tay' talked so much, was free—gloriously free. He was not under the fear of the hatred Dou-gow', as most all of the young men of Pau-lan'-tee were, and it was this full freedom of the young and handsome stranger that appealed strongly to her imagination.

"Oh, to be a man, En-tay'! A man free to go far out over the earth; to sleep under the stars on the mountain-top. Why was I not born a man? If I were a man—I would be a hunter, En-tay', and never, *never* would I stay long within the walls of a house. I despise houses!"

En-tay' looked questioningly into the face of her companion.

"For many days you have not said words like that. It is like your old self, my real Mah-wee'-nah, that speaks. But you are *not* a man—so, the next thing to *that* would be to run away with a brave, free hunter, and be his wife, and hunt with him on the mountain-tops. Almost I believe that you are happy that the Pan'-gua hunter has come. Tell me, is it not true?"

"It may be I shall not weep if I should see him," came the reply. "But what have I to do with him, and what has he to do with me? He has come to your home, not to mine. Is it not you who know his name, and all these things you have told me about him?"

"Yes, but you are not sorry I have told you, and you are not sorry he is here. His name is Che-loo'—say it, Mah-wee'-nah. I want to hear how it sounds in your mouth, and I want to see if your eyes do not tell me that you think it is a nice name."

"Who can be more foolish than you, silly one? I will *not* say it. If it is nice or if it is not—I will not say it. What is his name to me?"

The reply did not deceive En-tay'. Since their chance meeting with the young Pan'-gua hunter, on the mesa-trail, she had harbored a secret desire to interest her friend in him. To her, Che-loo', of all men she had known, seemed nearest the kind she would choose for her beloved and admired Mah-wee'-nah. She had secretly hoped that he might one day come to the mesa, for she firmly believed that no young man could look upon Mah-wee'-nah and not try to see her again. She believed Che-loo' had partly, if not mainly, come for this purpose. Dou-gow', she well knew, wished to take her friend for his wife, and though she believed he would not succeed, she knew that he would leave no stone unturned and no scheme untried, to win her. She also knew that Dou-gow''s rival would have to be one

A TEST OF SKILL

who had no fear, and whose love for Mah-wee'-nah would make him dare to do anything to get her.

"I will say no more to you about this Pan'-gua hunter. I see you will not like him, poor man, and I suppose I must say to him, 'Go back to your hunting, out over the far hills, and have no more nice thoughts of this Mah-wee'-nah girl, for she—'"

"It grows late, and we are walking like snails. Let's run and catch up with little Con-chi," broke in Mah-wee'-nah. Knowing that En-tay' had told her all she knew of Che-loo', she was aware that further talk of him would amount to no more than idle teasing, and she was in no mood to be teased.

While the two Pau-lan'-tee maidens were filling their sack with corn in the fields of Ah'-mot, Che-loo' was descending the ladder in Cha'-za's back room, after leaving his pack in his carefully barred room. He was now ready to go down the trail to help the old man with his harvest. The day had gone well with him, better than his experience of the night before had promised. The cool morning, after a good night's sleep on the roof, had brought him to see the wisdom of Cha'-za's counsel, and he had decided to let the matter of the stolen sky-stone rest for the present—but only for the present. He wanted time to think of some way of bringing justice to the thieving Me-te'-lo.

In his dealings with the moccasin-maker he had quickly let him know that he would brook no unfair bargaining, and Me-te'-lo had displayed none of the evil traits of which Cha'-za had warned him. This, Che-loo' laid to the fact that, knowing his own guilt, and the ease with which he had made the theft, the moccasin-maker felt inclined to deal more fairly with his victim.

Man'-yah, the friend of Cha'-za, who had proved to be the friendly man whom he had met on the trail with Klee'-tso, the war-captain, had told him much that he needed to know and, much to his comfort, had treated him as an equal. Perhaps Cha'-za had told Man'-yah something of the secret symbol with which Ne-chō'-ba had entrusted him.

So it was with a light heart that he made his way to the middle trail and descended to Cha'-za's cornfields. As he neared the foot of the wide path a pleasing scene was spread out before him. In the golden light of the late afternoon sun the broad fields, ripe for harvest, extended out into the reclaimed desert. Countless patches of yellow melons, small regular heaps of dried bean-vines, and rows on rows of ripe maize, told of a year of plenty, and the matured fruits of the fields waited to be carried to the houses on the mesa-top, there to be stored for winter use. Here and there, on the outer margin of the fields, were small strongly built shelters. In these the owners of the outlying fields took turns in keeping watch against the crows, and a more serious guard against thieving bands of desert men who occasionally fared forth at night to reap where they had not sown.

Several Pau-lan'-tee harvesters, both men and women, were in the fields threshing beans and husking the ripe corn for the bag and burden basket. Che-loo' found Cha'-za seated by a large pile of blue maize, busily husking the last few ears that would be needed to fill the two buckskin bags he had brought to the fields.

A TEST OF SKILL

The old man was singing nonsense in a high key, and as there were men at work near at hand in an adjoining field, Che-loo' was quick to realize that Cha'-za would expect to be treated as the fool.

"Ha-la'-ni, old Cha'-za! You sing like the crow!" he called out as he neared the pile of corn.

"Hoa! Child of the desert. You chatter like Squee-kin, the sand-rat!" shouted the old man. "If you come to the fields of Cha'-za, for Cha'-za you will work." Then, in a lower tone, "Fill the bags. I will return quickly."

The speaker rose and, holding to his childish chant, crossed the fields to where two young women and a little boy were laboring over their corn. In a short time he returned carrying a small filled bag, and set it down beside the larger one which Che-loo' had been filling in his absence.

"This we will carry with the rest," he announced in a low voice, as he fell to work filling the second bag.

As the two bent to their task, Cha'-za mumbling like a half-wit, a stout, loutish fellow came up to them, and without a word picked up the small bag that Cha'-za had just set down. Instantly the old man also grasped the bag and with sudden effort jerked it from the hands of the newcomer.

"Give the bag to me, old fool. Dou-gow' says *he* will carry it up the mesa for her," explained the man angrily as he started to take the bag from the other's hands.

Cha'-za backed away, wild-eyed and mumbling.

"The bag is in Cha'-za's care, and Cha'-za will keep it! The Black Witch take the hair from your empty head if you touch it!"

Che-loo' leaped to his feet, and stepped between the two, facing the stranger.

"You have heard the words of Cha'-za. The bag is in his care, and he will keep it." The words, spoken without anger, bore a decided note of warning, and the man was quick to see that to take the bag by force was out of the question.

"We shall see," said the loutish one threateningly, and he strode away to the men in the adjoining field.

"We must fill the bags and be gone quickly," said Cha'-za, as he set to work furiously. "It is not good that you should have spoken to that man. I could have kept the bag from him. There may now be trouble. Dou-gow' is a bad one to cross; but I am the fool, none quarrel long with me." The rapidly spoken sentences came in a guarded voice, and betrayed the speaker's agitation. "If they come, say nothing. I will talk," he concluded.

Che-loo' made no reply, but he felt that his host was giving him ill return for his prompt assistance. He could not understand about the little bag. Just why Dou-gow' should want to carry it was a mystery, and, for that matter, it was just as inexplicable why old Cha'-za should want to take charge of it, since it evidently did not belong to him. It was unlike men, at least any men he had known, to make a fuss over who should carry a sack of corn. Suddenly he remembered another small bag that Cha'-za had carried for two girls whom he had met one day—on the mesa-trail. He looked over the fields and seeing the two young women, quickly drew his own conclusions.

Shortly the two bags were filled and they were hastily tying them when the man returned, this time accompanied by two others. As the trio stopped beside them, Che-loo' very deliberately finished tying the bag he had filled, and laying it over the small one that had caused the dispute, he rose to his full height. He found himself looking into the eyes of a man whom he instinctively knew must be Dou-gow', the murderer, traitor, and, for the present, supreme ruler of Pau-lan'-tee.

The man's appearance fitted perfectly with his evil reputation. The cruel face, robust figure, and easy bearing seemed to radiate power and absolute self-confidence. Just now his wide mouth betrayed mild amusement, if not good nature, but his eyes, small, black and piercing, so held Che-loo''s attention that he was merely aware of the man's general appearance. To the other men he gave no heed. In the first brief moment after their eyes met, Che-loo' was held by curiosity, for he expected the other to speak. Then he felt a new and irritating sensation sweep over him— the glittering eyes, which he suddenly realized were like those of some great snake, were evidently trying to belittle him or make him cower under their dominant stare. He felt an intended menace in their steady, unblinking gaze now fixed on his eyes as fingers might be fixed on a throat.

No one spoke and he was aware that the attention of all were upon him and the man before him, as if entertained by this strange conflict of personalities. Evidently Dou-gow' was playing an old trick that they had enjoyed before. Did this Pau-lan'-tee tapop think he looked—"rabbit?" A wave of hot anger arose in Che-loo', and then as suddenly he became cool— strangely cool, as he gazed steadily into the eyes of his antagonist. Supreme confidence in his own powers settled upon him as he looked, more and more calmly, into the evil eyes. He was vaguely aware that Cha'-za had been keeping up an incessant mumbling, and now his foolish words grew louder, as if he were trying to break the spell that held the two silent men before him.

Che-loo' was held by one purpose: he would force this man to lower his eyes. With splendid self-mastery, he allowed no muscle of his face to change under the cold, fixed stare of Dou-gow'. After what seemed a long time, Dou-gow' folded his arms, but the gesture, meant to display calm deliberation, disclosed marked uneasiness. A sneer replaced the amused look that he had tried to retain, his eyes wavered, then suddenly shifted, sweeping Che-loo' from head to foot. He had lost to this young stranger from Pan'-gua, and the three men who stood by knew it. In the face of the mumbling Cha'-za was a look of mingled worry and fear.

"Who is this young whelp of the desert?" asked Dou-gow', turning to one of the men.

"I am Che-loo', son of Mat'-so, of Pan'-gua," announced Che-loo' promptly. "I have not heard your name, but it is strange welcome you give to a friend of Pau-lan'-tee."

For a moment Dou-gow' was silent, thoughtful. So the young Pan'-gua did not know whom he had stared out of countenance. That made a difference. Perhaps this youth would not have had such insolent self-confidence had he known. The thought eased Dou-gow''s pride, and might, to some extent, excuse his own defeat in the eyes of his two companions. As for Cha'-za, the Fool, he was not to be considered.

A TEST OF SKILL

"I—am—Dou-gow'." The words were spoken with deliberate emphasis.

"It is plain that we have both shot wide the mark," replied Che-loo'. "None had named you to me—and you thought *me* some whelp of the desert. It was not in my thought to wrong the Governor of Pau-lan'-tee."

If Dou-gow' expected the youth before him to show fear or great embarrassment, upon hearing the dread name, he was disappointed, for the cool, even voice betrayed no such emotion.

The third man of the three stepped forward and confronted the young trader with insolent look of appraisal. He was of about the same height as Che-loo', broad of shoulder, and his close-fitting doeskin shirt did not hide the bulge of the heavy muscles of his chest and arms.

"It may be the young Pan'-gua is more bold with his eyes than with his arms and legs." The words were uttered with the superior air of one who might be high in authority. "If he was thrown on his head, we could tell by the sound whether his bold eyes look out of a gourd—or a melon."

Dou-gow', and the loutish youth beside him, laughed—the youth loudly, and Dou-gow' with a scornful chuckle. He enjoyed this ridicule of the overbold young Pan'-gua. The youthful upstart would soon learn a lesson.

"My head is neither gourd nor melon," said Che-loo', eying the man quietly. "But who is it that would try to throw me?"

Cha'-za ran between them.

"No—no! The Pan'-gua has vowed to help Cha'-za

with the corn. It is late—Chi-nil' will *not* throw the Pan'-gua on his head. He must help—"

"Go, Fool!" exclaimed the man, as he pushed Cha'-za roughly with a strong sweep of his right arm. The old man staggered back a pace and fell on his hands and knees in the soft earth.

Che-loo' caught the name—Chi-nil'—and saw the wisdom of the old man's kindly warning and attempted intervention. So the man who spoke of throwing him on his head was Chi-nil', known far and wide as the Pau-lan'-tee wrestler. The man's rough treatment of the aged Cha'-za did not diminish Che-loo''s hot anger, but this was not betrayed in his calm voice or bearing.

"Cha'-za says your name is Chi-nil'," he remarked, as though the name meant nothing to him. "I tell you, Chi-nil' of Pau-lan'-tee, your words are big, and your talk strong talk—but it is like loud wind in the trees. I cannot remember of any wind that has thrown me on my head."

For reply, the wrestler permitted a broad, evil grin to spread slowly over his face. Other opponents had seen that slow sinister smirk and suddenly become doubtful of their ability to stand against the Pau-lan'-tee wrestler, but it seemed to have no such effect on Che-loo'. Dou-gow' was now satisfied that this tall, stolid-appearing young Pan'-gua had no idea that he was facing the most skilful wrestler of the mesa. The result would be very short and highly amusing. The Pau-lan'-tee began pulling off his doeskin shirt. Che-loo', already bare above the waist, stood with folded arms, calmly waiting.

As the wrestler's shirt came off, the heavy muscles of his strong torso were revealed to Che-loo''s apprais-

A TEST OF SKILL

ing eye. He thought the muscles of the chest and shoulders appeared just a little too round and smooth for hardened sinew. This softness of muscle might denote fat, and fat would mean shortness of wind. He decided at once what course to follow with this formidable adversary. He would test his strength, then he would remain on the defensive, and make an effort to cut down the wrestler's wind and endurance before attempting any aggressive action of his own. To keep from being thrown in the first few minutes of the struggle would be his aim. If the powerful muscles of his opponent could be held to an ineffectual effort for a short time, he might at least escape being thrown.

With the easy assurance of a man about to toss a sack of corn to the ground, Chi-nil' walked up to his innocent Pan'-gua victim with bent arms lowered for a quick grip. To his surprise, but one arm—his right—went where he had directed it, for he found Che-loo''s right arm below his own left. Still with easy confidence, he made a sudden trial of an old trick of twisting his opponent's body at the instant of attempting to lift him from his feet. Though he found no apparent resistance, the trick somehow failed, for the Pan'-gua remained solid on his feet, back arched as at the start. With another quick motion, he tried to lunge closer to Che-loo', that he might lower his hold to a more effectual position. The move was easily foiled; the Pau-lan'-tee found his arms higher than they were before. Suddenly pulling inward and downward at the same time, the wrestler exerted his whole strength, and though the strain on Che-loo' was great, the move gained nothing for the Pau-lan'-tee. Che-loo' believed he now knew the full strength of his antagonist. Alert, feet braced, but not too far apart, he seemed immovable.

"Throw him on his empty head!" shouted the loutish youth.

"Hold your barking tongue!" commanded Dou-gow'.

Other men, seeing the contest in progress, joined the small audience, and Cha'-za, who had drawn his bags of corn farther up the field, sat on one of them, outwardly the mumbling fool, but inwardly fearfully thoughtful, as he watched the outcome of the unfair struggle. Things were going from bad to worse.

Again and again the Pau-lan'-tee exerted his strength and skill, and one trick after another was tried, only to be anticipated and foiled by the stolid and unaggressive young Pan'-gua. At last it dawned on the wrestler that this innocent-appearing contender was, in truth, a wrestler and one who might possess a skill equal to his own.

Che-loo' now noticed that his opponent's violent efforts were beginning to tell on him. Perspiration gleamed on his brow and his breath was perceptibly shorter. The surrounding men remained silent, wondering, as their great faith in their champion began to waver. With feelings of exultation Che-loo' saw that the renowned Chi-nil' no longer possessed a strength or skill that need be feared. Evidently he had rested too long on his reputation, and had not—of late—had a sufficient number of contests to keep him fit.

Suddenly the wrestler forced his opponent backward, and then, with a mighty effort, freed himself and stepped back panting, but made as if he had merely wished to get a new grip. Instantly Che-loo' rushed at him, giving the Pau-lan'-tee no time for needed recovery of breath. The wrestler was now forced to take the defensive, but was wholly unprepared for the terrible grip of the young Pan'-gua's arm and hand. Up to this point in the contest Che-loo' had not put his full strength to the test—now both swiftness and skill were exerted at the same instant. With quick inward pull, and a half-step toward his opponent's left side, he easily broke the grip of the Pau-lan'-tee's right arm, and a second later, with a twisting upward swing, the mighty Chi-nil"'s body rose in the air and was thrown heavily to earth as a bag of beans might have been tossed from a strong man's shoulder.

Che-loo' stepped back and folded his arms, as the wrestler staggered to his feet, white with anger and gasping, for the sudden fall had driven most of the air from his lungs. The innocent Pan'-gua had tricked him.

An exclamation of utter disgust escaped from Dou-gow'.

"Where is your great power as a thrower of men that you let this Pan'-gua whelp throw you to earth like a bag of dry bones?" he exclaimed, with a hard bite of anger in his words.

The defeated wrestler, now either too angry or too dazed to realize what he was doing, again rushed at Che-loo'. Instantly Dou-gow' was between them, pushing them apart.

"Back, you fool!" he commanded the wrestler. "The Pan'-gua will break your neck if he throws you again." And with strong right hand against the Pau-lan'-tee's neck, he forced him backward.

For a moment Che-loo' stood waiting, but Chi-nil', the wrestler, had no thought of opposing Dou-gow', and with sullen and silent anger walked away, followed by the Governor, with the amazed and loutish youth bringing up the rear.

CHAPTER X

A FLAME TO THE ARROW

A hidden flame in the pulse may leap
From a fire as old as man,
And a spark may lie
In a maiden's eye,
Or the touch of a maiden's hand.

WHEN Dou-gow' and the defeated wrestler had gone, the few remaining harvesters, who had witnessed the contest, looked at Che-loo' with open wonder and approval. "You are one who wrestles with great knowledge," said one. Then they grinned discreetly, and returned to their fields to talk much of the unexpected fall of the renowned Chi-nil', and the marvelous strength and skill of the surprising young Pan'-gua.

As Che-loo' came up to Cha'-za, who remained seated on his bags of corn, he noted an expression of deep concern on the wrinkled old face of his friend. There was no one near them now.

"You received hurt by the hand of Chi-nil'?" asked Che-loo', as he noticed that Cha'-za made no move to rise.

"No, he did me no harm," came the scornful reply. "But this is an ill thing that has come to pass." The old man rose and regarded Che-loo' thoughtfully. "At another time, the throwing of Chi-nil' would have been good—but now—" and he shook his gray head as if in solemn warning. "You make Dou-gow' drop his eyes—that is bad; then you make his friend to look like a dog which has been beaten with the stick. *That* is bad medicine. You must give Dou-gow' a wide trail, for it is strong in my mind that he will make trouble come upon you quickly, if you remain longer on the mesa."

"I am a friend of Pau-lan'-tee," came the reply. "Must I have fear of one who is enemy of both your people and mine? Am I a rat that I should let this dog Chi-nil' bark so loudly at me, and then shake me in his teeth, because he is friend of Dou-gow'?"

The old man shook his head half sadly. "Ne-chō'-ba sends you to me with the ancient pact of friendship, and so you become my good friend, but he does not let me know you are wolf, bear, and Chin-di all in one, all with the skin of a rabbit to hide you from the eyes of men." A sudden chuckle, wholly unexpected by Che-loo', escaped the old man. "Always Chi-nil''s head has been high, like the top of the tree—now, he is little, like the sage. When Dou-gow' gave him the sign to quarrel with you it was in Chi-nil''s thought to send you on the Long Sleep. Two men has he sent. When he says 'throw on the head' he means to twist the neck—so." And Cha'-za laid his head suddenly on one side and opened his mouth.

"Humm!" grunted Che-loo' with interest.

"You are like Mat'-so," went on the old man. "You fear nothing. That is good, but"—and here Cha'-za lowered his voice almost to a whisper—"do not draw the bow again at one who has a thousand arrows to your one. Dou-gow' can strike in the dark, and with many hands. Keep in your thoughts that four of his hands belong to Klee'-tso and Me-te'-lo. He has tried Chi-nil', and Chi-nil' has failed. He may now use one of the others."

The old man bound the small bag of corn to one of the two larger ones, preparatory to lifting the combined load to his shoulders.

"That is too great a weight for you," warned Che-loo'. "Let me carry the small one with my sack."

He saw at once that his suggestions was useless, as Cha'-za carefully tied the last knot and swung the load deftly to his back. Then the old man spoke.

"I have given word, and the bag remains with me. We do not take the same trail up the mesa. I will follow the middle one, you will take the one to the right. It is better so." Che-loo' understood, for as he looked toward the foot of the mesa, across the last low light of the setting sun, he saw that Dou-gow' and his friends were already half-way up the middle trail.

He picked up the bag he was to carry, and without further words the two took their separate ways toward the village. Though outwardly calm, Che-loo"s thoughts were greatly disturbed. The encounter with Dou-gow', so unexpected, and so unlike anything that had ever come to him before, set his mind on a strange trail of thought. He had never heard of two men staring at each other without a word. He remembered, now that he came to think of it, that Cha'-za had said something about the former Governor, Ko-lee'-pah, as being the only man who could look into the eyes of Dou-gow' and make him look away. Perhaps it was one way that Dou-gow' had of making men fear him. Che-loo' felt no elation over his victory in the strange contest, it had seemed too foolish and without purpose.

Although he had no fear of Dou-gow', he knew that he should take Cha'-za's advice, and try to avoid any further meeting him.

As to the contest with Chi-nil', he had enjoyed that, every moment of it, though he might have acted differently had he known that the wrestler intended to do him harm. So these Pau-lan'-tees, at least those who had set themselves with Dou-gow', thought to bring trouble upon him, did they? Steal from him, bring fear upon him with a cold stare of the eyes, and break his neck in wrestling! These unpleasant thoughts caused him to remember the warning of his father about crossing Dou-gow', and that he was to return to Pan'-gua if he found the evil Governor set against him. If he was to heed his father's warning he must now return quickly, but he reflected that he had made no promise.

There was the thieving Me-te'-lo yet to deal with. He had ordered him to make new moccasins for him, and with tomorrow's sun they would be finished. He decided on a simple way to get even with the maker of moccasins. He would ask for them, put them on, then he would tell the thief that the sky-stone he had taken would pay for them. Just what Me-te'-lo would do or say about that would remain to be seen. That little matter settled, he would return to Pan'-gua. In the meantime he hoped to find a way to let Cha'-za know that three Pau-lan'-tee men had given Ah'-mot into the hands of the Apaches, and that the tracks of these three men had been found in the desert. He now felt sure that two of the three men were Klee'-tso and Me-te'-lo, as Cha'-za had seen them near the Black

Canyon on the day the Cacique was lost, but as to the identity of the third man there was, as yet, no evidence.

Near the top of the mesa he encountered a little boy who was wearily plodding his way upward with, for him, a heavy load of corn, in a very small bag, that seemed about to fall from his very small shoulders.

"Ha-la'-ni, big man!" said Che-loo' very seriously, as he came opposite him. "Give me your corn to carry for a while, and you run ahead and find a flat stone to rest upon until I catch up with you." With that he reached down with his free hand and lifted the sack from the very willing youngster, who looked up with a bright smile.

"I can run fast without the corn!" exclaimed the boy as he started running up the trail, and a moment later his little bare heels disappeared around a sharp bend.

At the turn Che-loo' heard voices, women's voices that sounded vaguely familiar, and the next moment he faced Mah-wee'-nah and En-tay' resting beside the steep path, and listening to an exciting account of a good Pan'-gua man, from the little brother.

En-tay,' who was not tongue-tied this time, jumped to her feet and confronted Che-loo'.

"You are good to carry the corn for my little brother, Che-loo' of Pan'-gua, and I see you help poor old Cha'-za too." Then, with a gesture toward Mah-wee'-nah, "She is my good friend Mah-wee'-nah. Her father is lost, and we have been down to get corn from his fields."

Che-loo' suddenly remembered the little bag of corn that both Cha'-za and Dou-gow' had wanted to carry, and found he disliked the evil Dou-gow' more than ever. The little brother of En-tay', perhaps fearing he was not fully obeying the kind Pan'-gua man who had asked him to find a flat stone to sit on, ran hastily up the trail.

This afforded the quick En-tay' the excuse she had hoped for. "Here, ushie!" she called out as she ran, rather slowly, however, after the fleeing brother. "You must not run away and leave the good Pan'-gua to carry your corn all the way. Come back here!" But she was glad, for once, that the ushie did not obey, and she continued after him, leaving the two most interesting of all the earth-born alone together. Not until she had reached a large flat rock, near the head of the trail, did she stop to wait for her friend, and here the weary little brother was willing to wait for the good Pan'-gua.

The unexpected meeting had occurred so quickly, Che-loo' had not had time for embarrassment. He lowered Cha'-za's heavy bag of corn to the ground, glad to have a moment's rest after the long climb. Mah-wee'-na rose and, with hands behind her back, leaned against the mesa wall.

"It must be very good to be a man with great strength, and—the thought to help others," she remarked.

Che-loo' folded his arms, and avoided her eyes. "To carry corn is nothing," he replied, greatly pleased and surprised to find that he could again listen to the low soft voice and not feel like running away. "Your friend has said that your father is lost. Are you the daughter of the Cacique?" He looked at her now, timidly.

"Ah'-mot is my father," came the low reply, and

A FLAME TO THE ARROW   147

Mah-wee'-nah bowed her head in sudden thought of her loss. The bright gleam of a small blue feather shone in the great mass of her dark hair.

A feeling of pity came into the heart of Che-loo', as he caught the note of distress in the girl's simple reply. He wished he could tell her that he had seen her father alive, and that he was among friends. The feather, his feather, was still worn in her hair. In some way he could not have explained, it made her seem nearer to him.

"You must not have fear that—that he is lost for always," he remarked kindly.

"Though five suns have risen since he went away, there is a feeling within me that he may still be among the earth-born," she replied with a brave show of hope.

"You feel what is true—I know he—I mean you must not believe he is, for always, gone from you." Che-loo' had meant this limping remark to be no more than a word of encouragement, but the confidence with which he spoke, and his earnest voice convinced Mah-wee'-nah that he knew her father was alive, and might be restored to her. The mystery of his visit, hinted at by En-tay', flashed into her mind.

With sudden impulse she stepped up to him, and forgetful of all but the possibility that her beloved father yet lived, she grasped his arm. "You know something of my father!" she exclaimed. "Tell me if you know that he lives—and will he come back to us! Tell me!"

At the touch of the girl's warm hand on his flesh, Che-loo' felt a shock pass through him: a wild and strange emotion. He caught his breath and stared at the face before him, now more beautiful than ever, as she looked at him, wide-eyed and self-forgotten in her excited interest in her foster father.

He felt strangely exalted, though his head was in a whirl, and he hardly knew his own voice as he replied:

"If he is yet among the earth-born, and my thoughts say he is, I know he is with friends." Scarcely had he spoken when a feeling of guilt seized him and he realized what he had done. He had broken his word to Ne-chō'-ba. "I have said what I gave vow I would not say!" he told her. "It was for good reason I gave the vow. You will keep my words—and give them to no other ears?" he asked. She caught the self-accusation in his voice, and realized that it was through kindness to her that he had broken his strange vow.

"Never, never will I tell!" she promised earnestly. Then she realized that she had touched his arm, and she stepped back as a flush of sudden embarrassment swept over her face. But the joyous import of his words quickly lifted her above her momentary confusion.

"You have brought to me great happiness," she told him, her face radiant with joy. "The Cacique is not my real father, but I could not have more love for him if he were, for always he has been so good to us. I will not ask more about him, if, if you must not tell me."

Che-loo' suddenly recalled the story of the Dawn Woman, the story of Ko-lee'-pah, and Dou-gow's evil act against his beautiful wife, the mother of the girl beside him. He could understand now why she was so different from any girl he had ever seen.

"Then you are the daughter of Ko-lee'-pah, who was

A FLAME TO THE ARROW 149

Governor of the mesa, and Tee'-lah his Apache wife!" he exclaimed.

"Yes, but it is strange that you should know of my parents, and can so quickly name them."

"I know about them, and I know more." There was anger in his voice now. "I know the murdering Chin-di who gave your mother bad medicine, that made her talk much, that he might make a lie about her being a witch. She was no witch. And I know of how your father Ko-lee'-pah went—" Che-loo' caught himself, felt suddenly embarrassed, and stopped short. This strange girl was causing him to forget his vows and promises. He had given vow to a dying woman that he would give her words to none but Cha'-za. He was glad for one thing, he hadn't mentioned the name of Dou-gow'.

"What are you saying? What is this that you know, and who was it who did this evil against my real father and mother?" The soft voice held more of awe than curiosity. What a strange man was this young and handsome Pan'-gua! Strange, and yet she was newly aware that he was no longer a stranger. Perhaps it was his remarkable knowledge of her parents, and of her foster father, that had caused this feeling of friendliness, for she now felt as though she had known him for a long time.

"I have no more words to say now. I have said too many things," said Che-loo'. Then after a pause, "At some time, I shall tell you all you ask." "And I shall ask many things—many," she replied, smiling up at him. Had the two been less absorbed in each other they might have heard the sound of cautious, very cautious, footsteps of one who had stolen up the trail to the sharp turn that was immediately below them. The spy had come in time to overhear Che-loo's angry remark about Ko-lee'-pah and the beautiful Tee'-lah, and had found it startling and well worth hearing.

Silence, a silence that was perhaps not altogether meaningless, fell between Che-loo' and Mah-wee'-nah. Then, suddenly realizing that the last of the sun's afterglow was fast fading, she exclaimed:

"Oh, it grows dark! I did not know the day was so nearly gone!" And she started swiftly up the trail as Che-loo' lifted Cha'-za's bag of corn to his shoulders and tucked the smaller one, belonging to the ushie, under his arm.

Seeing that she was leaving him far behind, and feeling, perhaps, that she had not shown him sufficient gratitude for the good news he had given her, Mah-wee'-nah stopped and when he drew nearer called softly back:

"Good be with you,—Che-loo' of Pan'-gua. It is *I* who run away *this* time. The second sun from this, I will again go to my father's fields, when the sun is low." At this an evil grin spread over the face of the hidden spy.

"I will be in the fields of Cha'-za on that day," replied Che-loo', forgetting all thought of an early return to Pan'-gua.

So swiftly, now, did she run, that in a moment she had turned a bend in the path and was gone. As he went gaily up the trail, a song rose to the lips of Che-loo', a wild, joyous song of the hunt which he had always loved to sing loudly, and it was with difficulty that he now kept it from ringing out for all the great village to hear. To him the trail was no longer steep, and Cha'-za's bag of corn was as light as a sack of feathers, and the little bag under his arm might have been a pebble from the trail. His thoughts sang with the song on his lips, but they were not thoughts of the hunt.

During the evening meal Cha'-za eyed his young friend narrowly. He saw that a marked change had come over him, a change that was causing him to act strangely gay, if not foolish. It might possibly be the thought of returning to his home in Pan'-gua that was responsible.

"You were a long time on the trail," remarked the old man soberly.

"Yes, the trail was very steep," came the reply. "Beautiful is that trail, Cha'-za, and I like it much. It is good to be in a village that has steep trails. Give me more of the stew. You are a good cook, a good cook, Cha'-za," he went on gaily. "We will go on the hunt, you and I, and get a fine buck for you to put away for winter."

"Sometime, it may be, I will go on the hunt with you, but now—now, you must not stay longer in Paulan'-tee," replied the old man quietly.

"It is now in my thoughts to stay here until three suns, maybe four, have come and gone. I like Paulan'-tee," announced Che-loo' brightly.

Seeing Cha'-za's look of worry, Che-loo' grinned broadly, showing his even white teeth. "Have no fear, Cha'-za. I will keep my eyes open, and will no more have words with Dou-gow', or the men you have named."

"Why do you stay longer on the mesa? Is there

more you can learn for the ears of Ne-chō'-ba?" asked Cha'-za bluntly.

"Yes, there may be much," replied Che-loo', glad of an excuse for his announced intention of remaining longer.

The reply did not satisfy the old man. It did not explain the sudden change from a serious-minded Che-loo' to this gay person who was bent on taking all things lightly. This strange and double-natured young Pan'-gua was now presenting the most annoying problem Cha'-za had ever faced. He owed it to Ne-chō'-ba to advise and, if possible, protect him from trouble that seemed certain to come upon him if he remained longer on the mesa, but a youth who appeared very innocent, but was wise, slow and indolent, but was in reality an experienced wrestler with astonishing speed and strength, was surely a difficult person to manage. And now a new and different side of his youthful guest was presenting itself. He was acting very happy, like some little child who had been given something it liked very much—liked very much. That last thought brought a quick suspicion into the old man's mind.

The young Pan'-gua had been a long time on the trail. Could Mah-wee'-nah and her friend have taken the right-hand trail, and met Che-loo'? Cha'-za hoped not, for that would be worse, far worse than all else that had happened. And the girl? Yes, he could see it—she would be almost sure to admire the young Pan'-gua.

"Did you know that Ah'-mot has a daughter?" asked Cha'-za.

"Yes, the woman I saw on the desert told me that the Cacique took the little daughter of Ko-lee'-pah to keep as his own. Why does the question come to you?"

"Have you seen this daughter of the Cacique?" questioned Cha'-za.

Che-loo' turned the question over in his mind. Why not tell Cha'-za?

"Yes," he said honestly, "twice have I seen her. Once near the foot of the mesa, when I was on the hunt. Once again this day. You carry pinyon-nuts for her, and bring up the corn for her—is it an evil thing that I should look upon her?"

For some time the old man ate absently, and as absently studied the flickering fire. Then, as if repeating something that he had said over and over in his mind, he remarked:

"I have done for her many things, to protect her from one of whom she is afraid. *I* am Cha'-za, the Fool. If a young man, a stranger, should be a friend to her—great evil would come upon him quickly—and it might come upon her too."

"Your words are clear, and easy to be heard," replied Che-loo'. "You are full of years, and wisdom. I am young, and the daughter of the Cacique is young. Dou-gow' is an old Chin-di. If her heart is against him, it may be that only a stranger can save her from his evil hand."

Cha'-za shook his gray head impressively. "One fool in Pau-lan'-tee is enough!" he exclaimed. "Tomorrow's sun should find you far on the trail to Pan'-gua. To remain here, you will walk under the paw of a mad bear, under the teeth of wolves. Hear the words of Cha'-za, son of Mat'-so. Stay no longer on the mesa. There is nothing you have not done to make anger in the heart of Dou-gow'. You may watch him, yes, but you cannot watch those who do his will." The old man lowered his voice to a whisper, "I have one who has always an eye on Dou-gow', and knows much of what he does. There are many who can give strong protection to the Cacique's daughter. Go back to Ne-chō'-ba, and tell him that our eyes are open against the Governor—but do not stay longer here."

Even as he looked into the face of his youthful guest Cha'-za saw the futility of his words. The same tolerant smile was on Che-loo''s mouth, a smile more determined and final than any words could express.

"I cannot leave the mesa quickly," replied Che-loo', more seriously now. "I have yet to settle with Me-te'-lo, who is making moccasins for me. Not until tomorrow's sun is old will they be finished." After a pause he went on, "Tell me one thing, Cha'-za. I have had a vision in my thoughts, a vision of three evil wolves who carried away the leader of their pack, and gave him into the jaws of three wild chin-dogs of the desert that the chin-dogs might eat him up, and one of the three wolves might be made leader of the pack. If these three wolves had names, tell me, if you can, what their names would be?"

Cha'-za pondered the question, and recalled Che-loo''s sudden guess about the two men he had seen near the Black Canyon. Then he asked:

"In your vision did you see the three chin-dogs of the desert eat up the leader of the wolf-pack?"

Che-loo' had not expected this question, and he saw that to answer it truthfully, he would have to reveal more than his promise to Ne-chō'-ba would permit.

"My vision of the wolves came to its end, in what I have said, but it may be that the three chin-dogs were sent on to the Silent Others, even before they could eat up the wolf."

"Hum!" grunted Cha'-za very thoughtfully. "It may be so. Then the three wolves might be named War-Captain, Moccasin-Maker, and Governor. But why do you make the question, if you saw them in your vision?"

"In my vision I saw but their tracks, and so could only tell that they were wolves," came the reply.

A sudden knock sounded on Cha'-za's door. The old man got to his feet, and mumbling about long-eared witches that poke about doors at night, he answered the summons. As he opened the door, a voice in the dark, low and guttural, spoke in command or salutation, but Che-loo' did not hear the words. Then, as the door opened wider, he thought he saw a half-outline of the bent figure of Gool, the Witch-killer, but he was too far away to be sure of it. Cha'-za either stepped out, or was pulled out, so quickly Che-loo' could not tell which had caused his sudden exit. Voices from without rapidly died away, and all was silence, though the door remained partly open.

He rose and going to the entrance looked out into the night. There was no one in sight, and after a long moment of waiting he thoughtfully closed the door and returned to Cha'-za's fire. He reflected that the old man was well able to take care of himself, but he wondered if the strange caller could have been the hunchbacked shaman, and, if so, what Cha'-za could have to do with him.

For some time he waited, expecting the old man to return. A feeling of oppression came over him, and the house walls seemed too close and too silent. The open desert and the forest had sounds, constant little friendly sounds, but house walls needed human voices or they were forbidding. He took down the ladder that led up to the passage, and hid it beneath Cha'-za's blankets, then he went out into the night. He passed but few people in the dark streets, and none whom he knew. To look for his aged friend would be useless. Finding the trail that led him up the mesa at sunset, he descended it, taking in the cool air in deep draughts.

At the spot where she had stood he stopped, and folding his arms looked up at the stars, the little sky-brothers of the blue night. The Moon God would rise later, but now the great field of yellow stars gave ample light.

Che-loo' was strangely happy. The spot on his arm, where her hand had touched him, burned as if warmed by the soft glow of a friendly fire—a sacred fire that would never be extinguished. Into his thoughts came the prophetic words of the Dawn Woman. "The flame has not yet kindled upon you, but when the fire comes to you, it will bring great trouble on some in Pau-lan'-tee." Was this spot on his arm, and this strange feeling within him, the fire?

CHAPTER XI

IN THE DARK

The fire-sticks whirl
In the knowing hands,
And a spark glows bright on the wood,
The spark turns flame
And the growing fire
Burns bright as a good fire should!

LATE one afternoon a keen-eyed boy on a housetop in the little village of Pan'-gua, saw something far out in the desert that caused him to descend to earth with all possible speed. Being near the house of Ne-chō'-ba, he hurriedly entered the door of the aged Cacique without knock or call.

That worthy old man, idly watching his daughter prepare the evening meal, was disturbed by the sudden and unannounced entrance of the young caller.

"A—ee! Son of Toh, you jump in the door like a hungry dog that smells new meat!" he exclaimed. "What witch of the Chin-di is at *your* heels?"

"Many Che'-pahs, men and women, are coming, umo, and they carry one who is badly hurt. On a litter of poles he is carried—and a Che'-pah runs ahead of them to tell us of it!" exclaimed the boy excitedly.

"Hum!" grunted Ne-chō'-ba as he slowly rose and wrapped his blanket about him. "Your words clatter on the tongue as though you talk of Apaches instead of our good friends the Che'-pahs. If one is sick of a wound, we will make place for him."

The two walked out into the plaza to learn that others, including some of the village dogs, were aware of the Che-pahs' approach.

The four men who carried the Dawn Woman on the comfortable litter had found easy going after leaving the country of canyons where Che-loo' had found the frail woman and her little son, but the long and weary journey had told heavily against the strength of their human burden. In her almost feverish haste to reach Pan'-gua, she had urged them forward, in disregard of her own welfare.

Within the comparatively short time that elapsed between the arrival of the man sent in advance, and the entrance of the Che'-pahs with the litter, Ne-chō'-ba and the efficient Mat'-so had chosen and prepared comfortable quarters for their unexpected guest.

With kind hospitality the Pan'-guas welcomed her and her escort of rough men and shy women, and saw that she and her son were given comfortable room in the house of Ne-chō'-ba's eldest daughter. The Che'-pahs refused all invitations to remain for the night in the shelter of the village, preferring, with the inclination of true desert people, to camp by the pool beneath the golden stars, but there was no refusal of the abundant food which found its way to them from many of the good wives of Pan'-gua.

Much to the surprise of those about her, the Dawn Woman was no sooner laid on her new and more comfortable couch, than she asked to be left alone with Mat'so and Ne-chō'-ba. When the wondering women who had attended her were put forth, the aged Cacique

IN THE DARK

and the Governor waited expectantly upon her words. With effort she raised herself on her elbow, and addressed Ne-chō'-ba—

"Is Ah'-mot living?"

"Why do you ask in Pan'-gua about the Cacique of the mesa?" countered the old man, startled in spite of himself, by the unexpected question. Mat'-so's eyes opened wide with surprise.

"Have no fear, and waste no words, Ne-chō'-ba," came the reply. "Tell me quickly if he yet lives—if he does, the time may be short." As she spoke she reached into her bosom with trembling hand and drew out a very small doeskin bag, and held it in her hand expectantly.

"Yes," said Ne-chō'-ba quietly. "He still lives."

"Thank the Shiuana above us, that I, Dez'-pah, am come in time!" She lay back and closed her eyes, breathing heavily against the exertion of her talk and the suppressed excitement that had held her. "Take this," she commanded weakly, holding out the little bag. "Let Ot-si'-pah pour it into a gourd of water, and make tea of it, quickly. When it is cool, give it to Ah'-mot, slowly—give half of it, and with the rising sun give him what remains."

Mat'-so took the little bag, and looked questioningly at Ne-chō'-ba. The woman opened her eyes.

"Why do you wait, Mat'-so? Is there fear that I, Dez'-pah, give you bad magic for the Cacique of my people? Go! Do as I have said. I know well the evil spell that has held Ah'-mot, and the murdering Chin-di that gave it him." A sudden laugh, mirthless and near-hysterical, escaped her. With an effort she choked it back, and calmed herself. "The Shiuana do strange things. I, Dez'-pah, the hunted one, the outcast wife of a dog, live—live to undo the evil work of the Chin-di, Dou-gow'—live to save the one he has thought he sent on the Long Sleep that he might be made Cacique in Ah'-mot's place." Again the dry laugh rose to her lips, more feeble now, and was again suppressed. She closed her eyes, and became so still the two wondering men beside her feared the spirit had begun its journey to the Silent Others.

"Go, do as she has said," commanded Ne-chō'-ba in a low voice, "I will remain. When Ot-si'-pah has made the tea, bring her here."

For some time after Mat'-so had gone, the exhausted Dez'-pah seemed scarcely to breathe. The aged Ne-chō'-ba, standing above her, lifted his eyes in a prayer to the Great Spirit of all-knowing, asking that strength be given to his frail guest.

After a time the Dawn Woman slowly opened her eyes and looked up at the quiet face of the aged Cacique.

"Ne-chō'-ba, I am not long here. Soon I will be with Nan-tah'-ha, my good sister—mother of your children. I would leave with you my son, Nah'-lee, that he might become Pan'-gua. But his heart is with the Che'-pahs whom he has always known as friends and brothers. Maybe it is better so." She paused and again reached into her bosom, and produced a very small white arrow, the dread Pau-lan'-tee symbol of the Black Witch who condemns those who do evil.

"Why do you, who are of a people who fear it, have the arrow of the Black Witch?" asked the amazed Ne-chō'-ba.

A strange smile lighted the face of the Dawn Woman.

"I have no fear—a Che'-pah, who knew not its meaning, made it for me, and it must go with me on the Long Sleep. When life has gone from me let it be laid in my hand—it is my wish, Ne-chō'-ba. The white arrow is the thing of which Dou-gow' has greatest fear, and—in the land of the Silent Others—it will be my protection against him."

"It will be as you wish," promised Ne-chō'-ba gently.

"You will question in your thoughts how it is that I know that Ah'-mot is here," continued the woman. "And how I know that an evil spell is upon him." She paused and motioned for the old man to stoop down, that it be less effort to talk to him. Ne-chō'-ba calmly seated himself on the floor beside her, and betrayed none of the alarm her strange knowledge of Ah'-mot had created within him. He had, until now, felt sure that no one, outside of Pan'-gua, knew where the Cacique of Pau-lan'-tee was, that any one else should know of it made the situation grave, if not dangerous.

"I came to Pan'-gua that I might, once more, hear the tongue of my own people, and be with you, my old friends. As you well know, I could not come before. He would have easily found me here, and made great trouble come upon you, and would have found a way to send me on the Long Sleep before my time. Now, he can come. He is too late to lay evil on the head of Dez'-pah. On the desert, as we journeyed, one came to me in the night, and spoke when none others could hear. He told me Ah'-mot was in Pan'-gua. He said he knew that Dou-gow' has secretly given Ah'-mot to eat of a bad medicine, a bean of evil magic that casts a spell on the eater and at last sends him on the Long Sleep. Then he gave me the little bag of yellow powder, and told me that tea made of it would break the witch-spell, and that Ah'-mot might live, if the good tea could be given to him quickly." The speaker paused, and again closed her eyes wearily.

"Who is this man?" asked Ne-chō'-ba quietly.

"I cannot name him. I gave promise, but I know he spoke truth, and I know that with him the secret of Ah'-mot and Pan'-gua are safe." The voice of the speaker had sunk to little more than a whisper. She fell silent, and in a few moments her more quiet breathing told that she was asleep.

Ne-chō'-ba rose quietly and for some time looked sadly down on the wan features of the once gay and handsome Dez'-pah, the happy younger sister of his wife Nan-tah'-ha, now long gone to the Silent Others.

Fond memories thronged the old man's thoughts, memories of joyous days on the great mesa—days of great ceremonies: feast days—long seasons of peace and security. He recalled how he and his wife had been sorrowful when they had learned that the happy Dez'-pah had become the wife of his enemy, Dou-gow'. She had paid, paid dearly for her blind faith in the evil young war-captain, for such he was at that time. Ne-chō'-ba wondered if Dou-gow' knew that his wife was still among the earth-born.

Quietly now he moved to the door and at the threshhold met Mat'-so and his wife Ot-si'-pah. At a sign of silence, they remained outside with him, and he softly closed the door.

"She sleeps," announced Ne-chō'-ba. Then to Ot-

IN THE DARK 163

si'-pah, "In a little time you can go in to her. You have made the tea?"

"Yes," came the reply. "By now it is cool enough to give him."

"Come, Mat'-so. I will go to Ah'-mot. Get the tea and bring it to the Council-house," commanded the old man.

While the two yet walked together for a space, Mat'-so asked, "Who, think you, told Dez'-pah about Ah'-mot?"

"Gool, the Witch-killer," replied Ne-chō'-ba.

In the afternoon of the day following Cha'-za's sudden, and somewhat mysterious, exit from his own doorway, Che-loo', with his trader's pack, was about to leave his house for the street, when the old man climbed the ladder leading to the back passage, and hearing him coming, Che-loo' waited expectantly. A moment later his caller entered the front room, and seeing that the old man was moved either by great fear or excitement Che-loo' put down his pack. Without a word Cha'-za went to the door and, unbarring it, looked out as if to make sure that no one was on the roof outside. After closing and re-barring the door he turned to his guest.

"I have told you to return to Pan'-gua, but my words were like silence to your ears. There is now something *more* than words. Trouble is already near your door. You have told a woman, on the trail, that you knew who it was that made a witch of Tee'-lah, wife of Ko-lee'-pah, and that the evil one secretly gave her bad medicine—and that—"

"She told?—Told my words!" broke in Che-loo', in sudden anger and amazement.

"No, she told nothing—and, like you, she did not know that a spy was near you—sent to have open ears for every word you said to her," went on the old man grimly. "There could not have been a worse one to hear your words, for he was one of the two men who helped Dou-gow' against Ko-lee'-pah and his wife, and one of the two who so easily found the owl-feathers hidden in the Governor's house. The spy was on the trail below you, and quickly took your words to Dou-gow.' Dou-gow' sent him for Klee'-tso. When Klee'-tso came, Dou-gow' had made his plans against you."

"Then the spy was Me-te'-lo?" said Che-loo'.

"I did not name him," replied Cha'-za. "This night, while you sleep, Dou-gow' and Klee'-tso come here to throw you from the roof out there—over the edge of the mesa. It will be easy to say that you walked over the roof and fell while you were asleep. They have learned that you sleep outside your door, like a desert man, and they will wait until you and all Pau-lan'-tee are asleep, then they will come over the roofs and take you quickly. *Now* do my words seem as nothing?"

"How is it that *you* know they will do all this?" asked Che-loo'.

"*That* is not the string to *this* bow of trouble," came the reply. "I know, and I know that what I have said is true."

"I give you thanks, Cha'-za, for the warning," replied Che-loo'.

"You will now return quickly to Pan'-gua, while there is yet time?" inquired the old man hopefully.

"I shall not sleep on the roof—*this* night," replied Che-loo' evasively.

"Twice since yesterday's sun has an ill omen come in my path," said the old man solemnly. In the night two times did the smoke from my chimney come back into the room—and with the dawn, as I went down to see my traps, I heard plainly the wind sounding the witch's cry over the rocks of Moan-tauck, the Pau-lan'-tee place of the dead. Two ill omens they were, and they come not far apart. The witch cry over Moan-tauck never comes except when some one on the mesa is soon to go on the Long Sleep. Always it is so." So intense was the manner of the old man, so wide his eyes, and so serious his voice, Che-loo', for the moment, caught something of his fear, but superstition had never held a place in his mind for long, and now he merely smiled.

"*Now* is the time for you to go," warned Cha'-za, half angrily.

To run away from the mesa was the very least of Che-loo's desires. The possibility of danger, and the chance to try his skill and strength against these men, these enemies of his people, had for him a fascination that Cha'-za could not understand had he told him of it. He turned to his host.

"Cha'-za, when I am old, it may be I will be wise— and fearful of all things. Now, I cannot have it in my thoughts to run away from enemies, from cowards who fight, two against one, in the dark. Have no fear—I shall sleep, this night, within the house, and my door well barred."

For a long moment the old man looked at him, and slowly, almost sadly, shook his head. Then, without another word, turned to depart by the way he had come. When he had gone Che-loo' sat down to think over the situation that confronted him. Evidently Cha'za had some spy of his own, who possessed secret means of learning about much that Dou-gow' said and did. There could be no doubt of the seriousness of the old man's warning. Dou-gow' and Klee'-tso would come for him, and he must stay within his house, like a rat in a trap.

Before he left the mesa he must have the moccasins Me-te'-lo had made for him, or he could give no account to his father of the valuable skystone which the thief had stolen. A sudden wave of anger swept him as he thought of the moccasin-maker—a spy and thief, as well as an enemy of his own Cacique. An idea leaped to his mind, and gradually began shaping, itself into a plan. He decided to begin its operation at once. If he were successful—it might reveal who the three men were who gave Ah'-mot to the Apaches, and it would, at the same time, make Me-te'-lo pay for his thieving, spying tricks. He grinned broadly at the thought of it. If he failed—well, he must not fail.

Leaving his pack in his room, he went to the rear passage and descended to Cha'-za's house. He was glad to find that the old man was absent. In the street he made his way to the home of the moccasin-maker, and by good, or ill, fortune found Me-te'-lo seated among his buckskins and an assortment of footwear.

"Ha-la'-ni!" said Che-loo', as he entered. "Are the moccasins ready for my feet?"

For reply Me-te'-lo took down a pair from a near-by peg on the wall and held them in his hand. "Have your eyes seen better than these?" he asked, a half-smile on his evil face.

"They are good to the eye, but it is the foot that wears them," replied Che-loo'. "I have nothing with me to trade for them. At my house I have fine sky-stones—one very fine, very large—like the one worn on the necklace of Ah'-mot when he was taken away from the mesa."

Me-te'-lo's smile suddenly gave place to a questioning stare that did not escape Che-loo'.

"I show my fine sky-stones to few men on the mesa," he went on. "When day is gone I will again be in my house. I will then get for you a fine stone, as fine as your eyes have seen." He held out his hand for the moccasins, but, as he expected, the suspicious Me-te'-lo did not give them to him.

"I will bring the moccasins with me, and will come for the sky-stone," came the reply.

"It is good," said Che-loo' indifferently. "At the setting of the sun I eat in the house of the old fool Cha'-za. After that, I will be alone in my house."

"I will come," replied Me-te'-lo. "And I will give you good bargain—*good* bargain."

On his way through Cha'za's house to the rear passage, he noted that the old man had returned, in his absence, long enough to put the evening pot on the fire, and the appetizing odor from its steaming contents made him hungry. Up in his own room he looked about him thoughtfully. The Dawn Woman, who had been right about so many things, had said, "You must make prayers to the Shiuana that they may give you eyes to see." He took his knife from its sheath and held it out, for this would be a prayer of battle.

Then he raised his eyes in silent invocation that the Shiuana might aid him.

His prayer finished, he looked thoughtfully at the knife. By ancient pact he could not draw it against the blood of a Pau-lan'-tee. He must conquer this enemy without weapons. Stepping to his pile of bedding, he hid the knife beneath it.

More confident now—he considered his plan. It was well begun, but that was the least of it. Going to the rear room, he took down a number of rawhide ropes, that Cha'-za evidently used for his bear-traps, and selected two—one about five paces in length, and the other much shorter. He coiled them up separately and laid them on the floor in the center of the room. Then he piled up small wood and dry bark in his fireplace ready for lighting when the need of light should come. He had worn his doeskin shirt all day. He now took it off, and laid it on top of his pack in a corner, and as though preparing for a wrestling match, he swung his arms about repeatedly and lifted his broad chest to loosen his muscles.

Below, in the house of Cha'-za, he found the old man busy over an earthen bowl of thin batter prepared for maize-cakes that would be cooked on a smooth flat stone now heating in the fire. Evidently resigned to what he believed to be the foolhardy stubbornness of his youthful guest, Cha'-za now acted as though nothing had occurred to disturb their peaceful relations. During the meal the old man was quick to see that the mind of Che-loo' was not on his food, or things immediately at hand. The gay and foolish Che-loo' of the evening before had given place to a more sober young warrior who seemed years older.

IN THE DARK

"Cha'-za, I want to use one of your old blankets—one that you do not value in trade," announced Che-loo'.

"You use more cover when you sleep under a roof, than when you sleep under the sky?" asked the old man.

"No, but this night I have need of an old blanket, and it will be put to good use," came the reply.

The old man rose and selected a blanket from the number he had, and dropped it on the floor at the foot of the ladder leading up to the passage. Then he resumed his seat.

"It is good," said Che-loo'. "I will bring it back, or give you good trade for it. This night a man will come to my house to trade. It may be I can make him say words that I will want you to hear. When I go up the ladder, I want you to follow, and remain in the back room quietly, that the one who comes will not know of it. Will you do it?"

Cha'-za looked at Che-loo' dubiously. What did this strange youth have in mind now? "Why will the words of this man be for *my* ears?" he questioned.

"His words may be of Ah'-mot," replied Che-loo'.

"Hum!" grunted Cha'-za. "I will come."

"I give you thanks for the food, umo," said Che-loo', rising. And making a small torch of juniper-bark that lay near the fireplace, he lighted it and picking up the blanket proceeded up the ladder, followed by the old man. In his own front room he lighted the wood he had prepared, and soon a blaze, aided by the whitened walls, gave abundant light. Cha'-za, doubtful of the wisdom of his own actions, but very curious as to who was coming and what the caller would say, waited silently in the dark among his traps.

Che-loo′ selected a spot on the floor, and carefully spread the borrowed blanket on it. He then picked up the longest coiled rope and after making a running noose in one end of it, re-coiled it and ran the folded loops through his belt at the back where it would be hidden from any one standing in front of him, but could be reached quickly without effort. He now unbarred his door, that it might be readily opened from the outside, and seated himself on the ledge opposite. He had not long to wait, for he soon heard sounds of some one ascending the ladder from the street, and this was followed by steps on the roof.

Instantly he was on the alert to catch, in one glance if possible, the expression and physical attitude of his caller. The success or failure of his bold plan would depend almost entirely on his ability to overcome Me-te′-lo the moment he was within the room. The manner of the moccasin-maker's entrance, his position when he paused before entering, would be of the utmost importance to the young Pan′-gua wrestler, who was accustomed to appraise quickly the position of the arms and legs of an opponent. There came a bold knock on the door.

"Enter!" called Che-loo′.

The door opened and Me-te′-lo stepped over the threshold, the new moccasins held on both hands. Che-loo″s eye caught a tiny flash of light, as though reflected from the sharp point of a knife hidden directly beneath the moccasins.

"Ha-la′-ni!" said Me-te′-lo, smiling.

"Good!" replied Che-loo′ calmly, as he rose and

IN THE DARK

took a step toward, but just a little to one side of, the moccasin-maker. He stretched out his left hand as though to receive the moccasins. Then, with a sudden leap, he caught the unsuspecting caller about the body, pinning his arms to his sides and forcing his hands downward.

Me-te'-lo gave a grunt of surprise as he staggered backward, and the moccasins fell to the floor. So sudden and unlooked-for had been the attack, Me-te'-lo was wholly unprepared, but instinctively he held to the knife, and now made effort to free his arms that he might use it. To force Me-te'-lo to drop the knife was now Che-loo''s one purpose, and to do this he knew he must keep to one side of his antagonist, and so out of the way of the weapon.

"Drop the knife, or I throw you on your head!" warned Che-loo'.

For reply Me-te-lo, in a sudden attempt to free himself, twisted his arms at the same instant Che-loo' gripped him the tighter. A quick, smothered cry, as if more of fear than pain, escaped him, and the knife clattered on the floor. In the excitement of the moment Che-loo' believed the cry was one of anger caused by losing the weapon, but the sharp ears of Cha'-za caught the strange quality of it and, being unable to see the antagonists, believed Me-te'-lo had received a mortal wound from the young Pan'-gua.

At the sound of the falling knife Che-loo' changed his position, and a moment later, exerting all of his strength, he threw the moccasin-maker face downward on the floor. Before Me-te'-lo could turn and rise to his feet, Che-loo' had leaped to the door, closed and barred it. Making sure that the coil of rope was still in his belt, he now waited for the half-risen man to make the last motion of getting to his feet. A look of terror shone on the face of his antagonist, and Che-loo' believed that the mighty, and much-feared, Me-te'-lo had turned coward. Instantly Che-loo' was again upon him, and this time the noose of the rope was thrown about his adversary's body.

The actions of Me-te'-lo were now those of a wild man; the contorted muscles stood out on his face, and his powerful hands gripped Che-loo''s flesh like the jaws of a wolf. Hoarsely he shouted:

"Let me go! You Chin-di's whelp—let me go!" and staggering backward, pulled Che-loo' with him. Then, by sheer strength of his mighty arms, he threw the young Pan'-gua from him, and was again almost on his feet before Che-loo' could regain his own feet and prepare for another onslaught. The rope, which was still over Me-te'-lo's head and under one arm, hampered him, but he made no effort to free himself from it, knowing that every second counted in his defense against the surprising speed and strength of the youth with whom he had to deal. Though a powerful man, Me-te'-lo had none of the skill of the wrestler, and once again he was thrown to the floor, falling so heavily the breath was partly driven from his great body. Before he could make the first move to rise, Che-loo' had forced the rope about him for the second time, and had drawn it tight enough to bind his arms to his sides. With great effort he turned Me-te'-lo face downward, and, seated on his back, he finally made the rope secure, though the twisting body of his adversary made this well-nigh impossible.

He then rose to his feet, breathing heavily against

IN THE DARK 173

the exertion. From the margin of the dark doorway at the back of the room, the gray face of Cha'-za peered out in amazement. Me-te'-lo, now helpless, rolled over on his back and a look of wild terror shone in his bulging eyes.

A stream of vile epithets poured from his mouth, ending in the oft-repeated, "Let me go—witch of the Chin-di!"

"So! You bring me a knife, as well as the moccasins!" said Che-loo', calmly picking up Me-te'-lo's weapons. "But there is blood upon it! Did you first cut yourself with it, to make sure it was sharp enough for me?" Looking down, he noticed a small red spot on Me-te'-lo's leg where, in the struggle, the knife had pricked him.

"You steal my sky-stones—you spy upon me, that you may carry my words to the ear of Dou-gow', and you come here with a knife ready to send me on the Long Sleep—but now, I give you a chance to trade. You like *well* to trade—so, I give you good bargain." Standing over the bound figure on the floor, he held the knife point downward. "Do you go—on the Long Sleep—or do you tell me quickly the names of the two men who were with you when you gave Ah'-mot into the hands of the Apaches?"

Me-te'-lo started visibly, and his mouth opened in amazement. He began to speak, but his voice shook, and his words were too low to be intelligible.

"Talk! Say words that I can hear!" commanded Che-loo' threateningly, and he stooped lower with the upraised knife.

"No! Put the knife away!" screamed Me-te'-lo.

"I will tell! It was Klee'-tso—Klee'-tso was with me. There was no other."

Within the little back room, old Cha'-za, wide-eyed and keenly attentive, sucked in his breath in amazement, as much at the question as its answer.

"One more man was with you! What was *his* name?" Che-loo'"s words were spoken with slow emphasis.

"You are a witch—a witch of the Chin-di!" gasped the terror-stricken man, as he made an effort to roll away from the young Pan'-gua with the raised knife.

Che-loo', disgusted at the fear displayed by the supposedly brave man, stood erect and tossed the knife onto the seat ledge at the side of the room. Then, picking up the smaller coil of rope, he stooped quickly and before Me-te'-lo had time to resist, he bound his feet securely together.

"You have told me a part of the truth," said Che-loo', rising. "For that—I will give you no harm." Picking up Me-te'-lo bodily, he laid him down on Cha'-za's blanket and wrapped him up. With his bonds hidden, the moccasin-maker now appeared like one who has prepared himself for a night's repose.

"Let me go," said Me-te'-lo, with a voice less strong, "and I give you the moccasins, and will give back the sky-stone, and much good weaving I will give." The words were spoken as though in last effort, and not with any hope that they would succeed.

"I have the moccasins—you have the sky-stone, so you have good bargain," replied Che-loo', unbarring his door. "Do as I say and no further harm will come to you. If you do not—I have means to make you silent."

IN THE DARK

The fire of small wood had burned itself down to a glow of embers, giving but faint light. Opening the door, Che-loo' looked cautiously out. The cool night air was welcome to his nostrils. Save for the barking of a few of the village dogs, and the faint yap-yap of coyotes far away in the desert, all was quiet. Che-loo' returned to the man on the floor.

"Tonight, your two friends, Dou-gow' and Klee'-tso, come in the dark to throw me from the roof, over the edge of the mesa. When they come they will find you, on the roof, in my place. Tell them, that you have told me, and the ears that have been listening to you from the room behind us, that you and Klee'-tso were two of the three men who gave your Cacique into the hands of the Apaches, and that we will soon know the third."

To this Me-te'-lo made no reply. Perhaps he was satisfied with the assurance of freedom. The listening Cha'-za sat wondering. Che-loo' now carried the moccasin-maker to the roof and laid him carefully across the open doorway on the spot where he was accustomed to sleep. He bent close to the ear of his prisoner.

"I shall be just inside the doorway where my hand can reach you. Make no move—make no sound before your friends come." No reply came from the bound figure.

As he sat, silently waiting, just within the doorway, Che-loo' thought of what he would do when Dou-gow' and Klee'-tso arrived. The Shiuana had heard him, he had conquered this Pau-lan'-tee without a knife, and in spite of the knife drawn against him.

Suddenly he was aware that Cha'-za was in the room. So silently had the old man moved, he had not made the slightest sound. Dimly Che-loo' could see the gray head, and outline of the face a few feet away. No sign passed between them as they sat in the silent watch.

Time passed slowly. One by one the village dogs ceased barking. Small clouds passed over the sky, and in their wake moved larger ones, blotting out most of the stars. All objects became mere masses with vague outline.

Faintly came the sound of creeping feet, as if from some adjoining roof. Very cautiously Che-loo' moved a little farther back into the deeper shadows of the room. Again came the faint sound, this time nearer at hand—a sound of crawling made by cautious hands and knees.

After an ominous moment of silence came a rush as Dou-gow' and Klee'-tso caught up the bound figure of Me-te'-lo and ran toward the adjoining roof. In a moment they were swallowed up in the darkness. Che-loo' jumped to his feet and, with straining ears, stood waiting for the two men to discover their mistake.

Why did not Me-te'-lo cry out—let them know that it was he—and not Che-loo' they were about to throw to his death?

Immediately came again the sound of running feet as the two murderers returned to Cha'-za's roof, and in a moment were down the ladder and running swiftly in the silent street below.

Che-loo' seemed rooted to the floor. "Cha'-za!" he whispered hoarsely. "They have thrown Me-te'-lo over the mesa wall! They have sent him—on the Long Sleep!"

CHAPTER XII

THREE AGAINST ONE

> The vines are dead, the harvest done,
> The crows fly o'er the field,
> And red-men thank the Mother Earth,
> Who gave the goodly yield.

CHA'-ZA busied himself hurriedly with the smoldering coals of Che-loo'′s fire.

"Close and bar your door!" he commanded in a low voice. "We have work to do before this night is gone!"

Che-loo' seemed not to hear, and stood as though dazed by what had occurred.

"Why did Me-te'-lo let them throw him from the roof without word to let them know who he was? Why didn't he cry out?" he questioned, a note of alarm in his voice.

"Close your door!" again commanded Cha'-za more emphatically.

Che-loo' obeyed, and as he slowly laid the bar in place he realized that Cha'-za was now the calm and wise one of the two. When he turned to the old man, now silhouetted against the glow from the live coals of the fire, Cha'-za rose.

"The Black Witch of the Long Silence had laid its hand on Me-te'-lo before Dou-gow' and Klee'-tso came," he explained.

"That could not be," said Che-loo'. "I did him no harm."

"Why, think you, did he cry out as from a mortal wound when his knife pricked him? I will tell you why. It was his own hand that sent him on the Long Sleep. The poisoned knife, meant for you, was by accident turned against his own blood," explained the old man calmly. "It is not a new trick, and—I think Me-te'-lo has used it before. Come. The dawn must not find the body of the moccasin-maker wrapped in my blanket, bound with my trap-ropes, and on the rocks below my house." And he moved toward the dim doorway of the little back room.

Feeling his way in the darkness, Che-loo' followed, his troubled thoughts trying to adjust themselves to the new situation. So *that* was why Me-te'-lo was so fearful, and why he had acted like a madman, and begged to be set free. It might be days before the body of the man would be found, since there were no trails nor fields on that side of the mesa, and few people would have occasion to climb among the rocks and drifts piled against the foot of the mesa. And what would the two murderers think when he, Che-loo', faced them alive and unharmed?

"Come without noise," whispered Cha'-za from the foot of the ladder.

Out in the street they kept within the shadows, and Che-loo' marveled at the catlike tread and long swift stride of his aged host. In the dim shadows at the foot of the trail, he followed close on the heels of his guide, who seemed to know every passage and by-path among the dense brush and rocks that lay in black masses all about them.

THREE AGAINST ONE 179

The first chill winds, that always precede the desert dawn, were blowing up from the plains as they silently reëntered Cha'-za's door, weary yet glad that their gruesome task was finished. Cha'-za barred his door, and threw down the ropes and blanket.

"Now there will be great wonder in Pau-lan'-tee. Me-te'-lo will be found on the rocks beneath the house of his good friend Klee'-tso," he announced. "My eyes will be glad to look at the face of Dou-gow', when he sees *you* again. He will be sure you are a witch; but his mouth, and the mouth of Klee'-tso, will be shut tight by their own guilt, and they can say nothing." A dry chuckle followed the last remark.

"Why do you not ask me to return quickly to Pan'-gua?" asked Che-loo', for he had been expecting the old man to tell him that now was the time to go.

"When it is plain to my eyes that the Shiuana mark a man with strength and favor, Cha'-za will no longer give him counsel," came the unexpected reply. "When tomorrow's sun is in the midst of the sky, nine men will meet secretly. I have told them they would see you, and from your mouth hear the vision of the three wolves. We might have more to tell them, now that Me-te'-lo has named two of the wolves—but of that we cannot speak. Like Dou-gow' and Klee'-tso, our tongues are tied. What can *we* know about Me-te'-lo, or what he said before he fell from Klee'-tso's roof to the foot of the mesa?"

"We can know nothing," replied Che-loo', smiling broadly.

"Go up to your house and sleep," commanded Cha'-za. "Some one will miss Me-te'-lo, it may be soon, though he has no family but a sister who lives in another house, and fears him. Until he is found,—we know nothing."

The sun was near the zenith when Che-loo' awoke. The strange events of the previous night came to his mind like memories of a troubled dream, and he reviewed them with solemn interest. Below he found Cha'-za waiting for him beside a flat basket of dried meat and warm maize-cakes, and as they ate, the old man talked lightly like one who has had some burden lifted from his heart. Che-loo' had never seen him so happy. He wondered at this, considering all that had just occurred, but he soon began to guess the probable cause.

"The Shiuana hear our prayers—at last their ears are open toward Pau-lan'-tee," announced Cha'-za. "Many seasons have we, who are against Dou-gow', made prayers and much secret ceremony, that it might destroy his power for evil, and the power of the two men who have been as one with him. Now, *now* we have a sign, a great sign, that they have heard us. You come to the mesa with the good magic of an ancient pact of friendship. It is good magic,—always friendship is good magic. The Shiuana guide your feet, and now one enemy, a man more feared, and more evil than Klee'-tso, has gone on the Long Sleep—slain by his own hand, and thrown to the earth below by the hands of his own friends. The witch that made evil in the heart of Me-te'-lo is the one that sent him to the Silent Others—the witch of greed. He planned to poison you with a scratch of his knife before Dou-gow' and Klee'-tso could come. Then he could take all of your sky-stones and buckskins without trade or witness. It

THREE AGAINST ONE 181

may be he thought to play your trick, and lay your body out on the roof so that Dou-gow' and Klee'-tso would believe *they* had sent you on the Long Sleep when they had thrown you from the roof. When the Shiuana guide the feet of a man, they make his enemies' weapons to turn back upon them. It is *good*—and great is the sign that our prayers have gone to open ears."

Che-loo' could now see how great had been Cha'-za's interest in the welfare of his people. For this cause he had been willing to be known as the fool. The death of Me-te'-lo, one of the three chief enemies of Pau-lan'-tee, had raised his spirits with renewed hope of a better government on the mesa and he was happy.

"Are Dou-gow' and his two friends the only enemies of Ah'-mot, and the good men of your Council?" asked Che-loo'.

"No, there are many, but few of them are strongly against us, for they have only followed Dou-gow' and Klee'-tso because they have fear of them, or think to have great advantage by it. When they are in our hands, all will be well," explained the old man, rising. "I go now," he continued. "You know where Man'-yah lives. Take your pack and go to his house as if to trade. He will expect you, and will take you to the place where the nine men will be. When I have gone, wait a little time before you follow."

"It is good," assented Che-loo'.

Soon after Cha'-za had departed, he secured his pack and started for the house of Man'-yah. After his long sleep within closed walls, the outdoor air and bright sunlight seemed good to him. Many men greeted him in a friendly manner as he passed through the streets.

Though he did not know it, word of his brief and decisive encounter with Chi-nil' had spread rapidly over the village. His reputation as a wrestler was now established on the mesa, and thus many smiles and salutations followed where only cool welcome had been accorded him when he had arrived. He crossed the plaza and entered one of the streets that opened from it.

Four men were standing beside a doorway, and the back of one of them looked familiar. When he was nearly opposite the group, the man turned and Che-loo' looked into the eyes of Klee'-tso.

The war-captain stared with a look of blank amazement that instantly changed to one of terror, and he jerked himself backward against the house wall as though struck by a blow. His eyes bulged with fear, and his mouth sagged open—speechless. The Pan'-gua witch had risen from the dead! For a brief space Che-loo' paused, as he coldly eyed the guilty man, then without a word he walked slowly on. He heard the noise of a door closed violently, and looking back saw that Klee'-tso had disappeared, but his three companions remained in the street, a look of astonishment on their faces.

Man'-yah answered his knock and welcomed him as one whom he was pleased to see. "Leave your pack here, for we go where it could not be carried," he explained. "We will go to the Council-house by a back way."

As they passed through the second room Che-loo' encountered Man'-yah's daughter En-tay', who smiled and nodded as though greatly pleased to see him. As he passed her she stepped close to him and whispered:

"She likes you *much!* Is it not nice?"

Che-loo' replied with his brightest smile, and a decided nod of his head, as he continued after her father. Then he suddenly felt guilty of being very foolish to thus disclose his feelings.

He followed Man'-yah out of the house and into a second building which appeared to have been long abandoned as a dwelling-place. In the last of its deserted rooms they ascended a long ladder, and from the second floor ascended still another, and finally came out on a wide flat roof. Here Che-loo' looked quickly about him and saw that the place was completely hidden from the view of the rest of the village. Lofty windowless walls rose on three sides, the fourth being open to the desert, as the wall on that side, like the rear wall of Cha'-za's house, had been built on the very edge of the mesa. Along the open side ran a low guard-wall, of about the height of a man's waist. A small red door was set in one of the high walls, and toward this they made their way.

"This place, where we go, is the old Council-house," explained Man'-yah. "It is here the Great Council always met before Dou-gow' became Governor. He likes to meet in one of the estufas on the plaza, where people can see him come and go, but the older men like *this* place."

While Che-loo' and his guide were entering the ancient red door, to meet the nine men seated in secret Council, En-tay' was on her way to the house of Mah-wee'-nah, bubbling over with the news that she had just spoken to the handsome Pan'-gua about a very interesting matter, and had received a very interesting and definite reply. At Mah-wee'-nah's door she stepped back with a low exclamation. Dou-gow' was just leaving. The Governor smiled his friendliest smile at her as he passed into the street, but En-tay' returned a look of annoyance. Once within, she slammed the door, and ran to the mother of her friend.

"Where is Mah-wee'-nah?" she asked breathlessly.

"Gone to the spring for water," came the sad-voiced reply. "Dou-gow' came to us with kind advice, and sorrow for us in our great loss, and—" here the mother paused to weep silently—"and Mah-wee'-nah acted angry, and went quickly away with the olla, saying to me, 'I go for water,' but the wicked child said no word of greeting to our good friend the Governor." Again came more weeping.

"I don't blame her," said En-tay', rising. "I hate the old—I don't like him any more than Mah-wee'-nah does."

"Foolish one!" exclaimed the woman half angrily. "Do you not know that the Governor can bring great evil on those who do not please him? You must tell Mah-wee'-nah that she *must* like Dou-gow', for he—he *wants* her to like him. He—he has told me that she must, or—"

"Or what?" demanded En-tay'.

"Or all might not go well—with us," came the tearful confession.

"The old Chin-di! I shall tell Mah-wee'-nah to hate him—to *hate* him, and I know one who will protect her from that old wretch!" With that, En-tay' almost ran out the door, while the weak and troubled woman looked feebly after her.

At one of the springs, not one that she usually visited, lest Dou-gow' should attempt to find her, Mah-wee'-nah sat staring sadly out over the desert toward the distant hills, beyond which lay Pan'-gua.

Here En-tay' found her, and crept up to her so noiselessly, Mah-wee'-nah was taken by surprise.

"Why do you look with so much sadness in your eyes? You who have been so very happy. For two long days have you been smiling much, and never have I seen you so gay, but *now*—Is it old Dou-gow' who comes to your mother with his soft evil tongue and big lies? Is it?"

Mah-wee'-nah smiled up at her friend, and then made room for her on the rock beside her. "I have no fear of him. He may make my mother to fear, but I know that he cannot harm me," replied Mah-wee'-nah. "You say he tells lies. Do you think he always tells lies—when it is about people that he speaks—?"

En-tay' looked questioningly at her friend. Here was something to look into. Evidently Dou-gow' had said something about somebody that had caused her friend to be sad. What could it be?

"Yes, he lies about *everything!* I do not think he knows how to say words that are true," she announced boldly, and with some exaggeration, "If he tells me something, I will say in my heart, 'I wonder if that is true!' That's what *I* would do."

"He has said to my mother, so that I could hear plainly, that a young Pan'-gua had been on the mesa to make trouble, and to spy on people, but that he had gone away quickly, and would never again be permitted to return to Pau-lan'-tee," said Mah-wee'-nah.

"Then he tells bigger lies than—than all this mesa, and the desert too! I have just *seen*—our friend, Che-loo' of Pan'-gua, and right now he is with my father, and I saw him close and I said to him—you won't be mad, Mah-wee'-nah, if I tell what I said?"

"I will not be mad—silly one. Go on—what did you say to him?" and the changed and eager voice of her friend filled En-tay' with delight.

"I whispered to him, 'She likes you much, is that not nice?' And he said—shall I tell what *he* said—?"

"I shall throw you in the spring, if you do not!" threatened Mah-wee'-nah, grasping the arm of her friend, and looking as angry as she could.

"He said, 'I like her too, *very* much I like her—' And—"

"I don't believe one word of what you are saying!" interrupted Mah-wee'-nah. "You say that to tease. He would *never* say such words. He does not talk that way."

"No, he did not *say* words *just* like that, but he smiled—oh, the nicest smile—and nodded his head hard, for he was close to my father and was afraid he would hear—but if you had seen his smile, and his big nod of the head, you would know well that he *meant* all that I have said, and more—much more."

"I can think that he smiled and nodded his head—yes, that would be like him. Are your words true—did he do that?" insisted Mah-wee'-nah.

"Yes," affirmed En-tay' solemnly. "And I heard lots more about him this day. Did I not tell you that he is very strong, and without fear? Some men have told my father that he threw Chi-nil'. My father asked Chi-nil', and Chi-nil' said yes, he did, but that the Pan'-gua was a great wrestler, and did not let him, Chi-nil', know it. What do you think of *that*?"

"It may be good that he is strong, and can throw

THREE AGAINST ONE

Chi-nil′, but it is not good that Dou-gow′ is against him," replied Mah-wee′-nah. "What Dou-gow′ said to my mother tells plainly that he is very angry with—with our friend from Pan′-gua. If Dou-gow′ knows he has talked with me, he may try to bring harm to him quickly. Will you tell me, if you hear men say things about him? You will tell me, En-tay′?"

"To you I tell all that comes to my ears," she affirmed, "and I hear much that others do not."

With filled water-jar the two returned to the top of the mesa, talking on the subject nearest their hearts.

Che-loo′ did not remain long at the meeting of the nine men. He repeated for them an account of his vision of the three wolves, as he had told it to Cha′-za, and to the many questions that followed, he gave the same answer—"That is all of my vision. It is for you to think if it has meaning." And with that the men had to be content.

Above the ancient Council-house, high on the roof, a man lay beneath a wide and colorless blanket. Since before the dawn his silent figure had been hidden from all vision, excepting that of the birds that flew above the lofty mesa. With straining ears, held at the top of the low chimney-pot, he heard many words that were wafted up to him by the draft from the room below. When the men had all departed he still lay beneath the colorless blanket, knowing that he must wait until the deep darkness of night would permit him to slide over the wall, and silently drop into the hands that would be reaching up to break his fall.

From the house of Man′-yah, Che-loo′ returned directly to the house of Cha′-za. An idea had come to him, a happy idea that had been born of the brief message from En-tay'—"She likes you *much*." Behind his barred door, he took out his bag of sky-stones, and very carefully selected a number that would match perfectly if strung together. To these he added the large and beautiful stone like the one stolen by Me-te'-lo. A pleased smile lighted his face—a smile of self-satisfaction. Would she accept them? And would she wear them openly, for all to see? That last question was the very great and very important one. Once they were worn about her throat, all Pau-lan'-tee would soon know that she had given her word to be wife of the fortunate man who had given her so beautiful a gift. Most of the stones were drilled for pendants or ear ornaments and with a sharp drill he could, in a very short time, make the necessary holes in the others. He remembered seeing one hanging on Cha'-za's wall, and though the old man was not at home, he took the liberty of borrowing it and was soon at work with a song in his heart that kept time to the whirr of the drill.

When the pleasant task was finished, he opened his door and looked out to observe the time of day, and found the sun was low in the west. He hurriedly put all of the stones into a small doeskin pouch and tied it to his belt. Then he barred his door, and going below found Cha'-za standing with some tangled thongs in his hand, and two empty grain-bags on the floor in front of him.

"You go to your fields for corn?" asked Che-loo'.

"Beans and melons this time," replied the old man.

"I will go with you," announced Che-loo'. "Melons are not easily carried. With me to help, you can take a larger bean-bag than that."

THREE AGAINST ONE 189

For reply Cha'-za exchanged the small sack he had selected, for a larger one.

"If you are to go, we must keep our eyes open and our mouths closed. Your enemies are set strongly against you, and remember that all traps are not made alike."

Below in the fields they found few men at work, and none were near at hand. Almost all of the harvest had been stored away for the winter in the various homes on the mesa-top, and in most of the fields lay great heaps of dried bean-vines and cornstalks waiting to be burned or scattered later by the winter winds.

Che-loo' scanned the few groups of men, looking for Dou-gow' or Klee'-tso, but they were not among them. The bags were filled now, and Cha'-za, as Che-loo' had expected, announced that it would be better if they did not go up the mesa together. The old man knew that it was not a time for them to appear to be on too friendly terms. For Che-loo' to help to gather his crops would appear all right in the eyes of any who might be watching them, as it would be seen that the young Pan'-gua took this way to repay the old man for his hospitality, but to be seen together too much might create a suspicion that would make trouble for them both.

When ready to depart Cha'-za gave his final word of warning. "Keep your eyes and ears open. There will be no time when you are not watched. Me-te'-lo was not the only spy that Dou-gow' had."

"I shall keep your words in my thoughts," replied Che-loo'. "And will be up the mesa before the day is gone."

"You will follow me, on the middle trail?" questioned Cha'-za.

"I shall take the right-hand trail—as before," came the reply.

The old man looked at him questioningly for a moment; then without more words he slowly turned with his load of melons and made his way toward the mesa.

When he had gone Che-loo' looked toward the fields of Ah'-mot, where on their previous trip, Mah-wee'-nah and her friend had filled the fateful little bag of corn that Cha'-za had carried for them. Stacks of bean-vines and scattered rows of standing corn interrupted his view, and he walked back a short distance to a small rise of ground. He thought of the little pouch of beautiful sky-stones at his belt, and a feeling of embarrassment came over him. Could he, after all, have the courage to give the sky-stones to her? He hadn't thought it would take courage. The idea, at first so simple and joyous, suddenly seemed an almost impossible thing to carry out. What if she refused to accept the gift? He did not doubt she had refused many others. From the higher elevation he could see that the two girls were not in the field, nor could he see them anywhere. He wondered if Mah-wee'-nah had forgotten, or if she had been unable to come.

Thoughtfully, now, he started back to the sack of beans that he must carry up the mesa. Suddenly, while passing one of the heaps of dead vines, a man leaped from the ground behind it, and the next instant Che-loo"'s feet were pulled from under him. As he fell, two more men leaped upon him and before he could make effectual resistance, he was tied hand and foot.

"Quick! Pull him behind the stack!" commanded

THREE AGAINST ONE

one of the men, and he was drawn nearer the vines, where he could be hidden from any who might chance to be looking from the mesa. One of the men stooped and picked up the little pouch of sky-stones that had dropped from Che-loo''s belt.

"Give that to me, Bor'-sa!" said the man who had given the first command. "Klee'-tso has said I am to bring all of his things to him." And when he had received the little bag, he stooped down and took Che-loo''s knife from its sheath.

"What do we now?" asked the man addressed as Bor'-sa.

"You know what word has been given us!" said the first speaker sharply.

"Yes, but if we carry him back to the shelter now, we will be seen. Must we stand here waiting until dark, like three owls?"

"Your head is like the gourd!" exclaimed the first speaker. "Throw some bean-vines over him, and tie them on him so they will not fall off. Then we will drag him back to the shelter, and none will know but that we move the vines and not a Pan'-gua spy."

During this conversation Che-loo' had uttered no sound. Now he spoke.

"I am no spy, and I give you word for the coward Klee'-tso, who fears to fight me alone. Tell him—"

But before he could complete his remark an armful of dried vines was thrown over him and he had to close both mouth and eyes quickly against the fine dust that came sifting down over him. The three Pau-lan'-tees laughed loudly at the sudden ending of his message to Klee'-tso.

"We will tell him your words, and he too will laugh much!" exclaimed one of the men.

Anger seized Che-loo', and he made no further effort to speak. When the vines, that now completely covered him, had been loosely tied to him, his shoulders were lifted by two of the men, one under each arm, and he was dragged over the ground. Though he could not see, he knew he was being taken to one of the little sheds that stood on the outer margin of the fields. After a time his captors stopped, let him down to the earth again, and removed the dusty vines.

He found himself just inside one of the little shelters. Only two of the men were with him now; the third had disappeared. One of the two men untied his feet and commanded him to stand up. Che-loo' drew his feet under him, and although his hands were still bound, he was able to get to his feet. At the back of the shelter a stout post arose to support the small roof-timbers. Leading him up to this, his captors bid him turn his back to it.

"Do as I say and no harm comes to you for the night," said the man who seemed to have charge of his capture as well as his few belongings.

"Being bound, I must take your words," replied Che-loo' coolly. He then turned his back to the post and was soon bound to it, hand and foot.

"I go, Bor'-sa," said the man who had been in charge. "Do not go far from the shelter, and until it is dark you will act like one who works in his fields with the corn and beans."

"It is good," came the reply.

The first speaker walked rapidly away toward the mesa, and Che-loo"s guard began at once to make pre-

THREE AGAINST ONE

tense of working among the few cornstalks that stood along the margin of this outer field.

The open end of the little shelter looked eastward, and from where he was forced to stand Che-loo' could just see the far eastern corner of the mesa. The trail he would have taken was near the opposite end, and he wondered if Mah-wee'-nah and En-tay' could be on it waiting for him. Time dragged along, and the sun's afterglow that had been reflected against the eastern sky was fast fading into the early twilight that would last but a short time before night dropped down. He wondered what his captors intended to do with him. He knew that Dou-gow' and Klee'-tso were capable of anything, and had given ample proof of their desire to send him on the Long Sleep.

The man Bor'-sa was now some thirty paces away, but in plain sight. As Che-loo' watched him the guard turned suddenly, as though attracted by some one approaching, and in a few moments Che-loo' heard the sound of steps drawing near. Perhaps old Cha'-za had become suspicious, during his long absence, and had come down to look for him; or it might be some other friend to whom he could cry out. While speculating on all this, the great, stooping figure of Gool, the Witch-killer, ambled into view, and the hunchback walked up to the guard. A feeling of anger and disgust arose in Che-loo' at sight of the hunchback. So the vile shaman was also to be used in the plan of Dou-gow' to get rid of him! The hunchback did not so much as look in the direction of the shelter, but his great, bent body completely hid the man Bor'-sa, who was evidently engaged in low but earnest conversation with him.

A sound, immediately at his back, now caught Che-loo"s ear and he listened intently. Some one was creeping up at the back of the shelter.

A moment later he heard the slight noise as of some one trying to get his hand between the loose poles that formed the back of the little shelter. Turning his head as far as his bonds would permit, he tried to see immediately back of him. A knife, with unusually long blade, was slowly thrust into view, and now moved unerringly toward the thongs that bound him. A number of strokes of the blade was required for each thong, and from the manner of the cutting Che-loo' knew that the hand that held the knife was not that of a strong man. His hands were now free.

"Take the knife, and free your feet," came a whispered voice.

In a moment he had slashed the ropes that held him, and was about to step from his place of confinement when his guard, passing around the hunchback, made as though to approach the shelter. Instantly Che-loo' backed up to the post, and held his hands behind him as though bound, but the long knife remained in his grasp. When yet some distance away, the Witch-killer again engaged the guard in conversation, and now, so it seemed to the watchful prisoner, he deliberately moved his great body between the guard and the shelter. In a moment Che-loo' was out and running swiftly back of the shed, and careful to keep it between himself and the two men whom he was rapidly leaving behind. He knew the deep twilight would soon swallow him up among the corn-shocks and the vines. The big knife was too large for his sheath, and he stuck it in his belt as he ran.

THREE AGAINST ONE 195

The whispered voice of his liberator had sent mingled joy and fear into his heart. After a few moments of rapid running he saw a dim figure far ahead of him running toward the mesa. He increased his speed, and overtook her as she neared the foot of the right-hand trail.

"Mah-wee'-nah!" he called. She stopped, panting hard against the long run, and in a moment he was beside her.

"You saved me—from those men! You are good—to do that. I cannot say the words that are in my mind to say," he announced, trying hard amid his tumbling thoughts for some way to express himself.

"Come!" she commanded. "We must not stop here! There may yet be danger, and we can talk as we go—but we must speak low, for always there are ears to hear."

Che-loo"s heart pounded in his breast, and not from the light exertion of running. He longed for the kind of speech that would enable him to tell this girl—this one beautiful woman of all the earth-born—how he regarded her.

"How did you know that I was out there, tied to the post? And where did you get the great knife? You should not—"

"I saw the men throw the vines over you, and take you away," she interrupted. "I watched them and saw the little house where they stopped. Then I sent my friend En-tay' to say to my mother that I would not be home until the day was gone. I hid in a place by the trail until the sun had set—and that's all, and now you are—are here," she explained.

"You should not have come where there was such

danger—and all alone,—just for me. My thoughts say—always, that you are good, and beautiful—like the flowers in the forest, you are beautiful, and I would not have let you come out there, alone—if I had known."

She stopped walking, and laughed a low teasing laugh. "And could you have stopped me—if you *had* known, and you all tied up to a post?" she questioned. Even in the semi-darkness, he could see the teasing light in her eyes and the smile that revealed her white teeth.

"Of all Earth Women, you are the best, and the most wonderful!" he exclaimed.

"You mean, that you want to thank me for helping you—Che-loo' of Pan'-gua?" she questioned. "Is that what your words mean?" She seemed to enjoy his embarrassed attempt to tell her what, in truth, she wanted most to hear.

"Yes, I give you thanks, great thanks—but my words mean a bigger thing than that—much bigger than thanks. I—I like you very much, and I will—always!"

The falling darkness made him more bold, and he stepped nearer to her.

She stood with her face averted, and for a long moment made no reply.

"You like me—because I helped you?" she whispered.

"Before this day—long before this day, I have liked you more than all Earth Women—I think that always I have liked you." He suddenly remembered the pouch of sky-stones that he was to have given her, and knew that here, with cover of darkness to hide his embarrassment, he would have the courage to offer them to her. He felt he could, with great joy, break the necks of the three men who had robbed him.

"When I came down to Cha'-za's field, I brought something, something very good, for you to wear—and you would like it. The three men stole it from me—but I will get it again." He paused awkwardly, and silence fell between them. He wished he could see her face.

"A Pau-lan'-tee girl does not wear things that a man gives to her, unless—she is the woman he is to—to have in his home." It was her turn to feel embarrassed, but Che-loo' saw nothing of that.

"I know. That is why I—I thought you might take my gift. There is *no* other woman—that can ever be the one woman in my house."

"Was it a bluebird's feather?" she asked, with great show of innocence. Then, for the first time, she heard him laugh—a low pleasing laugh that, she was sure, could only come from a good heart.

"*No.* It was something that you would like *much*—it was sky-stones—the kind you would like if you would take them and wear them," he explained, more at ease now.

"I wore your bluebird's feather, and it was a good omen," she said encouragingly.

A joyous hope leaped to his heart.

"Will you, then, wear a gift from me—for all to see—Mah-wee'-nah?"

Heavy steps sounded near at hand. Some one was running toward them from the fields. Che-loo' whirled, the great knife grasped in his hand.

"Quick! This way!" whispered Mah-wee'-nah, pulling him to one side where great black rocks loomed in the darkness. Crouching among them they waited in silence. Che-loo' raised his head to look toward the foot of the trail, where the approaching man would have to pass if he intended to go up the mesa. A moment later the massive figure of the Witch-killer came black against the sky. The man paused and looked carefully about him, then he stood perfectly still and seemed to be listening. Though it was perhaps not altogether necessary, Mah-wee'-nah put out her hand and touched Che-loo''s mouth, as a signal for silence.

CHAPTER XIII

SIGN OF THE BLACK WITCH

There are trails that climb the sunny hills,
And trails where the tall trees bend
O'er the shadows deep
Where the "Silent" sleep—
For, at last, all trails must end.

AS Che-loo' and Mah-wee'-nah waited in silence among the great rocks at the foot of the mesa, the Witch-killer slowly turned and made his way around the cliffs as if intending to ascend one of the other trails. When he had gone, they arose and Mah-wee'-nah sprang to the trail and began running upward as fast as she could go. Che-loo' ran after her, and not until she had neared the top would she pause or make reply to his many efforts at conversation. But at last, from sheer lack of breath, she was forced to slacken her pace.

"I must go quickly now, to my home," she panted. "My mother will have people search for me if I am not soon in my house."

"You did not tell me—what I asked, about the gift," he protested. "Will you not say, now, if you will have it, and—"

A figure—a small figure this time—arose beside the trail a little way ahead, and a moment later En-tay' stood in front of them.

"Oh, I am *glad* it is you!" she exclaimed. "And that nothing evil happened to—to him, and that he is free. Oh, Mah-wee'-nah, was it not good you had one to help you who is so strong and—"

"Is my mother angry, that I have not come?" interrupted Mah-wee'-nah quickly.

"I found her in the house of your aunt," replied En-tay'. "And I said to her that you would be at my house, and that was all right. Cha'-za has come to our house, and he looked for—for him,"—she pointed at Che-loo'—"and I told him you were both on the trail, somewhere, for I did not want him to go down in the fields, to that place and get into great trouble. I will go back now, and tell him that you come, and you—Mah-wee'-nah—you must come to my house." With that she turned and fled up the short stretch of trail that lay between them and the top.

En-tay''s mention of the help Mah-wee'-nah had received, and the thought of the big knife with which she had cut his bonds, now filled Che-loo''s mind.

"Who gave you the knife?" he asked, as he drew it from his belt, fingering the curiously carved handle of bone.

"I will take it, and return it to the one who owns it," she said quietly, as she held out her hand.

Carefully he gave it to her. "You cannot tell me—who it is?" he questioned again.

She remained silent for a moment, as if deciding on a reply. "No, I cannot tell. Sometime I will tell you."

"Then I do not want to know," he replied. "But I give him thanks that he let you have the knife."

"You know, now, that there are men on the mesa who are trying to bring harm to you. One here, who is very evil, is strong against you, and you should not stay longer in Pau-lan'-tee." Then she added in a low voice, "If my father lives—all things will be well. I do not ask you to tell me now—but I think he *must* be wounded—and in the care of your people."

"I cannot give answer to that—but I will not say that your words are wrong," he replied. Then, after a pause, "You *want* me to come again to the mesa?"

She hesitated. "Yes," she replied. "But now is an evil time. We must not have more words about the gift for me—not now. People must not see you with me in Pau-lan'-tee, and you should not stay longer on the mesa where you are in great danger. It may be you will want to come again—when evil men do not hold council over Pau-lan'-tee."

They were at the top of the mesa, and soon would have to part. He tried to think of something nice to say to her, something that would sound as wise as her words had sounded to him, but he felt strange and confused. Mah-wee'-nah stopped and spoke hurriedly.

"I will go now to the house of my friend En-tay', and you must leave me here and walk some other way. It is better so." Then she added in a lower voice, "May the Shiuana be with you—my good friend!" And before he could think of anything to reply she had vanished into the shadows of the village.

When she had gone he instantly thought of many things he should have said to her. He was suddenly angry with himself and felt he had been foolish, empty-headed. He had not even told her that he would return to Pau-lan'-tee. With very disagreeable thoughts he went on his way to Cha'-za's house, and was not surprised to find that his host had not returned; but the old man had left a share of the evening meal in the pot, and dried plums and maize-cakes lay on the wide, flat basket. Che-loo' ate but little, and sat looking moodily into the fire. The day that had promised so much had turned out badly.

After a time Cha'-za entered and, in answer to his questions, Che-loo' told him all that had taken place in the fields, with the exception of his conversation with Mah-wee'-nah. The old man frowned and gave a low exclamation.

"The man Bor'-sa must have learned that you had escaped from the shelter, for he is now on the mesa looking for Klee'-tso. Do nothing to get the things the men took from you. Klee'-tso is an evil man, but he is not a thief. You will again have your bag of sky-stones."

Having given this good advice, Cha'-za went to a corner of the room and, after pushing aside a flat stone, returned with a knife in his out-stretched hand. "This you will use, until you have your own."

"I give you thanks, umo," said Che-loo', taking the proffered weapon and placing it in his belt. "Who, think you, gave the knife to the daughter of Ah'-mot, that she might cut the thongs that bound me?" he asked.

"I could not speak with truth," replied Cha'-za. "It might have been any one of the nine men who met with Man'-yah, or some other, but I know not."

"The knife was large—and the handle of bone, deeply carved," said Che-loo'.

"Hum!" grunted Cha'-za. "There are more knives than people on the mesa."

SIGN OF THE BLACK WITCH

The following morning Che-loo' slowly awoke out of dreams, golden dreams of a maiden tall and beautiful, who danced with him on the mountain-top to the tune of a hunting-song. The night's rest had dispelled his gloom of the evening before. He would go back to Pan'-gua, but—he would come again soon. He arose, pulled on his moccasins and went below.

"A good day comes, Cha'-za!" he called out at the foot of the ladder.

"A—ee—if it is not a bad day, it may be good," came the reply; "but the dawn is red, and on the trail a feather of the crow blew across my path. No farther did I go, but came straight back to make a change of the traps I had with me, and to burn sacred meal on the hearth. An ill omen is in the black feather and the red dawn. It will be a day for wide eyes and open ears."

"I will keep your words," replied Che-loo'. "If an ill omen begins this day, I will have a care."

Cha'-za picked up the fresh traps he had selected and went to the door.

"I am not long in the desert. There is food for you —I have eaten."

With this brief announcement he departed, mumbling his meaningless jargon for outside ears, and leaving Che-loo' to his meal and his meditations.

One by one the events of the previous night passed through Che-loo''s mind, and he suddenly remembered that Cha'-za's bag of beans must still be lying where he had left it in the field. He wondered if the old man could have carried it up during his absence the night before. He rose and went up to the little storage-room and looked about in the dim light. There were sacks of corn, and the melons that Cha'-za had carried, but the bag of beans was not there. He must go down to the fields and get it. Men might see the beans lying unguarded on the ground and laugh at both himself and Cha'-za, if they did nothing worse.

He went on to his front room to make sure that he had barred his door, and suddenly noticed that his trader's pack was not in its accustomed place. The door was barred but the pack was missing. He looked about him in sudden alarm, then a guilty laugh escaped him. He remembered that he had left it in the house of Man'-yah. His thoughts had been so filled with the idea of the sky-stones, and her to whom they were to be given, he had gone off without it. The words of the Che'-pah hunter came back to him, "You trader like a squaw." Well he knew, well enough, that he was no trader. He unbarred his door and went out on the roof. The sun was up and the early morning air was fresh and cool. He decided to go down and get the bag of beans, then he would go to Man'-yah's house for the pack. He hoped Man'-yah would not be there to laugh at him. He went on to the broad ladder and down into the street.

As he passed the many houses he heard women singing the grinding-song as they kept time with the metate stones that ground the blue corn into meal. Fat children played with lean dogs, and sacred turkeys gobbled and reluctantly made room for him as he passed through the narrow streets. He wondered if *she* ground the corn for her mother and if she sang when she ground it. He was sure that her songs would be good to hear.

Down in the fields all was peaceful and quiet. The far, blue hills, soft in the September haze, gave him a sudden desire to hunt—to run free over the desert and the slopes of high mountains. But one old man was at work in the fields and he some distance away. Che-loo' felt lonely. The events of the evening before seemed remote, as though they had occurred long ago.

The bag of beans was lying where he had left it. Swinging it to his shoulder he returned to the trail and slowly plodded his way upward.

He disliked the thought of it, but he knew it was now time for him to return to Pan'-gua. He would come again to the mesa as soon as he could, but now he must go back and tell Ne-chō'-ba all that he had learned, and he had learned much—all, in fact, that his Cacique had wanted to know.

His knife and the sky-stones would give him reasonable excuse for returning to Pau-lan'-tee. He did not ask himself just why he wanted an excuse.

As he approached Cha'-za's house, he saw the old man peering at him from the partly-closed door as if waiting for him.

"Bring the beans in here," commanded Cha'-za. When he had stepped within and had dropped the heavy bag the old man closed his door. "Have a care when you go up to your house," he warned. "One whose word I know to be true has just told me that while we were away Klee'-tso went up to your house by the street ladder, and he carried something in his hand like a small sack."

"He has brought my stolen sky-stones, and feared to come while I was here," said Che-loo', confidently.

"I think not," said the old man. "That is not the way of Klee'-tso. He came for no good. I have in my thought one reason why he came, but we shall see. We will go up by the front way, and we will have open eyes."

Arriving at Che-loo"s door, Cha'-za pushed it open cautiously, and then stepped within. Che-loo' followed wonderingly. He had learned to have great respect for the old man's caution and wisdom, and was willing now to let him have his way. Cha'-za stood still and looked carefully around the room.

"Ah—ee l" he exclaimed in a low voice, as he pointed toward Che-loo"s bedding. "There is the little gift he brought for you."

Extending from the folds of the blanket was a rattlesnake, its venomous head raised as if studying the enemies who had interrupted its attempt to crawl out of its hiding-place. Che-loo' closed the door and removing his belt approached the snake.

"A long stick is better," advised Cha'-za.

"It is not in my thought to kill it," announced Che-loo'. "I will show this coward Klee'-tso how I fear his snakes," and he began waving the end of the belt slowly back and forth above the raised head of the reptile. After a few moments the snake began to lower its head and to crawl farther from the folds of the blanket. Che-loo"s hand shot down and a second later he lifted the writhing serpent, now helpless in the grasp that held it just back of the open jaws.

"You will take out its teeth?" inquired Cha'-za.

"Yes, if you give me help," replied Che-loo', and he deftly held the snake's mouth open with careful fingers. "Get a sharp stick, and bring it here and I will show you—"

"Save your words," interrupted Cha'-za. "It is a trick I have often seen the Che'-pahs do, but you are the first stone-house man that I have seen to lift a living snake."

With the sharp point of the stick Che-loo' pried the two poisonous fangs from the upper part of its mouth, and looked about him for a place to keep the now harmless reptile. His eye caught the empty water-jar with the stone lid. "I will keep it here until I again pass Klee'-tso's door," he announced. "I will then show him how I fear his crawling witch with the rattling tail."

Cha'-za made a wry face and nodded his head, then he carefully threw down the bedding, piece by piece, to make sure no more of the poisonous snakes were hidden in its folds. He made careful search of the rest of the room, looking in all corners and behind all movable objects.

"You think there was more than one?" questioned Che-loo'.

"It is well to be sure of it," came the reply.

"It is good you were warned of Klee'-tso's visit," remarked Che-loo' when they had descended to Cha'-za's back room.

As the old man was about to make reply there came a soft knock on the door, then it immediately opened and En-tay' stepped within, closing the door behind her. Her eyes were bright with excitement, and her breath came short, as though she had been running.

"Cha'-za, my father wants you to come soon to our house," she announced; then she stepped nearer to the two men and added in a whisper, "Dou-gow' and Klee'-tso have gone down the trail with a hundred men, and while I was on my way here some one told me that the men go to Pan'-gua to make fight."

"The one who says such words is a fool with an empty head!" exclaimed Cha'-za, as he opened the door and passed quickly into the street. En-tay' started to follow him, but turned back before passing the threshhold.

Che-loo' stood as if stunned by the news. For the first time in his life fear gripped him, and all of his self-confidence seemed to leave him. Dou-gow' with men in Pan'-gua would mean one thing—a search for Ah'-mot—and if the Pau-lan'-tee Cacique were yet alive, he would be found and there would be fighting in Pan'-gua, with great trouble for his people. They would have no warning of the Pau-lan'-tees' visit, and would be wholly unprepared. A pang of guilt smote him. He had talked too much, and in some way Dou-gow' must have learned that Ah'-mot might be alive and in Pan'-gua. All this passed swiftly through his mind while Cha'-za was departing, and En-tay' was turning back to the room.

"I did not tell Cha'-za, but I have heard one thing more," she whispered quickly. "There are three men on each of the trails, and they are told not to let you leave the mesa. A—a friend told me that, and he is sure the men have gone to your village of Pan'-gua, for his brother is one of the men that is with Dou-gow' and Klee'-tso. Not always does Cha'-za know all things. And—the old Chin-di, Dou-gow', has made Mah-wee'-nah's aunt and her mother shut Mah-wee'-nah up in a room, so that she cannot see you while Dou-gow' is away—and they are very fearful to go against Dou-gow'. I must go quickly—" and she turned and walked rapidly away while he stood pondering her words and wondering what he should do. He went up the outer ladder and on over to the adjoining roof, where he had stood on the evening of his arrival on the mesa. Carefully he scanned the desert in the direction of Pan'-gua. There, just beyond the shallow canyon, through which he and his two companions had chased the wounded buck, he could plainly see the long column of men moving over the plain. By sunset the following day, they would enter Pan'-gua. He must get there before they did—but how?

He had made a great mistake in telling Cha'-za, and the nine men, of his vision of the three wolves. He had been a fool. The vision could mean only one thing to them, and that was that he knew more about Ah'-mot than he dared tell. In some way word of this had gone to the ears of Dou-gow'.

He went into his house, and sat down to think. To attempt to pass the three men who guarded each trail would be useless, and might result in his being bound and kept a close prisoner. To get down over the mesa wall would be impossible. Would it? Could he not climb down—? He went out again to the low retaining-wall at the edge of the roof and looked over. He believed that a rope thirty paces long would let him down to the topmost rocks of the high drift that sloped down sharply at the foot of the mesa. If Cha'-za would let him make a hole in his wall, near the floor of his back room, the rope could be still shorter and he would have a way to tie it securely. This would also hide his operations from any spies who might be watching his house from any of the roofs opposite. He returned to his own house, and after closing and barring the door, went into the little storage-room. Bringing out all of the ropes he could find he sorted them over and saw at once that all of them tied together would not reach much more than half-way down the mesa wall. But Cha'-za had friends, and his friends must have ropes. Carefully he tied together those that he was sure would bear his weight. He *must* get down to the desert, and once there he might have a chance to overtake the Pau-lan'-tees and get to Pan'-gua ahead of them—if they did not get too great a start.

Coiling the long rope, he went down the passage to Cha'za's back room and examined the wall. While he was thus occupied Cha'za entered and carefully barred his door. Without a word, he walked back to Che-loo' and stood regarding him thoughtfully.

"Dou-gow' has heard that Ah'-mot is alive, and in Pan'-gua. Is it true that Ah'-mot lives?"

"I have talked as a fool talks," replied Che-loo' bitterly, "but you are Cha'-za, friend of Pan'-gua and Ne-chō'-ba. This will I say to you: If Ah'-mot lives he is with those who will try to heal him of any wounds given him by his Pau-lan'-tee enemies. Now, I must return quickly to Pan'-gua—I must get to my people before Dou-gow' and Klee'-tso."

Cha'-za shook his head. "It is too late for you to go—now. There are guards on each trail."

"It is not too late if you give me help." He grasped the old man's arm. "Cha'-za, I *must* go, and go quickly. I know about the men who guard the trails—I have a way, if you can get more rope for me. I have here enough to reach half-way down the mesa wall, and if you can get more rope I will show you how I can go down over the wall."

The old man fell silent, and Che-loo', impatient to be doing something, thought he would never speak.

SIGN OF THE BLACK WITCH

Without a word Cha'-za threw a thin blanket about his shoulders and went to the door. "Soon I will return," he said.

"If I can make a hole in your wall, near the floor there in the corner, where it is dark, I can go down from the mesa without being seen by eyes that may be watching your house from the roofs, and I will not need so much rope."

"It is good," replied Cha'-za. "Bar my door after me, that no one may come and learn what you do. I will knock twice when I come." He passed out into the street and Che-loo' barred the door.

He had all but completed the hole in the wall when the two knocks sounded. When the old man entered he dropped his blanket to the floor, disclosing coils of stout rawhide rope wound about his waist. "This will be all that you will need," he remarked. "It is well for you to reach Pan'-gua before Dou-gow'. Ne-chō'-ba should have warning. Dou-gow' has long waited for a chance to strike at your people, because he has hated Ne-chō'-ba."

Che-loo' made no reply, as he worked, almost frantically, to complete the hole through which he must pass. He felt that Dou-gow' and his men were getting too great a start. The hole finished, he rose and tied the ropes securely together, and to one end he bound a long stout piece of wood as an upper anchor. Then he put the opposite end through the hole and carefully played out the rope as far as it would go. Cautiously putting his head through the hole, he looked down over the great cliff that he must descend. The far end of the rope lay in a small coil on one of the great rocks at the mesa's base.

When he rose, Cha'-za was busy filling a little bag with dried meat and maize-cakes.

"You will leave your pack. I will take care of it for you," said the old man.

"I will be back for it before three suns have come and gone," announced Che-loo'. "I must be back before Dou-gow' and his men return, for they must not know that I have gone to Pan'-gua to warn my people to hide—" he stopped short.

"To hide the wounded Ah'-mot?" questioned Cha'-za.

"If he is wounded, so that his mind knows nothing more than a child knows, must he be found in Pan'-gua, and by Dou-gow' and Klee'-tso, who caused his wounds?" asked Che-loo' desperately. "Do you not see that I must be here when Dou-gow' returns, and that none must know that I have left the mesa?"

The old man slowly nodded his head, and Che-loo' could see that his words had caused his aged host to marvel at the situation that confronted him.

"There is wisdom in your words, but you cannot return by the way you are leaving," said Cha'-za.

"I have a way," replied Che-loo'.

The little bag of food was now tied to his belt and he stood ready to depart. On his hands and knees he backed through the hole, and when all but his arms and head had disappeared, he looked up at the old man.

"I give you thanks for all you have done, umo."

"May Ah'-hool be with you!" replied Cha'-za simply.

A moment later Che-loo' was gripping the stout rope as he moved downward over the mesa wall like a spider dangling on a strand of its web. When his feet were at last on solid ground he looked up to see the kindly face of his host peering down from the hole in the wall. He waved a farewell to the old man, and made his way down to the desert.

The first faint light of dawn, the following day, found Che-loo' far beyond the forest in which he had encountered the Apaches while on his way to the mesa. It had been midnight when he had overtaken the Pau-lan'-tee war party, camped in wooded hills, and cautiously he passed around them under the protection of the heavy night shadows. Bright moonlight had served him well, enabling him to keep his steady and rapid gait through even the roughest country. His long experience as a hunter was standing him in good stead. Although it was very evident that Dou-gow' was hurrying the men toward Pan'-gua, he was not making them travel both day and night as he, Che-loo', had done.

He stretched himself on the ground for a brief rest. Near at hand was the little spring where he had met the gaunt coyote, while on his way to Pau-lan'-tee. Having slaked his thirst, and eaten some of the food Cha'-za had given him, he felt the heavy demand for sleep steal over him. He fought this off and soon rose to continue his forced journey across the expanse of desert that yet lay between him and his home village.

Once again some one on a house-top in Pan'-gua—a man this time—saw something in the desert that startled him, but the man did not stop to tell Ne-chō'-ba about it, as the boy had done, but slid down the ladder and ran out into the open plain.

"What evil comes to you?" called Tō'-bah-yan, as he

ran toward Che-loo'. "I saw you from the house-top —you are spent, like a buck after a long chase. Where is your bow-case and trader's pack?"

"In Pau-lan'-tee," replied Che-loo', smiling wearily. "But I will tell you about it, when I have rested. It is good to be again in Pan'-gua."

As the two approached the village walls, the sound of women wailing for the dead came to Che-loo"s ears. He stopped and gripped the arm of his old hunting companion.

"Who is it that has gone on the Long Sleep?" he commanded.

"One called the Dawn Woman," replied Tō'-bah-yan, and for a moment he wondered at the look of relief that came over the face of Che-loo'.

"You feared it was Ah'-mot, but *he* still lives and it is said he grows stronger each day," said Tō'-bah-yan.

"That is good," Che-loo' replied.

They now entered the village and it seemed to Che-loo' that all of the people of Pan'-gua must be in the crowd gathered in front of the house of Ne-chō'-ba's daughter.

"They wait for sunset," explained Tō'-bah-yan. "It is then this Dawn Woman is to be carried to the Pan'-gua place of the dead."

"I go to my father's house," said Che-loo'. Find him and Ne-chō'-ba, and send them quickly to me. I have word that they must hear. Tell no others I have come home. I have good reason."

"It is good," replied Tō'-bah-yan as he turned away toward the crowd. Che-loo' had hoped to reach his house without being seen by the people whose attention was attracted by the ceremony at the house across the

SIGN OF THE BLACK WITCH

plaza, but he had scarcely greeted his surprised mother, and thrown himself on the familiar bed of skins and blankets, before the room was filled with curious neighbors who came to welcome him and ply him with questions. But not until Mat'-so and Nechō'-ba arrived and all the others had been put out would he speak of his visit to Pau-lan'-tee. Those people who had called out of idle curiosity went away grumbling. "Always he is lazy, and will not talk when he is in the village. He likes nothing but to hunt," and they went back to the curious crowd awaiting the burial of the Dawn Woman.

Alone with his father, mother and Ne-chō'-ba, Che-loo' quickly told of the approaching Pau-lan'-tees, and of why they were coming. "Tō'-bah-yan has told me that Ah'-mot lives," he said.

"Yes," replied Ne-chō'-ba, rising. "And he will live, though his right mind does not yet stay long with him. 'Mat'-so,'" he commanded, "put a man to watch from the roofs. I will go and tell the people that the Pau-lan'-tees are coming. While they have their eyes upon me you must get Tō'-bah-yan or some other, and take Ah'-mot out to the cave beneath the Shrine Rock. He must be safely hidden when Dou-gow' comes, for he will search every house in the village."

Mat'-so went to obey the command, and as Ne-chō'-ba was about to follow, Che-loo' called to him. "I, too, must be hidden from Dou-gow' and the Pau-lan'-tees. They must not know I am here to give you warning. Word must go to the people not to say that I am returned to Pan'-gua."

"Hum!" grunted Ne-chō'-ba, wondering a little at the commanding voice of this new Che-loo'. "You speak true, and you also must go to the Shrine. Can you go without being seen?"

"Yes, the back door will let him through a passage to the back of the village," said his mother. "He need not be seen if he keeps the houses between himself and the crowd."

"It is good," replied Che-loo', rising wearily.

His mother placed a large blanket about him. "You will need this in the Shrine."

When word was first given the people that the Pau-lan'-tees were coming to search their village for the lost Cacique, wonder and then anger swept over them, for, with the exception of the Council and a few others, none knew that the Cacique was hidden in the village, though they knew that he was missing from the great mesa. Ne-chō'-ba climbed a ladder to a low roof and, raising his hands, gained their attention.

"Hearken, my people!" he called. "The Pau-lan'-tees are our friends and brothers. They come at the command of one who is evil, but they will do no harm by looking within our houses. This evil leader makes great show of searching all villages—that he may seem to want to find the lost one. Let us show the Pau-lan'-tees kindness, even though our hearts are against the one who brings them."

"Yes, yes—it is so. Ne-chō'-ba is right," they thoughtfully assented.

"The Sun God touches the hills," continued the old man. "Now we shall go to bury her who has gone on the Long Sleep. This must be done before the Pau-lan'-tees are here, that we may be in our houses when they come."

The wail of the women began afresh, and the four

SIGN OF THE BLACK WITCH 217

men who were to carry the litter which was to bear the silent figure of the Dawn Woman on her last earth-journey, entered the house of Ne-chō′-ba's daughter.

The man stationed on the roof hurried to the ground, and found Mat′-so near at hand. "They come!" he said in a low voice. "They follow the draw a little to the north and they neared the village before I saw them."

"Let them come," replied the Governor. "We will not stop the burial of the dead. The Shiuana lead men to do strange things. Dou-gow′ comes, though he knows it not, to look upon the burial of his wife."

Out through the village walls passed the slow-moving litter, heavily draped with soft skins and bright blankets that the departed spirit might have ample covering in that far land of the Silent Others. The few wailing women, and old Ne-chō′-ba with Ti′-ee, the witch-doctor, led the crowd of spectators that followed. Northward toward the near-by hills the mournful column moved, and had gone but a little way when Dou-gow′ and Klee′-tso, followed by their men, came hurrying to the walls of Pan′-gua.

As they halted, Mat′-so went to meet them, and appearing surprised at their arrival, gave them a gesture of friendly greeting.

"My friends, you come to Pan′-gua like men in war. Have you been making fight with Apaches?" he called out.

"We come here for Ah′-mot, our Cacique," replied Dou-gow′, as he solemnly folded his arms. Then, as solemnly he turned to Klee′-tso, who stood at his side. "Take men with you and stop those who go to bury the dead. We may want to know *who* it is that is gone on the Long Sleep."

"Why do you come to Pan'-gua to ask for Ah'-mot?" asked Mat'-so, coolly.

"Because he may be here—hidden away in one of your houses, or—" he added slowly, "being buried among your dead. But we shall see." He turned to one of the men and gave command. "Take the rest of the men and make search of each house, and the estufa of the village."

When the man had obeyed, Dou-gow' strode after Klee'-tso, who had quickly overtaken and halted the slow-moving funeral procession. As the Pau-lan'-tee Governor came up, Klee'-tso turned to him.

"They will not say who it is that has gone on the Long Sleep," he announced.

"Then we shall see for ourselves," replied Dou-gow'.

The wondering bearers of the litter stared in silence, and the crowd that followed looked at the Pau-lan'-tee Governor in anger and amazement. Ne-chō'-ba stepped in front of Dou-gow'.

"So you have become so evil you no longer have regard for the dead!" The voice of the old man rang out in solemn accusation.

In the presence of the aged Ne-chō'-ba Dou-gow' lost some of his self-confidence. Ignoring the old man's remark, he pointed to the covered figure on the litter.

"Is the one you carry a Pan'-gua? If it is—no harm shall come, and we let you go on your way."

Ne-chō'-ba was taken aback by the unexpected question. He saw instantly that Dou-gow' suspected it might be Ah'-mot who had gone on the Long Sleep.

"No, it is not a Pan'-gua—but it is not the one you

SIGN OF THE BLACK WITCH 219

have in your evil thoughts," replied the old man quietly.

"Then it is *not* a Pau-lan'-tee?" persisted Dou-gow', with slow emphasis.

"It is a Pau-lan'-tee," admitted Ne-chō'-ba.

Dou-gow' gave a short, ugly laugh. "It could be but *one* Pau-lan'-tee—just as I thought. Klee'-tso!" he commanded sharply. "We will see this Pau-lan'-tee whom the Pan'-gua dogs bury in the rocks. Take the covering away, that we may know!"

Several of the Pan'-gua women stepped between the litter and Klee'-tso with angry protests; but Ne-chō'-ba waved them back.

"It may be that no one has better right than Dou-gow' to look on the face of the one we bury," he announced.

A look of triumph shone in the eyes of the Pau-lan'-tee Governor. Klee'-tso obeyed the command, and Dou-gow' stepped forward to where he could look over the war-captain's shoulder. As the covering was lifted from the figure of the Dawn Woman, Dou-gow' stared in amazement, then his eyes caught the little white arrow, dread symbol of the Black Witch who condemns those who do evil.

"Dez'-pah!" he gasped. "Dez'-pah!" and with outflung arms he backed away into the men behind him. Then, shaken with fear, he put a trembling hand to his eyes, and turning, walked away as if dazed by what he had seen.

The surrounding crowd, both Pan'-guas and Pau-lan'-tees, looked after him, amazed by his actions. Ne-chō'-ba tenderly replaced the covering over the silent figure, and as he did so the last strong light of the setting sun went out behind the peaceful hills, leaving the soft upward flare of gold and rose as a final gesture of the dying day.

Ne-chō'-ba broke the silence, and his voice was low and clear as he addressed those about him.

"Yes, this is Dez'-pah, wife of Dou-gow'. A good woman—driven from her people by the evil one who now fears to look upon her face. Keep my words— you men of Pau-lan'-tee, for you have had witness of their truth."

Safely hidden within the dry cave, beneath the great Shrine Rock, that stood like a gray outcropping of stone, a little way back of the village, Che-loo' fell asleep on his blanket; and seated beside him, Ah'-mot, the Cacique of the Pau-lan'-tees, stared at the low-arched roof, and like one slowly awakening from a troubled dream, wondered where he was, and who might be the sleeping youth at his side.

CHAPTER XIV

THE RATTLESNAKE

> Over the night the Wind Witch flies,
> And the chin-dogs howl in the plain;
> On the mesa wall
> The gray owls call
> Till the dawn-light comes again.

AFTER leaving the funeral procession, Dou-gow' had no further interest in the search of Pan'-gua. The sight of the fearful sign of the Black Witch, held in the hand of his wife, whom he had supposed he would never see again, had unnerved him.

Against the grumbling protest of the Pau-lan'-tee men, he gave them command to rest for a little time beside the pool of Pan'-gua and return to the great mesa. Even Klee'-tso protested, and said the men should camp for the night, as they needed the rest, and begin their homeward march with the dawn. But Dou-gow' had determined to remain no longer than necessary near those who had known and talked with his wife during her last days among the earth-born, for he feared she had told the Pan'-guas much that might now get to the ears of his Pau-lan'-tee followers.

A compromise came to his mind. "We will rest until the moon is up," he announced. "We are nearer the camps of the Che'-pahs than we are to Pau-lan'-tee, and the Che'-pahs will have much good meat and good water. It is there we will go."

This suited the men somewhat better, and when many of the kind-hearted Pan'-gua women brought them steaming meat and baskets of piki-bread they forgot to grumble.

At dawn Che-loo' woke with a start to find himself on his own familiar bed, under his father's roof. He had a vague recollection of being led from the Shrine cave, out into the moonlight, by some one who held him under the arms as he staggered sleepily back to the village.

He remembered that he had gone to the little secret Shrine, and that Ah'-mot, looking strong and well, but still muttering words without reason, had been led into the cave by his father and Tō'-bah-yan. Then he had fallen asleep. And the Pau-lan'-tees! He wondered if they had gone. He leaped from his bed in alarm. He must be back on the mesa before they were. They must have gone, or his father would not have led him back from the Shrine. He ran to the door, already unbarred, and rushed out into the dawn, that he might look toward the pool where the Pau-lan'-tees would camp. His father was coming across the plaza, evidently from the Council-house, a pleased smile on his face.

"Where are the Pau-lan'-tees?" Che-loo' asked excitedly, and before his father could reply, "I must be back on the mesa before they are, or they will know I left Pau-lan'-tee and came here!"

"Give yourself peace," commanded his father. "Go back to the house—your mother will soon cook the morning meal. Ah'-mot is again in his right mind and—"

"But I must go quickly!" interrupted Che-loo'.

"You do not know all. There will be trouble, great trouble, for Cha'-za and for me. My trader's pack, my bow-case, all are in Pau-lan'-tee. I could not again go on the mesa if it were known I came here."

"Quiet yourself," commanded his father impatiently, pushing him back into the house. "You can be back in Pau-lan'-tee long before Dou-gow', if you must go. He and his men have gone to the Che'-pah camps, and they did not leave here until the moon was up, near the middle of the night. They will not again be on the mesa before the third sun."

"Ah—that is good!" said Che-loo', suddenly relieved of his fears. "But I must start as soon as I have eaten, for it is not in my mind to run all the way back."

Over the morning meal he told his father and mother many things that had occurred on the mesa— of the ending of Me-te'-lo and of the hole in Cha'-za's wall through which he had escaped from the mesa— and they listened in amazed silence. Had his father not been present he would have told his mother of a very beautiful Pau-lan'-tee maiden, and the telling would have pleased the mother greatly.

"The body of Me-te'-lo will be found, and if I am away from the mesa when Dou-gow' returns he and Klee'-tso will say *I* am the one who sent him on the Long Sleep. This they will not do if I am there, for I have proof and witness that Me-te'-lo was ended by his own hand. I have the poisoned knife, and Cha'-za has secretly found in Me-te'-lo's house three dead snakes from which he took the poison for the knife."

"Hmm—your words are right," admitted his father. "You must be back in Pau-lan'-tee to bear witness."

Night still hung darkly over the desert when Che-loo' crawled from a shallow cave in the wall of a little canyon a short distance from the great mesa of Pau-lan'-tee, glad to be so near his journey's end. On leaving Pan'-gua a vague apprehension had come to him, a feeling that he ought to return to the great mesa quickly, and he had made good time. He carefully walked forward on the smooth sand that floored the little canyon, looking within the deep shadows for the water-hole that he had dug the evening before.

A faint sound as of some one whistling, evidently a signal, came to his ears from the direction of the mesa. Then from the same direction came the sound of some one running. Che-loo' stopped, and listened intently to catch the footfalls of the runner. A long, steady stride was carrying the man forward, and the sound of the rhythmic *pound—pound—pound* on the earth came clearer. Cautiously he climbed to the canyon's rim and, crouching behind some sagebrush, waited.

The oncoming man was running a little way out in the plain, and just as he came opposite Che-loo' he slowed down to a walk, and after a little distance stopped and again gave the three sharp notes of the signal. Out of the silence that followed came an answering whistle far down the canyon. The runner moved confidently forward now to join the one who had given the expected reply. Che-loo', with careful and silent tread, stole down the canyon rim toward the point where the runner had gone. Soon the faint murmur of voices came to his ears. On hands and knees he slowly made his way along the rim. The two men were down in the canyon, not far from him now. Crawling forward as far as he dared, he lay still and

THE RATTLESNAKE

listened. The questioning voice of Chi-nil', the Pau-lan'-tee wrestler, came clearly:

"Why is Dou-gow' not with you?"

To Che-loo"s surprise it was Klee'-tso who gave the answer. "He is with the Che'-pahs. I left him, with yesterday's sun, and came on quickly. I have only ten men with me, and they sleep back there on the rim. What word of the young Pan'-gua dog?"

"He has not been seen by any, since you left the mesa," replied Chi-nil'. "I have tried his door, but there was no answer—the door was barred."

"It is good!" exclaimed Klee'-tso, exultantly. "He is within his house—but could not give you answer. The gift I left for him, while he was out, has done well, and saved me the trouble of sending the young Chin-di on the Long Sleep—it was for *that* I returned quickly."

"But Cha'-za, what of him? He has said nothing. He would know of it very soon, and tell of it," said Chi-nil'.

"I think not. He is only half-fool, and he has great fear of all things. He knows enough to let some one else find the body of the Pan'-gua," came the logical reply.

"Ah—ah!" suddenly exclaimed Chi-nil'. "I had forgot to tell you—the body of Me-te'-lo was found at the foot of the mesa below your house, and he had to be buried quickly. There is much talk about you and Dou-gow'. It is in my thoughts that the Pan'-gua told many that you threw Me-te'-lo from the roof. I warned you to search the foot of the mesa to see who it was that you and Dou-gow' threw—"

"Hold your tongue—fool!" commanded Klee'-tso. "Even the rocks hear at night, and a bad omen came to me with the setting sun. Think you we would be searching the rocks below Cha'-za's house? Would not *all* suspect us?"

"But there is now much talk," persisted Chi-nil'. "And it is well that you come back."

Silence fell between the two; but after a time Klee'-tso spoke.

"You say the body of Me-te'-lo was found below *my* house. The young Chin-di did that—but nothing can be proved, and none can accuse *us*."

"Why is Dou-gow' with the Che'-pahs?" asked Chi-nil'.

"He feared to remain near Pan'-gua—and he had good reason. He went to the Che'-pah camps to please the men. I left them at the hills and came on quickly, as I wanted to make sure the young Pan'-gua dog never returns to his people. We found the Pan'-guas know nothing of Ah'-mot, for I questioned many of their women, and it is easy to tell if women know a thing. We know now that the young Pan'-gua learned about the matter while on his way to the mesa. He acts like a witch who knows all things, and there is but one ending for a witch." Bitter anger was in the speaker's voice.

Che-loo' marveled at the conversation of the two men, and suddenly wondered if, after all, it was Chi-nil' who was the third man of the three who had betrayed Ah'-mot. After a pause, the last speaker continued.

"Did the women keep Ah'-mot's daughter in the house, as Dou-gow' commanded?"

"No," came the reply; "they *could* not. I have

THE RATTLESNAKE

heard she beat down the door with a bar—and now the aunt greatly fears her."

"Hmm!" grunted Klee'-tso, indifferently.

So! Che-loo' smiled as he lay there in the darkness. Mah-wee'-nah was free! The news pleased him. Suddenly he was aware of the dawn winds sweeping over the sage. Carefully he moved backward, and not until he knew he was beyond hearing of the two men did he drop down into the canyon and run swiftly toward the great mesa.

At the head of the trail nearest Cha'-za's house, he moved cautiously, keeping within the shadows. Dawn was breaking with broad white light, and he hoped to find no more than one guard to contend with. As he moved upward he had begun to believe the trail had been left unguarded, when he heard the sound of some one breathing heavily—the slow regular breathing of one who sleeps peacefully.

Crawling past the slumbering guard, Che-loo' was about to rise and run for Cha'-za's door, when a second guard came up as if to relieve the one who slumbered on his post. The second man was so near, Che-loo' feared to move and there was no cover near at hand. He could easily overpower the man, but that would reveal the fact that he had returned to the mesa. Before he could think of what to do, the approaching guard saw him and leaped forward with drawn knife.

"So! You thought to escape, did you?" he called out. "Bor'-sa, you fool!" he shouted. "Wake up! The Pan'-gua was about to run down the trail. Go back to your house!" he commanded Che-loo'. "You can't sneak away from the mesa now that *I* am here."

The sleepy Bor'-sa staggered to his feet.

"A good guard *you* are," went on the new man. "A moment more and the Pan'-gua would have been on his way to the desert."

Che-loo' turned without a word, as though reluctant to obey the command given him, and made his way to the house of Cha'-za. Surely, the Shiuana had smiled on him in his moment of need!

The Sun God was high in the blue heavens before he and Cha'-za stopped talking of all that had occurred to each of them since they had parted. A stranger, looking in upon them, would have said that a grandfather had just found his long-lost grandson, and that the grandson was pleased to be found.

"The mesa is no longer with Dou-gow'," said Cha'-za. "There is much talk against him among the people, and it is true talk. When the body of Me-te'-lo was found the people quickly said Klee'-tso may know of this, since the moccasin-maker lay beneath his house, but now they believe it was the Black Witch that threw Me-te'-lo from the mesa because he was an evil man."

"I must go for my trader's pack" announced Che-loo', rising.

"It is up in your house," said Cha'-za. "Man'-yah came to help repair my wall, and brought the pack with him. . . . You have heard Klee'-tso's words to Chi-nil'," warned Cha'-za. "He will learn from the guards that you are *not* on the Long Sleep, and will quickly lay some plan to be rid of you. Before you went to Pan'-gua you were in danger, but not in so great danger as you are now. Is it well that you stay longer?"

"Think you that Dou-gow' and Klee'-tso would ask for better chance to slay me than with arrows while in the desert on my way to Pan'-gua?" questioned Che-loo'. "I will stay where I am."

"Ah—ah, your words may have truth in them," admitted the old man. "But you can no longer go out by night. Dou-gow' can throw the knife like a Che'-pah, and it does not need the light of the sun to do it."

"By ancient pact a Pan'-gua cannot draw knife against a Pau-lan'-tee, but I may forget that Dou-gow' is a Pau-lan'tee," said Che-loo'. "For he gives no heed to a pact of friendship."

"It is in my thoughts that Dou-gow' will not come near your hands," remarked Cha'-za. "He is one who uses caution, and he saw you throw Chi-nil'. Klee'-tso has no caution when he is filled with anger, and he will trust to the knife. It is in my thoughts that he has given vow to Dou-gow' that he will slay you."

The old man rose. "I go now. Stay in the house until I am here again. There are those who must be told that Klee'-tso has returned to the mesa without Dou-gow', and that Dou-gow' is a day's journey away. We are not yet sure who the third wolf was, but it may be that enough members of the Council are now ready to accuse Klee'-tso, and make him tell before Dou-gow' returns. If Dou-gow' and his hundred men were with Klee'-tso, all would stand against us—we must not have fighting among our own people."

"It is good," assented Che-loo'. "I have traveled much with little rest. I go up to my house and sleep."

"Sleep with one eye open," warned Cha'-za, as he turned to the door. It seemed to Che-loo' that he had no sooner become unconscious than he was awakened by a low knock on his door.

"Who knocks?" he called.

"I am Klee'-tso. I come with something that belongs to you." The voice of the war-captain was friendly, but this did not deceive his hearer.

"It is good," replied Che-loo', wide awake now and ready for action. He thought quickly of the situation that confronted him, as he very slowly unbarred his door. Klee'-tso would be armed, and had come, he was sure, to slay him, and no doubt knew that Cha'-za was away. His best defense would be quickness. He lifted the strong cottonwood bar from the two forked sticks that held it across the door and instantly decided what to do. Throwing the door open he stepped to one side, ready to thrust out the bar between the legs of his caller if the latter should have a knife in his hand. Klee'-tso fairly jumped into the room and with upraised knife leaped toward Che-loo' before the bar could be used as he had intended. As it was, he could only thrust the end of the short pole sharply at the stomach of his adversary. This was more effective than he expected and Klee'-tso's blow with the knife fell short. Instantly Che-loo' used the bar as a club and whirled it in front of him with such speed and power that the war-captain was forced backward toward the wall of the storage-room.

"Drop the knife or I break your head!" commanded Che-loo'.

Klee'-tso only snarled, and though backing away he watched for a chance to grasp the bar and run in on his youthful antagonist with the knife. With an incredibly quick lunge forward, he caught the swinging club with his left hand and again thrust at Che-loo' with the upraised knife.

Che-loo' caught the descending arm by the wrist; but

he felt the keen point of the knife enter his forearm. He dropped the bar and at the same instant grasped the war-captain by the throat and closed his hand with a mighty grip. Gasping and vainly struggling to break the strangling hold, Klee'-tso was forced back against the wall.

Cha'-za, who had returned and had heard the sounds of the scuffle, came up through the passage and entered the room.

"Close and bar the door!" commanded Che-loo'. "The bar is on the floor behind me."

Cha'-za, playing the fool, mumbled incoherently as he obeyed. When the old man turned back to the two antagonists he saw Klee'-tso's livid face and open mouth, and knew that his young friend would soon have the better of him. After a long moment the knife slid from the upraised hand and fell to the floor.

Che-loo' now grasped his adversary about the waist and, after a brief struggle, threw him heavily to the floor. There was little resistance from the breathless war-captain as Che-loo' turned him face downward.

"Cha'-za, bring me a stout piece of rope!" he commanded.

"Your arm bleeds," said Cha'-za. "It—"

"Bring the rope!" interrupted Che-loo'. "I can fix the arm when I have done with this dog."

When Klee'-tso's hands had been securely bound, Che-loo' permitted the mumbling Cha'-za to bind the cut on his arm with ashes and a piece of doeskin. This done, he motioned for the old man to go below, and lifted the bound man to his feet. Klee'-tso, half-exhausted and still breathing heavily, staggered backward, but after a step or two regained his balance and stood glaring at his captor. In a husky voice he called Che-loo' every vile name that came to his mind. Paying no heed to this, Che-loo' picked up the fallen knife and thrust it into his belt. Then, pointing to the post in the center of the room he commanded Klee'-tso to place his back to it. The war-captain hesitated, and Che-loo' put his hand to the handle of the knife. With a sneer Klee'-tso walked to the post.

In a few moments he was bound, hand and foot, with his face opposite the little door at the back of the room. As he stood up, after tying his captive's feet, Che-loo' noticed, for the first time, the stolen bag of sky-stones hanging from Klee'-tso's belt.

"I see my sky-stones have come back to me," he remarked coolly, and he untied the bag and fastened it to his own belt. "You have not brought my knife to me, but I have yours. It may be a fair bargain."

Che-loo' now went below to join Cha'-za. "What will you do with him?" inquired the old man.

"I may make him tell the name of the third wolf. I have an idea, and it may serve me double purpose," replied Che-loo'. "Can you get two more men to come and hear what Klee'-tso will say? I am told that two men must bear witness before your Council, and it may be they do not count *your* words, since some think you the fool," he added, smiling.

"Soon I will be back with two men of the Council," said Cha'-za, excitement gleaming in his old eyes. "I will take them up to the little room. Do not make Klee'-tso talk until we come." With that the old man hurriedly departed.

Che-loo' returned to the upper room, and went to the water-jar with the flat stone lid. He lifted the lid

THE RATTLESNAKE

—the jar was empty. His captive snake had probably grown hungry and had crawled out to look for flies. Che-loo' looked about the room, kicking at the pots and baskets that stood by the fireplace. The rattler crawled out, wriggling slowly across the cool earthen floor. Klee'-tso looked on with growing fear as he watched the slow-moving serpent gliding toward him. Taking off his belt, as he had done before, Che-loo' waved it over the reptile's head, just as he would do if the dread fangs were still in its jaws. The snake stopped and coiled as if ready to strike, but it watched the quietly swaying belt, and very slowly began to straighten out. With great patience Che-loo' continued to swing the belt.

With sudden, downward thrust of his hand Che-loo' grasped the serpent back of the head, and confronted Klee'-tso.

"You see, I have the little gift you left for me. The Che'-pahs say the snake with the rattling tail only bites a murderer. If you are one who is counted good among men—you are safe. If you are one who has sent a man on the Long Sleep—"

He did not complete the sentence, but passing around behind his prisoner he stooped down, and with his free hand pulled up one leg of Klee'-tso's leggings exposing a portion of the bare calf above the ankle. He then dropped the rattlesnake to the floor immediately behind the prisoner's feet. The sound of some one coming up through the passage came to his ears. He hoped Klee'-tso did not hear it. Evidently Cha'-za and his friends had come with all speed.

The snake coiled itself angrily behind Klee'-tso's heels, and Che-loo' now stepped in front of his captive.

"Who was with you and Me-te'-lo when you took Ah'-mot to the Black Canyon and gave him into the hands of the three Apaches?" he asked in a slow, even voice.

Klee'-tso stared at his young captor with mingled fear and sullen hatred. He was now sure that the young Pan'-gua was a witch, and it was this thought that put fear into his heart, but he had by no means lost his hope of freedom. He suddenly remembered that a snake will not strike at an object that is not moving. If he could keep his exposed leg perfectly still, the snake would not attempt to bite him.

"You talk like the fool," he replied at last. "I know nothing of Ah'-mot."

"We will know who is the fool," warned Che-loo'.

With the belt he struck at the coiled snake. The dry, angry rattle of the quivering tail broke the stillness of the room. Then with the point of his knife he suddenly pricked the upper leg of his prisoner. Unable to see either the knife or the snake, the sudden knife-prick took Klee'-tso by surprise and involuntarily he jerked his leg upward as far as the bonds would permit. Being the nearest moving object within range of its dull vision, the angry serpent struck at the exposed calf. Klee'-tso gave a low scream of fright.

"Take it away! Take it away! It bit me, you Chin-di!" he exclaimed hoarsely.

"You will now tell me who was with you and Me-te'-lo?" asked Che-loo'.

"Yes—yes—if you will let me go!" said the now thoroughly frightened man.

"You will go when you have told me," said Che-loo',

THE RATTLESNAKE

drawing his knife, as if ready to cut the ropes that bound his captive.

"It was Dou-gow'," said Klee'-tso, but he spoke so low Che-loo' knew the men in the little storage-room could not hear.

"Speak louder!" commanded Che-loo'. "Who was it with you and Me-te'-lo when you gave Ah'-mot to the Apaches?"

"Dou-gow'!" yelled the war-captain.

"Your ears have heard the words of your war-captain. Now you know who the third man was," called Che-loo' to the men in the back room.

"Let me go!" yelled Klee'-tso, tugging vainly at the thongs that bound him. Fear shone in his starting eyes, and ashen face.

Che-loo' unbarred the door, and opened it wide. Then, as Cha'-za and his companions entered the room, he cut the ropes that bound his captive. Without a look backward Klee'-tso plunged out of the door and, running to the ladder, slid down to the street. Che-loo' turned to the three men, two of whom kept their eyes on the coiled and still angry snake. Cha'-za laughed.

"It is only fear that bit Klee'-tso," he announced. "The snake is harmless. Che-loo' has taken out its—"

The old man suddenly stopped and stared wide-eyed at the floor near the corner of the room. Che-loo' and the men followed his gaze. A second rattlesnake was slowly crawling from the shadow cast by the trader's pack. The men moved back to be out of striking-distance of the two reptiles.

"You have taken the teeth from *one* snake—but here are two," said Cha'-za, addressing Che-loo'.

"We must know which one is harmless," said Che-loo', stepping to the newly discovered serpent, now worming its sinuous way toward the light of the open door. With his belt he attracted the reptile's attention and, going through the same performance he had used before, he soon had the writhing snake by its neck. He carefully opened its mouth—the fangs were gone! He held it out for Cha'-za to see, while the two men looked on in wonder at the unusual performance.

Cha'-za nodded his head understandingly.

"You used the wrong snake on Klee'-tso," remarked the old man.

Che-loo' dropped the harmless serpent to the floor, and with a stout piece of firewood soon dispatched the one that still lay in an angry coil back of the post. As the men watched him he opened the mouth of the dead rattler. The two evil fangs showed plainly in the upper jaw.

"Klee'-tso brought you one too many snakes," said Cha'-za dryly.

He then turned to the two members of the Council and explained what had occurred, and they nodded their heads in silent amazement. One of them addressed Che-loo'.

"Cha'-za has said you used the wrong snake on Klee-tso, but some think Cha'-za is the fool. *I,* who am wise, say you used the *right* snake. But it is plain that you knew it not."

"A—it is so," affirmed the other man, holding out his hand to Che-loo'. "You are the good friend of Pau-lan'-tee, son of Mat'-so."

Che-loo' grasped the offered hand and smiled.

The two members of the Council hurried away,

filled with the startling news that had come to their ears, but aware that it was not yet time to spread it abroad. Che-loo' cleared his room of the snakes, and this time made thorough search of every spot and space. Cha'-za sat, for a time in silence, on the wide ledge that served as seat and bed.

"No longer I shall be Cha'-za, the Fool," he announced so solemnly that Che-loo' looked at him with interest. "Dou-gow"'s day is done, and gone is the evil power that gave him strength," he went on. "Greed is the she-wolf that nurses the whelps of evil. Greed for power—greed for things to hold in the hand—greed for the smooth talk of many followers. It is better to be the fool. It is the hands of the Shiuana that have drawn the bow against Me-te'-lo and Klee'-tso—you were the arrow on their strings."

The old man suddenly bounced up like a boy, and shed his serious mood like one who casts off a heavy blanket that has been wrapped about him. "Ah—*ah!*" he shouted. "No longer will Pau-lan'-tee hear the mumble of Cha'-za, the Fool!"

"It is good, umo," said Che-loo, not knowing what else to say. Then he thought of his sky-stones that had been restored to him. "Have you good thread of sinew—good for the stringing of sky-stones that a necklace may be made?"

"Yes," replied Cha'-za. "Come, I have the finest. Think you I would not have means to mend my garments?"

With great care the old man selected a flawless strand of sinew, and his eyes twinkled as he handed it to his young guest.

"*That* will wear until her children are too big to

hold on your knee," he said, and before the embarrassed Che-loo' could think of a reply he had gone out the door and down the winding street. His gray head was held high and no longer did he mumble the meaningless jargon of the fool.

CHAPTER XV

THE END OF MANY THINGS

High and clear the grinding song
Is heard through the open door,
And men with bows and arrows go
To hunt the deer where the aspens grow,
And old men talk of the long ago—
For the harvest days are o'er.

WITH the finished necklace in the pouch at his belt, Che-loo' boldly set out across the great village toward the house of Man'-yah. He hoped Man'-yah would not be at home, as it was the daughter whom he wished to see.

It was the good wife, a maternal duplicate of the flashing-eyed En-tay', who answered his greeting at the door.

"No," said the mother, in smiling reply to his query, "En-tay' is not here. She has gone to help the Cacique's daughter who dries plums on her father's roof. I will show you the way to that house," continued the obliging mother, as she stepped out into the street beside him, "and it is very easy to find."

"I give you thanks," replied Che-loo' hurriedly. "I know the house—I believe—I—"

He stopped short, deeply embarrassed. He did not want to go to the home of Mah-wee'-nah. He had merely intended, after summoning all of his courage, to ask En-tay' if she would make it possible for him to see Mah-wee'-nah again.

En-tay"s mother looked at him quizzically, and mischief shone in her eyes. "She is like her daughter," thought Che-loo'.

"You are sure it is not Mah-wee'-nah whom you want to see?" she asked.

He smiled a little sheepishly, and became interested in the toe of his moccasin. Then he nodded his head. "Yes, I would see her—but she has asked me to leave the mesa—and not be seen with her in Pau-lan'-tee," he announced in a low voice.

The eyes of En-tay"s mother now fairly danced, and her broad smile came near to laughter. "If but a little of the words that have come to my ears be true, her words to you were not half so bad as you make them to sound. It is said that you know the ways of men and that you are without fear—but it is clear to my thoughts that when you have aught to do with women, you have fear and no knowledge."

While he was trying to think of some reply, En-tay' came up to them, walking rapidly. She stopped and, after a brief though friendly greeting to Che-loo', flashed a questioning look at her mother.

"He is here to have words with you—about some very great thing," explained the mother, and with a sly glance at Che-loo' she entered her door, leaving the pair to carry on their conversation alone.

En-tay' looked up at her caller expectantly. "My thoughts say that you want to talk of my friend Mah-wee'-nah—is it not so?" she asked encouragingly.

"Yes," he admitted, and then he suddenly thought to change his plans. Why not ask En-tay' to deliver

THE END OF MANY THINGS

the gift for him. "I have something for her—a—a gift," and he looked away to hide his embarrassment. "She has told me to go back to Pan'-gua, and that I must not be seen with her here in Pau-lan'-tee. If I am to keep her words—I—I have no way to give her a gift."

He suddenly took the little bag from his belt, and held it out to En-tay'. "Will you give it to her?"

She took the bag and made a shrewd guess as to what it contained. "What shall I say to her?" she asked, astonished by the unexpected request.

"Say to her—if she will not have it, she can—throw it away, in the desert—it cannot go to any other woman. You must not look at it. It is only for her eyes—unless she will show it to you. You will give me promise?"

"I give you promise," replied the excited En-tay'. This was going to be a most interesting errand, and she could hardly wait to deliver the gift to her good friend and witness the results. "You are not afraid she will be very angry and throw away your gift?" she asked with dancing eyes and an exaggerated seriousness. But Che-loo' caught nothing of the teasing intent of the question.

"It may be—she will," he replied. "I have no true thoughts of it in my mind, but I—I could not give the gift to any other. I give you thanks." He turned quickly, and before she could think of anything else to say, he was down the street, walking rapidly toward the plaza by the way he had come.

At the house of Cha'-za he found Man'-yah just leaving the door.

"I have come for Cha'-za, but he is not here. Do you know where he is?" he inquired.

"I do not know," replied Che-loo'. "For some time I have not seen him."

Man'-yah reëntered Cha'-za's house with him and closed the door.

"I must find our good friend quickly," he announced. "The Council meets, to name men to take the place of Me-te'-lo and Klee'-tso."

"But Cha'-za is no longer a member of your Council," said Che-loo'.

"He soon will be one again. He is to be named in place of Me-te'-lo—but he does not know of it," came the reply.

"That is *good!*" exclaimed Che-loo' delightedly. "You speak of Klee'-tso—has he gone on the Long Sleep?"

"It is said by the witch-doctors that he will not see the rising of tomorrow's sun. Now that he has confessed that he was one of the three men who gave Ah'-mot to the Apaches—he can as well go on the Long Sleep from snake-bite, as by the hand of the Council. He told the witch-doctors that the snake was thrown at him by a very old witch that followed him through the street, and that the witch snatched up the snake as soon as it had bitten him. There are two men of the Council who say very different words about it," and Man'-yah looked shrewdly at Che-loo'. "We must now find Cha'-za," he continued as he turned to the door.

"I will go down the trail," volunteered Che-loo'. "I know where he sets his rabbit-traps. It may be he is there."

THE END OF MANY THINGS

The flat, white light of the midday sun shone down on the trail as Che-loo' descended it, and he thought of the many strange things that had occurred since the day he had reluctantly climbed the mesa with his trader's pack to hunt for the house of Cha'-za. He had learned to like the great mesa—since that day—and disliked the thought of going back to live in the little village by the pool.

Near the last sharp turn above the foot of the trail, the shouts and laughter of children came to his ears. As he rounded the bend he could see a group of boys and girls, with a few women among them, standing about a great rock. As he neared them he heard the voice of Cha'-za. Then as he came closer he was surprised to see the old man standing within the shadow of the rock, with a child in his arms, and a group of the smallest youngsters gathered close about him. Never before, to Che-loo''s knowledge, had children gone nearer to Cha'-za than the length of his arm, plus the long and much-feared staff. Children had been afraid of him. He wondered what had happened to change all this, but the old man's words explained.

"No—I shall tell no more stories now. Maybe some other time I will tell more—but keep this in your thoughts—Cha'-za is no longer the fool, and no longer will you hear him say strange words, and swing the long stick. Three evil witches made Cha'-za to be the fool. Now two of the evil witches have been slain, and the one that is left will have no more power over Cha'-za. Go now, and tell your mothers, and tell all of the children, that Cha'-za is a wise one who tells you stories, but no longer is he the fool." Thus did the shrewd old man make known the change that had been made possible to him in the overthrow of Dou-gow"s evil reign. None could bear the message more quickly or to better purpose than the children and the few women who had gathered about him. His talk and his stories having ended, he danced out into the crowd of happy youngsters with the little brother of En-tay' high on his shoulders.

When Che-loo' had gained his ear, he told him of Man'-yah and the meeting of the Council, but made no mention of the surprise that awaited his kindly old host. As he looked at the little brother of En-tay', whom Cha'-za was lifting to the ground, and idea came to him.

"Come with us, little one; I have something that you must do for me," exclaimed Che-loo', and lifting the boy in his arms, the three rapidly ascended the trail, followed by the happy shouts of the children who followed more slowly with the women who accompanied them.

Back at Cha'-za's house Che-loo' entered with the little brother while the old man continued on his way to the Pau-lan'-tee Council-house. From his pack Che-loo' took out his stock of sky-stones and selected three of the finest that were left. Wrapping them securely in a piece of doeskin he gave the little package to the waiting boy.

"Can you remember the words I will give you?" he asked.

The little fellow nodded his head emphatically. "I can remember lots of words. All that you will say," came the reply.

"It is good," replied Che-loo'. "Give the little package to your mother and say to her—the Pan'-gua

THE END OF MANY THINGS

says you are to give this to En-tay', because she has been good to the Pan'-gua. Can you remember to say that?"

"Yes," said the boy, and he carefully repeated the message.

"It is good," said Che-loo'. "When I again come to Pau-lan'-tee I will bring for you a bright katcina doll."

The boy ran away, excited by the the importance of the message he was to give his mother.

Che-loo' was awakened the following dawn by the sound of footsteps on the floor of the little storage-room. The old man is early with his traps, he thought, as he listened for the familiar rattle of small ropes and wooden gear.

"A good day comes, Cha'-za," he called out, but without rising from the wide ledge on which he had slept since his experience with Me-te'-lo. There was no reply to his greeting, but the steps continued as the feet that made them entered the front room, and a moment later the bent figure of Gool, the Witch-killer, was beside him.

Instantly Che-loo' sat up, and his hand went to his knife. As he was about to leap to his feet, the Witch-killer raised one open hand.

"I come in peace, and as a friend," he said quietly. "I have just had words with our friend Cha'-za—he told me I could come to make talk with you. I am not seen in the village by day—and it is best for you and for me that I did not come over the roof to your door."

Che-loo' sat amazed as he looked into the face of his visitor, now almost hidden in the dim light.

"Why do you want words with me?" he asked coolly.

"You once talked with one called the Dawn Woman," said the hunchback, seating himself farther down the ledge. "She told you about one who, long ago, was Governor of Pau-lan'-tee, and of his wife who was sent away from the mesa as a witch. I have come to ask that you give to me her words."

"Why do you not ask Cha'-za? He has her words, and they were given to me for his ears alone," replied Che-loo'.

"That is well known to me, but Cha'-za has said that he gave promise not to tell of it while the Dawn Woman lives. He has said that *you* might tell me."

Che-loo' suddenly remembered that he had not told Cha'-za that the Dawn Woman had gone to the Silent Others.

"How is it that *you* know that she gave me the words of this matter?" he asked with sudden suspicion.

"You told some one, on the trail, that you knew who it was that made the lie about the wife of Ko-lee'-pah being a witch, and you called the one who made the lie a Chin-di. Word of it came to my ears, and I asked Cha'-za if he knew, as I had thought you had the matter from him. He told me of the Dawn Woman, and that he was under vow not to tell her words."

"We are no longer under the vow, but Cha'-za does not know of it. The woman has gone on the Long Sleep," said Che-loo'.

"Then you will tell me who she said it was that made

the wife of the Governor a witch?" asked the hunchback, rising to his feet.

Che-loo' hesitated—perhaps there could be no harm in giving him answer—now that he was no longer held to secrecy.

The Witch-killer moved to the post in the center of the room, and leaned against it, and as he did so he threw back the buffalo mantle that he might the more easily rest his hand on his hip. From a sheath bound to his belt protruded the handle of a long knife, and the dawning light from the windows fell upon its curiously carved handle of bone. As his eyes rested upon it, Che-loo' was startled. There could be no mistake—it was the knife Mah-wee'-nah had used to free him from his bonds when he was held prisoner in the field.

"I have seen your knife before. You gave it to the daughter of Ah'-mot the night she helped to free me from the shelter, down in the fields. Is it not so?" he asked.

"It may be," came the reply. "You think, then, that I am come here as a friend?"

"Yes," admitted Che-loo', somewhat dazed by his discovery. "I will tell what you ask." And he told his caller all that the Dawn Woman had said.

When the account was finished the Witch-killer slowly nodded his head, and with a gesture of farewell, went out by the way he had come, leaving Che-loo' to ponder over two things—why had Me-te'-lo told the hunchback what he had overheard when he had spied on him, and why had Mah-wee'-nah thought to borrow the knife and ask the help of so vile a person as the Witch-killer.

He rose and went down to Cha'-za's house. The hunchback had gone, and the old man was making some fresh maize-cakes over the morning fire. Cha'-za, it seemed, could not—or would not, help solve the riddle of the two questions that bothered him.

Over their morning meal, the old man had much to tell his young friend, and enjoyed the telling. He told of the long session of the Council that had met to settle the grave matters that confronted it.

"I am again a member of the Great Circle, and was named to take the place of Me-te'-lo," he announced, with pardonable pride.

"That is *good*!" exclaimed Che-loo', as though he had not known that such news would be forthcoming.

"And our good friend Man'-yah is now war-captain of Pau-lan'-tee," went on the old man, happily.

"That, too, is good news to my ears," responded Che-loo'. "What of Dou-gow'?" he asked. "Will there not be a man named in *his* place?"

"Not until he appears before the Council to hear what will be said against him. He has not yet returned to the mesa, but he was expected with the dawn. He must be condemned by the Council before another can take his place."

"To condemn—does that mean to be sent on the Long Sleep?" inquired Che-loo'.

Cha'-za nodded his head. "It is an ancient law of all stone-house people that when a man betrays a Cacique or Governor to an enemy—that man is slain by order of the Council. Dou-gow' will not know what is known against him until he comes to hear what Klee'-tso confessed." The old man's serious attitude suddenly changed. "You have said that Ah'-mot is again strong, and that Ne-chō'-ba says he will soon have his right mind. Those are the words that will make all Pau-lan'-tee glad. Now that Klee'-tso, and the ten men who came back with him, have told the people that Ah'-mot is not in Pan'-gua, they again fear that the Cacique will return to us no more. I have told none what you said, and when people say 'Ah'-mot' to me, I look sorrowful and make my head shake slowly, but when they are gone, I smile. Great will be the day when he comes back to us!"

A loud knock sounded on the door, and immediately Man'-yah entered and looked at Cha'-za.

"Dou-gow' is here," he announced. "We have told him to come before the Council, in the old Council-house, at midday."

"Hmm!" grunted Cha'-za, rising. "What does he say?"

"He showed great anger. He asked why *we* should tell him what to do and where to go. We told him of Klee'-tso, but did not say what Klee'-tso had said of him and Me-te'-lo. The Council will do that. We asked if he had forgotten that by ancient law a Council could be called by its men, if both the Cacique and the Governor were not in the village. To that he could say nothing. He showed fear when I told him that Klee'-tso had gone on the Long Sleep of a snake-bite. He said, 'It is the Pan'-gua Chin-di that did that. The young Pan'-gua is a witch—a Black Witch. I will see the end of *him!*' We told him he could say that to the Council, who decided such things, and I could see fear and great anger in his face. He could not say many words, because he sees that something has gone greatly against him." Man'-yah turned to Che-loo'.

"I give you good warning, my friend, to watch Dou-gow' when you are in the streets. It is in his thoughts to send you on the Long Sleep when he sees you. Then he would try to make false proof that he had destroyed a witch. You must come before the Council to tell of Klee'-tso and Me-te'-lo. The men know of it, but must have your words. You will come with Cha'-za when the sun is half-way to the midst. We will do much before Dou-gow' comes at midday. It is better to hear your words when he is not there."

Man'-yah turned to the door.

"I give you thanks for your words," said Che-loo'. "If I use the knife in defense against Dou-gow', what does the Council say of it?" he asked.

Man'-yah hesitated, and looked to Cha'-za for help in making reply.

"Dou-gow' would be condemned, if *he* was the one who lived," said Cha'-za. "If you sent *him* on the Long Sleep the people would condemn you, for you are not Pau-lan'-tee, and the people have not yet heard of Dou-gow''s guilt against Ah'-mot."

"It is good," replied Che-loo'. "I will not use the knife."

Man'-yah looked speculatively at the youth before him and wondered if he had ever known fear.

Once again Che-loo' crossed the wide roof that lay in front of the ancient red door of the Pau-lan'-tee Council-house. He had not come through the home of Man'-yah, as before, but had followed Cha'-za through a narrow passage that ran from the street to ladders that led up to the wide roof.

This time he walked to the low guard-wall and

THE END OF MANY THINGS

looked over it at the great, peaceful desert below. Two crows were flying up to the mesa wall beneath, and their backs glistened in the sunlight as it glanced from their smooth, iridescent feathers. He turned back to Cha'-za waiting patiently by the red door.

Within the Council-house smoke hung thick above the men seated in the great circle, and Che-loo' wished the door could be left open, as the holes in the wall near the ceiling did not seem to admit enough air. When Cha'-za was seated, but one place remained vacant—that of the Governor who was soon to be deposed. Man'-yah, as highest in authority, took charge. When Che-loo''s eyes had grown accustomed to the low light in the room, he looked about him and was surprised to see the Witch-killer seated within the door, his curved back against the wall. Chi-nil', the wrestler, also was there, and Che-loo' noticed that an expression of haunting fear shone in his face. The Council must have learned that the wrestler had something to do with the guilt of the three men who had betrayed their Cacique. Man'-yah began a long recount of the disappearance of Ah'-mot, and while he talked Che-loo' studied the face of the Witch-killer, whose eyes were upon the speaker, and was aware that a change had come over the features of the hunchback shaman. At first he could not tell what this change was, then he saw that the two yellow fangs were gone, and the wide mouth seemed less sinister. The hair, too, was changed—it was no longer matted, but brushed neatly back from the wide forehead. "He was ashamed to appear before the Council with dirt upon him," thought Che-loo', and he wondered why Gool was there.

When Man'-yah called upon him, Che-loo' rose and gave the Council his account of the passing of Me-te'-lo, and the confession of Klee'-tso. As he talked, the men within the room listened with close and silent attention. A murmur of amazement swept over them when he told of the throwing of Me-te'-lo's body from the roof, and again when he described his fight with Klee'-tso and of the two rattlesnakes.

It seemed to Che-loo' that he had been in the stuffy room a very long time when the Council told him that he could go. He went out and attempted to close the door behind him, but some one within who, like himself, evidently wanted more fresh air prevented him from shutting it tightly, by thrusting a foot against it. Che-loo' looked down at the foot and was not surprised to see the pointed moccasin of the hunchback.

The brilliant light outside almost blinded him and he paused by the door until his eyes could grow accustomed to it. Some one was ascending the ladder, whose top projected from an opening in the opposite side of the roof, and a moment later Dou-gow''s head and shoulders appeared.

The warning of Man'-yah came to Che-loo''s mind, but he dismissed it, as he was sure Dou-gow' would attempt no violence at the very door of the Council-house. He stood still and waited. As Dou-gow' stepped to the roof he saw him, and stopped. A sneer curled his upper lip and his evil eyes narrowed. Without a word he moved away from the opening but keeping his face to Che-loo' and his back to the high blank wall opposite the Council-house. No more than seven paces separated the two men, who now silently regarded each other. The words of Cha'-za came to

THE END OF MANY THINGS

Che-loo"s mind—"He can throw a knife like a Che'-pah." Slowly the right hand of the Governor rose to his belt, and Che-loo' tried to decide quickly whether to rush at his enemy before the knife could be drawn or attempt to dodge the flying weapon when it should be thrown.

He hesitated a moment too long, for, like a flash, Dou-gow' drew his knife and whipped his arm forward with a quick motion—

In that instant a great brown figure leaped in front of Che-loo' and the flying knife struck the hump on the back of Gool, the Witch-killer, burying itself to the hilt. Almost too amazed to move, Che-loo' expected to see the hunchback fall to the roof, or to hear him cry out with pain, but instead, the bent figure rose slowly, higher and higher—the big buffalo mantle slid to the roof—the hump and the knife with it. Che-loo', too astonished to move, looked at the face of the tall, erect man who now stood where the Witch-killer had been. It was the face of Gool, but no longer was he a hunchback. Che-loo' looked at Dou-gow'. The small, evil eyes of the Governor stared from his ashen face and *terror* seemed personified in his cringing body as he sought to retreat as far as possible from the silent figure that confronted him. Not for a second did he take his staring eyes from the tall man before him.

"Ko-Lee'-Pah!" he screamed, as he reached the angle formed by the low wall and the corner of the house.

"For once there is truth on your lying tongue. Yes, I am Ko-lee'-pah," came the reply. "Many long seasons have I waited to learn the name of the murderer and maker of lies who brought the great trouble upon me, and sent my wife on the Long Sleep. Long have I suspected, but, until this day, was without proof."

"No! No!" shouted Dou-gow'. "You are a witch—a ghost from the Silent Others!" and he crouched lower in the angle of the wall, breathing heavily, like one who had undergone violent exertion.

The amazed members of the Council poured through the small doorway and crowded back of the tall man who, but a few moments before, had been known as the Witch-killer. With bent arms, like a wrestler prepared for a contest, Ko-lee'-pah rushed at the cringing figure—but the distance between him and his enemy was too great. With a loud scream, like that of a madman, Dou-gow' leaped over the low guard-wall, and his body hurtled downward over the towering side of the mesa.

The unexpected act of Dou-gow'—in taking his own life—and the equally astonishing change in the much-feared hunchback—seemed to render the men speechless. Then exclamations of awe and amazement swept the astonished crowd. But not all of the Council members were surprised by the sudden appearance of Ko-lee'-pah.

The former Governor turned to Cha'-za, and a look of great disappointment shone in his face. "The Shiuana have snatched him from my hands, Cha'-za," he exclaimed.

"And the Shiuana are always wise," replied the old man simply.

"You knew that this man was *not* a hunchback witch-doctor?" asked Che-loo', turning to Cha'-za.

THE END OF MANY THINGS

"For many seasons, Ah'-mot and certain others of us have known," said the old man. "I did not tell him the words that the Dawn Woman gave you— I did not want the blood of Dou-gow' on his hands. I knew the Council would bring an end to Dou-gow', and I did not want Ko-lee'-pah to know of the matter until after Dou-gow' had been condemned. But, the Shiuana often take such things from the hands of men. Now they have saved us the labor of sending the evil dog on the Long Sleep."

Che-loo' turned to Ko-lee'-pah and held out his hand.

"I give you thanks for what you did."

"It may be I saved you for another, as well as for yourself," replied Ko-lee'-pah; and Che-loo' flushed as he suddenly realized that the man before him was the real father of Mah-wee'-nah.

As the former Governor and the awestruck Council started down from the lofty roof, the sound of great shouting came up to them from the village streets. The noise increased mightily as they descended, but not until they neared the lower entrance could Che-loo' or Cha'-za learn what the people were shouting about.

"It is *Ah'-mot!* He comes up the trail with many men of Pan'-gua!" a woman called to them over her shoulder as she ran down the street.

Making their way through the excited crowd as best they could, Che-loo', with Cha'-za at his heels, finally reached the plaza, now massed with people, many of whom climbed to the quickly crowded roofs or perched like great birds on ladder-rungs. Che-loo', who could look over the heads of those immediately in front of him, saw Ah'-mot, the lost Cacique, lifted high and being carried through the excited throng on the strong shoulders of Mat'-so and Tō'-bah-yan. In their wake came Mah-wee'-nah with the almost hysterical mother, followed by En-tay'—while behind them were twenty or more men of Pan'-gua.

Toward one of the two great circular estufas they bore the Cacique, and in a few moments he was lifted down that he might climb the wide stone steps that led up to the low flat roof. When he had reached the top he insisted that he be joined by the three women and the men of his Pan'-gua escort. Here a seat of folded blankets and skins was quickly made for him, and he seated himself, and raised his hands for quiet.

After several moments of increased tumult, an expectant hush settled over the wondering and happy people—but on the outer margin of the throng the dogs barked and children voiced their excitement without knowing what it was all about.

In a voice whose strength and volume surprised Cheloo', Ah'-mot recounted all that he had experienced from the time he had been delivered to the Apaches to his return from Pan'-gua. At last he mentioned the names of his three betrayers, and at the name of Dou-gow' the people cried out in rage; and shouts of, "Slay him! Slay him!" went up.

Man'-yah, who had been forcing his way toward the estufa with Ko-lee'-pah at his heels, climbed halfway up the steps and called out to them:

"Dou-gow' is no more! His guilt has come upon him, and he has thrown himself over the mesa!"

Awed silence fell on the people, and astonishment shone in the face of Ah'-mot. Briefly then Man'-yah told of Ko-lee'-pah, who had, for so long disguised

THE END OF MANY THINGS 257

himself as a hunchbacked shaman, and who would again be Governor as he had never—rightfully—been deposed. At this a great cheer went up from the older people, who so well remembered the beloved Governor and his beautiful Apache wife.

Ah'-mot showed no surprise at this bit of news, and now called on Ko-lee'-pah and Man'-yah to join him on the estufa roof. Again the crowd gave vent to its mad joy, and it was some time before it could be quieted sufficiently for the Cacique to continue his talk.

"Now, my people," exclaimed Ah'-mot, "I would not be here—and I would not be among the earth-born but for the quick hand and brave heart of one man."

"Who? WHO!—His name! His name!" shouted the people.

Ah'-mot raised his hand for silence. "Peace! I will name him to you in good time!"

Che-loo' felt suddenly hot and then cold, and panic seemed to seize him. He looked about him, and took some comfort in the fact that of those men near him only Cha'-za knew who he was.

"And had it not been for this same man," continued the speaker, "the names of the three men who betrayed me to the Apaches might never have been known." Here Man'-yah whispered something in the ear of Ah'-mot and again the Cacique spoke: "I have just learned that in witness before the Council this same young man gave still more proof of his bravery and of his friendship for the Pau-lan'-tee people. This man is not a Pau-lan'-tee—he is a Pan'-gua—known to many of you here as Che-loo', son of my good friend

Mat'-so. If he is here I want him to come—that I may give him thanks for myself and for all of Pau-lan'-tee."

Wild shouts of, "The Pan'-gua! Che-loo'—the Pan'-gua!" went up from the crowd. This was a wild day of exciting things—a day of joy that would not be stayed—and there was need of a hero.

Che-loo' turned and fled through the wondering people who had stood back of him. Instantly Cha'-za was at his heels shouting:

"Here he is! Catch him—he runs away!"

But the panic-ridden hero was not to be halted immediately, and would easily have escaped into a narrow street toward which he was headed had it not been for a very stout old woman who all but blocked its entrance. Here he was forced to make a momentary halt to avoid a disastrous collision, and instantly the strong hands of near-by men seized him and, assisted by Cha'-za, they turned him about and, in spite of his resistance, forced him toward the estufa.

As he climbed the steps he looked up into the amused faces of his father and Tō'-bah-yan, and at sight of them he regained some of his courage—at least enough to hide the fear and tumult within him beneath a mask of forced composure.

And now the shouts of the people became almost deafening, as he reached the estufa roof and took the outstretched hand of the smiling Cacique. What happened after that he was never able to recall with any accuracy, but there was one thing—a very small thing to all but himself and one other, that made a joyous and lasting impression on his turbulent mind, and did much to restore his natural poise. Over the shoulder of the Cacique he caught the smiling eyes of Mah-wee'-nah, her beautiful face flushed with a double joy as she regarded him with open admiration—and about her throat gleamed the sky-blue stones of his necklace.

ENVOY

Time, with its happy seasons of corn planting—of gay summer ceremonies, and of golden harvest—moved peacefully over the great mesa. Again on its towering summit a little village stood beside the mighty one of Pau-lan'-tee—and it appeared as though it had never tarried for a time beside the little pool in the desert. Here the aged Ne-chō'-ba spent his last round of the seasons among the earth-born, content to see the old glad days return, and to witness the fulfillment of his last request—that he who had saved Pau-lan'-tee from its three great enemies and made possible the return of Pan'-gua to its old site on the mesa, should take his place as ruler of his people.

And when the young Cacique, often more concerned with the joys of the hunt than the solemn duties of the Council, takes his young wife with him to hunt on the mountain-tops, and camp beneath the wide freedom of the gold stars—the women of the great mesa smile indulgently over their pottery-making and say, "Why not? Is he not the bravest of men, and is she not the most beautiful of all earth-born?"

6494